Praise for Janet Gurtler

"Just right for fans of Sarah Dessen and Jodi Picoult."
—*Booklist* on *I'm Not Her*

"Fascinating and unique. A powerful look at the place where guilt and innocence collide into one confusing, heartbreaking, and life-changing moment."
—Jennifer Brown, author of *Hate List* and *Bitter End* on *Who I Kissed*

"An emotionally satisfying climax. Well done, sensitive, and real."
—*Kirkus Reviews* on *16 Things I Thought Were True*

"Gurtler gracefully negotiates the powerful emotions that accompany a changing friendship. Readers…will understand the difficulty of moving on from a toxic relationship that once felt like it would last forever."
—*Publishers Weekly* on *How I Lost You*

"Gurtler handles complex issues of race, identity, friendship, and fidelity with laugh-out-loud humor and engaging frankness…once you're in, you won't regret it."
—*RT Book Reviews* on *If I Tell*

"[A] timely heartbreaker…Gurtler pulls no punches."
—*VOYA* on *Who I Kissed*

Also by Janet Gurtler

I'm Not Her

If I Tell

Who I Kissed

How I Lost You

16 Things I Thought Were True

the **truth** about us

Janet Gurtler

sourcebooks
fire

Published by Sourcebooks Fire, an imprint of Sourcebooks, Inc.
P.O. Box 4410, Naperville, Illinois 60567-4410
(630) 961-3900
Fax: (630) 961-2168
www.sourcebooks.com

Library of Congress Cataloging-in-Publication Data

Gurtler, Janet.
  The truth about us / Janet Gurtler.
       pages cm
  Summary: When Jess's father orders her to work at a soup kitchen for the summer, she
meets Flynn, a classmate from the wrong side of the tracks, and discovers that sometimes
the person who should not fit in your world is the one who finally makes you feel as if
you belong.
  (alk. paper)
  [1. Dating (Social customs)--Fiction. 2. Social classes--Fiction. 3. Family problems--Fic-
tion. 4. Soup kitchens--Fiction. 5. Voluntarism--Fiction. 6. Conduct of life--Fiction.]
I. Title.
  PZ7.G9818Tru 2015
  [Fic]--dc23
                            2014042461

      Printed and bound in the United States of America.

            VP 10 9 8 7 6 5 4 3 2 1

For those who aren't where they want to be yet
but plan to get there.

chapter **one**

I have fifteen minutes to get home. It's a twenty-five-minute walk. I'm so dead.

If I were smarter, I'd run, rise to the challenge or something, but I'm not even moving at all. Instead, I'm stuck, my feet immobile on the sidewalk, all because of a pedestrian sign flashing a red hand at me, commanding me to stay where I am. The *Jeopardy* theme song plays in my head as I wait for the green light. Penny and I used to love watching *Jeopardy*. She always knew more answers. I wonder if she still watches. I gave it up when Penny and I stopped being best friends and Nance took her place.

"Hey, Jess," a girl says as she and a boy walk past. I wave and my cheeks burn brighter, because it's awkward and weird to be busted with my feet refusing to move until a light turns green. The girl is a friend of my sister; I don't know the guy. They obviously don't share my hang-up about jaywalking, and they cross the street without even glancing around for cars.

No matter how hard I try to shake it off, choke its hold, and squeeze it out, some of my lameness still lingers in my cells, part of who I really am. Or who I was. I don't know anymore.

"It's not a good idea to walk all alone at night," she calls back like she's a friggin' genius and I'm the poster child for bad choices. The light finally changes, and I step onto the road and walk, glancing down at my phone. My head is fuzzy and my heart pounds thinking about my dad at home waiting for me. I didn't plan to screw up again, but apparently it's kind of a gift, because I'm really, really good at it. Being late will equal no phone for a few days at least. My dad knows how much I hate to lose my phone.

I jump when a car toots the horn as it whizzes by. A boy screams something about my ass and whistles. My heart beats faster, and for a second, fear springs the hairs up on my arms and a swooshing sensation swells in my belly. Fear feels a lot like excitement. The fact that some pervert thinks I'm whistle-worthy might be the best part of my day. Of course, *pervert* is the key word. So he's probably not that picky.

"Does your stupidity not know any bounds?" I hear my dad say in my head.

I worry it doesn't. And wish he were away on one of his business trips so I wasn't in this bind. In lots of ways, things are easier when he's gone. I think about blaming Nance for my predicament. She does have a knack for getting me into these situations. Of course, I have a knack for letting her. Besides, responsibility for my own actions and all that. Blaming her will get me exactly nowhere.

Another car whizzes past, and I glance back to see if my sister's friend is still behind me, but she's nowhere in sight. They must have turned down another street or live somewhere close by. There's another car coming now, and it's driving slower. I know from every horror show I've ever watched that it's not a good sign. Man, I know from what happened to my mom it's not a good sign.

I force myself to glare at the car. It's an old rust bucket, "an eyesore" as my dad would say. Not the kind of car usually seen in this neighborhood. I frown and peer inside, keeping my expression fierce. When I see the driver grinning at me, I relax a little. He's about my age, and his smile reminds me of a floppy-eared golden retriever. Friendly. Wouldn't hurt a soul. The guy in the passenger seat stares off into the distance, as if he doesn't see me.

"Hey," the driver calls and leans forward to look at me with an even bigger smile. "Where ya headed?"

He's cute. Blond with overly spiky hair. I have an urge to offer him a treat. Scratch him behind the ear. His car is a total piece of crap, and the guys inside obviously aren't from around here, but they look harmless.

"Home," I tell him and glance at the passenger again. He's good looking too but in a totally different way. His hair is longish and black. His eyes are dark. He looks biracial or something. Exotic and almost pretty. He turns his head and looks right at me. When our eyes meet, my insides mush together. Fear or excitement? It's hard to tell them apart sometimes.

"Come on. I'll give you a lift," the driver calls. "I'm Braxton Brooks," he offers. "This is Flynn. He's not as badass as he thinks he is."

Flynn. I have an urge to say the name out loud. To feel the shape of the quick and hard sound on my lips.

"Screw you, Brooks," Flynn says, and I turn away so he doesn't see me smile.

The car drives slowly beside me.

"No strings," Braxton calls. "We're not serial killers or anything."

"You sure about that?" the passenger asks. His voice is deep and low.

I stop walking and narrow my eyes, a nervous sensation pooling in my stomach. When my gaze locks with Flynn's, goose bumps run up my arm and I'm as woozy as if my blood sugar plummeted. I get a sort of déjà vu vibe from him, as if we've met before.

"What's the matter? Are you drunk?" he asks.

"Not anymore." A heated blush melts my mouth into a frown.

"Chill, Flynn," Braxton says to him and leans forward to smile before returning his attention to the road. "We'll drive you home. Come on. We're from Tadita too. Not this neighborhood, but I know I've seen you around. You're not scared of us, are you?"

It sounds like a challenge, and I'm not going to admit to being scared. Still I hesitate. A tiny argument starts up in the back of my head. I don't recognize them. They don't go to my school. But they would get me home by curfew. Besides, rapists or murderers don't give out their names. I won't lose my phone privileges. I'll stay out of trouble. A swoop of adrenaline bungee jumps up and down in my gut as I consider my options. I don't want more trouble at home. I want my troubles at home to leave me the hell alone.

"You're not actually going to accept a ride from perfect strangers?" Flynn asks.

I glare at him. That's an even bigger challenge.

"It's a basic," he says. "Something you learn in kindergarten."

"Dude," Braxton says to him. "Quit dicking around." He leans forward. "Don't listen to him. We'll take you straight home. It's safer than walking."

The vodka coolers I drank at Nance's earlier still linger in my system though they're wearing off in the cool night air. I lift my chin to show him I'm not afraid. I might be a girl who can't cross the street when the light flashes at me, but I reach for the car door handle.

chapter **two**

The car smells like hamburgers. I give Braxton my address and a couple of directions and lean back against the backseat. He keeps talking, but my head is full and all it sounds like is blah blah blah. There's a hive of angry bees buzzing around my head, and I nibble on my thumbnail. His voice sounds far away. I feel removed.

My gaze drifts to the back of the passenger's head. Flynn. His hair touches the back collar of his T-shirt. For a second I have an urge to lean forward and touch it to see if it's as soft as it looks. Braxton keeps talking in a hum of words I don't understand as Flynn stares out the side window at the night air, ignoring me. Braxton is quiet then, and I realize he's asked me a question.

"Which way?" he asks again.

I look out the window. "Uh, turn right. It's halfway up the next street."

He whistles as he turns the corner. "Holy crap. Your family rob a bank?" Braxton jokes, laughing.

There should be a punch line, but it evades me.

"The one with the lights on," I say, pointing to my house.

He stops his car in front of the driveway.

"Uh, thanks. For the ride." I reach for the door handle.

Say something, I silently urge Flynn.

"You're lucky that's all you got," Flynn says softly.

Um. Not that.

"Chill," Braxton says and turns to me. "No problem." He glances quickly at his friend's profile, but Flynn stares out at our neighbor's house, his lips turned down in a frown.

"Hey. Can I get your number? I could give you a call sometime?" Braxton asks.

Flynn turns his head and glances back at me, kind of smirking, and raises an eyebrow. We stare at each other for a brief second, and then Braxton glances at Flynn and frowns. I drop my gaze, my hand still on the door handle. I don't want to give Braxton my number. I want to give it to his friend. I have an urge to crawl over the front seat and try to make him like me.

"Uh," I say.

"Don't stop here too long," Flynn says. "Someone will call the cops or a tow truck in this neighborhood."

"Dude," Braxton says. "You don't have a car, so shut up, man."

"You call this thing a car?" Flynn laughs.

I open the door, using the interruption as a way to avoid giving out my number without offending anyone. Avoidance is another one of my skills.

"Thanks for the ride. See you around," I say quickly, as if he never asked the question, and climb out and shut the door behind me.

• • •

I walk toward my room but stop in front of my mom's bedroom door. It's closed but I wrap my hand around the knob, push on it slowly, and look inside. There's a lump under the covers, but her face isn't visible. The hope I'd been holding in my heart—that maybe she was feeling better—squeezes out. She's been laying low for a couple of days. I pull the door closed and wonder how long this spell will last. It's unpredictable, how long she'll disappear for.

"She's still not feeling well, Jess," a voice behind me says softly.

I bite my lip and turn to look at my dad. Even this late at night, he's still dressed in business casual. His hair is styled with product, and I know he's handsome for a dad—I hear it all the time— but I wish he'd relax sometimes. Maybe put on a pair of sweats, Lululemons if that's what he needs. Forget to shave. Spill mustard on his shirt. Quit with the perfect.

"I heard a car. Did Carol drive you home?" he asks. Carol is Nance's mom, an old friend of Mom's. When she had friends, that is.

I shrug, the best way to lie without saying a thing. Carol left Nance and I alone so she could go to her boyfriend's for a sleepover. Nance's brother bought us a case of vodka coolers, with a markup for supplying underage drinkers. We drank until we felt silly and FaceTimed a couple of boys from the high school across town. Nance flashed her boobs and we both dirty danced for the camera until one of the boys' mom's shouted in the background and he abruptly hung up. I'd thought it was funny at the time. Now it seems stupid.

I think about the two boys in the car. Even more stupid.

"Jess?" Dad says.

"Yeah, Dad?"

"Everything okay?"

"Fine."

He clears his throat. "Okay," he says softly. "I picked up the Audi from the shop," he tells me. "It's parked out front. Try not to back into anything again, okay? They replaced the back bumper. She's good as new."

I backed into a streetlight and gave the Audi its first dent. As soon as he was home, he'd rushed it in to the shop to get it fixed.

"Yeah, I saw," I say and then force out, "Thanks." He likes his cars flawless.

"You're welcome," he says and clears his throat. "Allie's sleeping at Dana's house tonight. They both worked late," he says, as if I'm worried about where my sister is.

"Yeah?" I ask. She's not. She's at her boyfriend's. Doug Henderson. They've been dating for three years. Dad has no idea Doug's mom allows her to stay over all the time. I suppose she feels sorry for Allie and her messed-up home life. The family secret isn't much of a secret, no matter how much Dad pretends it is.

I wonder if my dad even knows the last time we had an honest conversation. He doesn't want to hear truth from me or from my sister, not really. He's not as good at Mom's job. She used to check up on us. She'd make sure we were where we said we'd be. I don't think he can fathom that the people he created could lie to him.

He walks down the hall to his bedroom then, the separate room he moved into to give Mom space to recover. Something else we don't talk about. He looks over his shoulder before he disappears into it. "I have to be at work early. Can you check on Mom in the morning? Text me and let me know how she is."

I nod and he pauses, as if he's going to say something more, but then he steps inside his bedroom and shuts the door behind him.

Stupid Allie for leaving stupid Mom in my hands tomorrow. I cringe and immediately guilt sticks to my belly. I wish every day for my mom to be back. The mom I used to know. I don't blame her for the way she is now; how could I? But still.

I miss her.

• • •

A greasy scent floats under my bedroom door. Bacon. Mom is obviously out of bed today. And apparently she's cooking. Out of bed and cooking means it's a good day. I haven't seen one in a while, so I push off my covers and stretch and head downstairs to the kitchen.

She's in front of the stove holding a spatula, staring down at hissing and popping bacon. She looks up and smiles when she hears me, and it almost reaches her eyes, but they're a little fuzzy, a little off. She meets me as I walk over and puts her arm around me. For a moment I let her try to convince me everything is fine. I lean against the warmth of her, and my heart fills with sadness, remembering days when her touch could convince me nothing bad could happen.

I step away, and she goes back to the stove. I lean up against the counter, bringing one leg up into a tree pose. My favorite standing position. Mom and Allie do it too.

"You want to make some toast?" she asks.

"Sure." The toaster sits permanently on the counter. Mom used to put the toaster away when it wasn't being used. Everything had its place. I open up a loaf of white bread and pop in a couple of slices. We eat white bread when Dad does the grocery shopping.

"Allie's at Dana's," I say.

"Yeah," she says softly. "I texted her this morning when I saw she wasn't in bed."

We don't discuss that she didn't know Allie was gone until the morning. We don't discuss that she was in bed all day yesterday with the lights off. Or why. We don't even discuss that she has her own bedroom now.

"Everything okay, Jess?" She piles the bacon on a plate and heads toward the kitchen table.

I snag a piece of crisp bacon as she passes and take a bite, suppressing an urge to blurt out what I did last night. Drank coolers, stayed at Nance's too late, and then got in a car with two boys I didn't know.

I imagine telling her I'm worried that Nance is a little too fond of flashing her boobs at boys and that her mom is too busy with her new boyfriend to notice. But it would send her back to her bedroom, so I keep chewing.

"Everything's fine," I tell her.

The toast pops up so I butter the slices and take them to the table.

"You sure you're feeling okay?" she asks. "You've lost weight. You're getting too thin."

"No. I mean, I'm fine. Fine." She used to be the kind of mom I could tell anything to. We used to have long talks. She used to want to listen.

"Okay," she says as I sit across from her. "But you're not dieting, are you? You girls are both naturally thin. You don't have to do that."

"Nope. No dieting," I tell her. "How about you, Mom?" I ask her softly. "You okay?"

For a second, our eyes meet. We stare at each other, and the pain that's nestled inside her soul shines out. It breaks my heart and I drop my eyes.

"I'm sorry," she says. She doesn't say what for, but I know.

For disappearing.

"No," I say softly. "You have nothing to feel sorry for." I don't look up because I don't want her to see that I'm lying. I do blame her sometimes. I want her to get over it. Go through it or around it or under it, like the hunting song she used to sing to me when I was little. Sometimes I hate who she is now. Weak. Afraid.

She's left us to deal with things, and I, for one, am really messing it all up. I want to be allowed to get mad at her like Nance gets mad at her mom. Fight with her. Yell at her. Tell her off. But I can't.

She stares down at her plate for a moment, playing with a piece of toast, then looks up. Tries to smile. "Do you need some spending money?" she offers. "It's almost time for back-to-school shopping. You and Penny could go."

I swallow my bitterness. She doesn't acknowledge that Penny and I aren't friends anymore. For years it was PennyandJess, the kind of best friends who could look across a room and know what each other was thinking. But I screwed that up. Now it's me and Nance, and I'm living a life I never would have imagined.

"Sure, I could go shopping," I say. Dad already gave me money for back-to-school shopping, but it's not like they'll discuss it. She stands and walks over to the counter where she leaves her purse and pulls out her wallet.

"Is five hundred enough?" she asks as she sifts through her cash.

"That'll buy me a pair of boots I have my eyes on," I say, testing her, pushing for a reaction.

"Really?" She looks up, but she doesn't even give me the crap I deserve. Instead, she sighs. "Things are so expensive these days. I used to get my entire back-to-school outfits from a thrift store."

I don't say anything. She grew up without a lot, but she made up for it by marrying Dad and also made a killing of her own selling real estate. There was a time she'd wanted Allie and I to have all the things she never did. The best schools, the best clothes. The best friends. I don't know what she wants now.

"You can take my credit card. You know the PIN, right?"

"Yeah, I do. Nance and I will shop till we drop." I emphasize Nance's name and sound angrier than I intend. I pick up a piece of bacon, chew on the end, and stare at my mom, willing her to see me.

She walks over and puts her gold MasterCard on the table beside me. "Put it back when you're done and leave me the receipts. Not too overboard, right? A couple of tops and a couple of pairs of jeans to go with the boots. Maybe a dress. Okay?"

"You know I don't hang out with Penny anymore. I'll be shopping with Nance," I say, spelling it out for her.

She sits and frowns down at her plate and sighs. "You know, I never really thought you and Nance would be such good friends," she says. "Penny…"

I hold my breath. Hoping she'll ask me about Penny. Listen to me. Maybe even offer some advice. Tears pop up in the corners of my eyes, and I blink fast to keep them from spilling out.

"I miss Penny," she says. "You and Nance are so different."

My breath sticks to my throat, waiting for her to ask, silently begging her to ask. I remember how much it hurt to cry alone in my room when I lost Penny. It ached even more because I suspected my mom heard me. And I needed her. But she let me cry all alone.

"How's Carol?" Mom asks.

I press my lips tight. She's gone too, I want to tell her. But her absence is different. She has a new boyfriend. She's finally over Nance's dad fooling around on her and moving out, and she's going on with her life, pretty excited to have new attention from the sounds of it. Nance doesn't see her mom much either, but we don't talk about that. She and I don't talk the way I did with Penny.

"Carol's okay." I press my lips tight. Blow out a big breath. "You know something, Mom?" I ask.

She blinks. Waiting.

"Me and Nance," I tell her. "We're not so different anymore."

Her eyes are getting cloudier and she frowns. We sit in silence for a while longer, both of us nibbling quietly at toast and bacon. Finally she pushes her plate away.

"I'm feeling a little tired. I'm going to go up and have a nap. Would you mind cleaning up, sweetie?"

"No." I stare at my plate, holding in tears, wanting to cry, wanting to yell. Make a scene. Do something. Instead, I push my own plate away and stand and start piling the dishes. "It's fine."

I'll clean up and then I have to get out. I'll choke on the quiet in the house.

"I'm heading to Nance's later when I'm done," I tell her.

She stands and moves away from the table, nodding. "Okay," she says. "Have fun."

"I'll drink to that," I mumble softly, but she's already gone, shuffling up the stairs. She doesn't hear me. Or maybe she pretends not to.

I watch her leave me. It feels like the hole inside my heart is growing bigger instead of healing.

chapter **three**

I twirl my huge key chain around and around as I head down the driveway. I only have a couple of keys, but my chain is a huge wad of ornaments. People started adding to my collection of key chains when they noticed I was collecting them.

I walk toward the dent-free Audi. Dad bought it for Allie and me. But Allie hardly even uses our car, since Doug drives her everywhere.

He and Mom each have a Tesla electric car; he has the roadster, and she has the sedan, though she hardly drives hers anymore. He pretends buying hybrids and electric cars makes him green.

I'm about to jump in the Audi when crying reaches my ears. It's feeble, as if trying not to attract attention. I glance around and spot Carly, the little girl who lives next door, sitting on her driveway, clutching a piece of pink sidewalk chalk, crying. She's an adorable kid, and the sight of her tugs on my dark heart. I'm no body language expert, but it looks like her entire world is crashing in. Like she's been deserted by everyone. I know that feeling, so I walk slowly toward her. When I reach her, I bend down so I'm at her level.

"Hey, Carly," I say softly. "Are you okay?"

She hiccups and rapidly sucks in breaths and blinks at me with her big eyes and manages to nod.

"Funny. 'Cause you look a little sad to me."

Her teary eyes reach inside and wrap around my heart. "I'm supposed to be brave. I shouldn't cry," she tells me. She glances around. "My parents are getting a divorce," she whispers. "I have to be brave."

My heart aches for her. Man, that sucks. "Being brave is hard sometimes," I tell her and look around, wondering what I can do. The mini sock monkey on my key chain stares at me. Impulsively, I unhook it. "But I happen to have a solution." I hand her the monkey. "This is a special monkey," I say. "Her name is Brave Monkey. She has powers. Magical ones. Keep her close and she will help you be brave."

Carly opens her eyes wider, and I stand up.

"I can keep it?" she asks.

"As long as you promise to take good care of her," I say solemnly.

She clutches the little sock monkey in her hand and nods, her eyes big and her expression serious. The monkey was a present and it's been on my key chain for a long time, but Carly looks like she needs it more than I do right now. I can always get myself another one to replace it.

"Brave," I tell her and wink.

"Brave," she whispers and nods again.

I pat her on the head. "See you soon, Carly," I say and walk to my car, watching her for a moment. She's talking to Brave Monkey, probably telling her the way things are with her parents. With a sad smile, I drive off toward Nance's.

When I arrive, I park in her driveway and open the door to hear music rumbling from the back deck. No one answers the front doorbell, but it's unlocked so I walk inside, slipping off my shoes and heading through the kitchen to the patio doors. Nance is stretched out on a lounge chair, and she waves and mouths hello to me but keeps talking on her phone.

I strip off my shorts and tank, down to my bathing suit, and spray myself with sunscreen. A second later, her brother struts out on the deck holding a twelve-pack of vodka coolers. I smile and he openly checks me out without smiling back, emphasizing how inappropriately tiny my bikini is. Serves me right. I glance down at my skimpy suit. Not exactly a suit for swimming laps.

He hands me a grape cooler and I take it, grateful for the drink even though I could do without him. I've known Scott since I was five years old, but he's still a jerk who enjoys making me feel like an entrée in an all-you-can-eat buffet. He takes his eyes off of me and scowls at Nance until she reaches for her purse and hands him some bills, and he hands over the coolers. I stretch out on the chair beside her and he turns back to me. "All grown up, hey Jess-A-cup," he says and chuckles. "Or should I say, Jess-C-cup."

I make a face at him, but my skin shivers under the hot rays of the sun. When he leaves the deck, I breathe a sigh of relief.

"I know, Dad," Nance is saying into the phone, and she rolls her eyes at me. "But Mom decided it wasn't a good idea."

I try to remember the last time my mom made a decision for me. It's a stretch.

Nance hangs up and turns to me. "Hey!"

I force a smile. "What's up with your dad?" I ask.

"He asked if I wanted to go to Vegas with him and his child bride.

Mom nixed the idea. She was worried I'd roam around the whole weekend in the land of free booze and single men. Plus they didn't invite Scott. Dad said it was because he's working, but Scott can get time off whenever he wants. I don't think the child bride likes him."

I don't blame her but say nothing.

"Party poopers." She checks her phone again and then snaps a quick selfie and puts it down. It'll show up on Instagram or somewhere later. Within minutes of posting, she'll have fifty comments telling her how pretty she is. "The child bride is pissed off because Scott's working at the golf club and Dad's still footing all his college bills. Plus he told her about the campus tour he's taking me on in September. Berkeley, Stanford, Brown, maybe Duke. She's pissed off I'm not picking a school in Washington. Honestly I think she's worried Scott and I are going to spend all the money before her child grows up. She doesn't understand that he'll never run out. He loves making money too much. It's a competition for him." She pauses. "Do you think she's kind of low class?"

It's not the first time she's asked, but I don't answer. I'm not stupid. There is no way to win that conversation, so I do what I do best. Ignore it.

"Ugh, colleges," I say. "I don't even want to think about them." The year ahead has so many big decisions. Exams, colleges, career options. Maybe even taking a year off to travel, which would probably make my dad lose his mind.

"You okay?" Nance asks. She flips onto her back and stretches her arms high over her head and points her toes. I glance at her wrists. The slight scars. She doesn't hide them.

"I'm fine," I tell her.

"Yeah?" She reaches for a pack of smokes under her chair and holds it out to offer me one. I don't smoke, but she offers me one every time as if she's convinced she'll convert me. "Liar."

"I'm fine," I say again. "I just don't want to think about school or trying to impress people next year."

"It's a big year. And we will rock it. But whatevs." Nance rolls her eyes as she reaches for the lighter and inhales and blows out smoke in my direction. "So you actually made it home on time last night? Your dad didn't freak?"

"Yeah. It was fine." I don't mention the ride home or the boys, even though it would both surprise and intrigue her. They were hot after all. And it was pretty daring.

"My mom was up this morning." I'm not sure why I tell her that.

"Yeah?" She watches me. "How's she doing?" she asks softly, and her cheeks suck in as she inhales from her cigarette.

"Okay." I don't think she wants to hear the truth. Not really.

She waits for more, but when I don't say anything, she sighs. "Our parents suck," she finally says, and her voice catches. "We might as well be orphans." She's staring at the smoke from her cigarette as it fades away. The serious expression on her face surprises me. "My therapist says I'm acting out to try and get attention. He thinks I feel unloved." She turns her gaze to me. Her eyes shine. As if she's daring me to deny it. Or agree.

"You're seeing a therapist again?" I ask tentatively and make a shield with my hand over my eyes and pretend to gaze at some clouds.

"Not again. Still." She inhales deeply and blows out smoke again and then laughs. Bitter, angry laughter. "My dad insists. We all have secrets, you know. Not just your family."

I should say something, ask more. Why? What's wrong? Obviously she has things she wants to say or talk about, but I pause too long. We hang out together for a reason. We don't over examine things. We find ways to forget them.

"You okay?" I ask, but insincerity stiffens my voice. My words sound cold and wrapped in bubble wrap.

She laughs. "Nothing a few vodka coolers won't fix."

"Seriously," I say. "Oh, wait, I have news!" I reach down to my purse and, with great flourish, pull out the credit card and wave it in the air. "Gold MasterCard. My mom gave it to me to go shopping."

Nance stares at it for a moment. Presses her lips closed and sits up straight. "Nice," she says. "I'm in. We can head to Seattle. How about the Shops at the Bravern? And then Alderwood Mall? I'll get some cash from my dad."

Her dad supplies her with cash for clothes on a regular basis. Nance calls it guilt money. For ditching her mom for a younger woman and a new baby.

"When do you want to go?" she asks.

"I don't know. It's supposed to rain in a couple of days." I tuck the card back in my purse.

Nance crosses her legs and lifts her bottle in the air. I raise mine and then we clink and pull back and bring them to our lips, tip, and chug.

I manage to finish the whole bottle in one go, but Nance still has half hers left when she drops it from her mouth. I grin and wipe off my mouth. "Beat that, beey-otch," I tell her and smile wider.

"You may beat me at drinking, but I beat you at life," she says and belches loudly.

"I love it when you talk dirty to me," I say, relieved the serious stuff is forgotten.

"You would," she retorts.

I reach for a new vodka cooler as Nance blows another smoke ring into the air. I watch it drift up and slowly expand until it's gone. The smell bothers me, but like many things with Nance, I put up with it and don't say anything. She leans back against her lawn chair and grins.

"So, liquor pig," she says. "Let's talk about boys."

"Boys?" I ask as if Nance asked a question.

"Hot boys," she says, and it makes me remember how Penny and I used to tease Nance about how guy crazy she was. At least that hasn't changed. My cheeks burn remembering how Penny and I swore we'd be mature teenagers, not girls who cared too much about makeup, clothes, and boys. We swore we'd never do stupid things just to be popular. Like drinking or smoking.

One of us was wrong.

"We need to find summer flings," Nance says. "Not Josh." Josh being my on-again, off-again something or other. We're off. For good, I hope. It's awkward.

"I'm over Josh," I tell her and swallow back a healthy amount of the new cooler, enjoying the buzz that's starting to lighten my head.

"Good. I mean, despite his 'good on paper' pedigree, Josh's not worthy of a summer fling." Nance takes a dainty sip of her drink and watches me over the top of the bottle.

"Good on paper?" I say.

"You know what I mean. There's a certain kind of guy that girls like us will be expected to date next year. But not this summer!"

I pretend to gag, but she shakes her head sadly and blows out a smoke ring.

"It's true. We're seniors this year, and everything we do matters. The right parties, the right people—we're going to need Josh-like boyfriends. Only Not Josh 'cause he smells like chlorine."

The first part sounds like Carol talking. Nance's mom worries a lot about what other people think. She's already nagging Nance about who's going to take her to prom. She wants it to be a boy with a good family name, to show the world she still has clout even if her husband left her. Her priorities are questionable, even to me.

Nance tosses the rest of her cigarette into her bottle and claps her hands together. "Anyhow, this is a summer for boys!" Nance says. "Last chance for summer flings."

"We're not going off to war," I say, rolling my eyes at her.

"No. We are going to be seniors. It matters. But first, boys."

I close my eyes and an image of Flynn fills my mind. I quickly open them, startled, and take a drink to wash his image away. Nance doesn't notice my distraction and continues on about summer flings and summer parties until she stops to light another smoke.

"Jennifer says there're lots of hot guys hanging out at Alderwood

24

Mall. We can go there to shop *and* check out the merchandise."
She wiggles her eyebrows up and down. "I can't believe Jennifer's
dad actually made her get a job this summer, though I love that she
showed him by getting one at the lingerie store. At least she gets to
dress slutty."

"My boobs aren't perky enough to work at a lingerie store," I say,
looking down at them.

"Oh, your boobs are fine."

I stick my tongue out at her, and we drink more and gossip as
time passes by.

Later, after going inside to pee, I stumble back to the deck and
Nance is on the phone, FaceTiming someone. I can tell it's a guy
by the way she's flipping her hair. She turns the phone to me.
"Say hi to Bryan," she says. I pirouette for him and then bow,
giggling, and almost trip. God. The coolers have definitely gone
to my head. I don't even like Bryan. He's a jerk, just like his pol-
itician dad.

I plunk down on my chair but Nance seems intent on chatting
him up. "Not fling material," I say too loud.

She laughs but shushes me at the same time.

"Bryan. Bryan. Do you have a trust fund?" I yell with drunken
gusto. "That's not going to get you Nance action this summer."

She waves her hand at me to shut me up. I listen for a while but
quickly get bored and pull out my own phone. There are no new
texts from anyone, so I flip to my eBay app. I'm addicted to watching bids on eBay.

I search dresses. After all, Mom said I could buy a dress.

I scan a bunch and then see one that makes my eyes pop. I laugh because it's so ridiculous and yet so perfect at the same time. It's short. Gold sequins. Ostrich feathers. Giorgio vintage. I imagine myself wearing it to school on the first day. Or better, to my college interviews. That cracks me up even more. Ostrich feathers at a college interview.

"Oh God. I totally want this!" I hold up my phone to Nance and point, but she's making prune lips at Bryan and ignores me. Ugh.

"Gross," I say and look down at the dress, really stare at it. "It is an important year," I say out loud to it in my snooty lady voice. "Everyone says so." I giggle some more. I've definitely had too many coolers. I imagine pirouetting in the dress. Maybe Josh is my date for prom. Ew. No. The Flynn guy! Taking a boy like him would get lots more attention. Not positive attention, but still. I laugh to myself and wonder how much the limit on my mom's credit card is. I glance down at the auction button. The Buy It Now button says it's $9,999. It's regularly $15,000. It's actually a total bargain.

I deserve something fun. There's so little fun in my life these days. My house is like a morgue most of the time. And okay, I won't wear it to school the first day, and definitely not on a college interview, but I could totally pull it off for prom.

I clap my hands together, imitating Nance, pull out my mom's credit card again, then click the Buy It Now button. I fill in the payment information with the credit card number and my home address.

"Whoo-hoo!" I yell to Nance when the payment goes through.

She takes her eyes off her phone for two seconds to look at me. "I bought it!" I tell her.

"Of course you did," she says and goes back to her phone.

I grab another cooler and move to sit beside her and stick my face into her phone screen. "She's not going to sleep with you, Bryan," I tell him. "Not this summer. You have too much money."

He smirks at me. "Yeah? Well, least you can do is show me your boobs."

Nance grabs my hand and swings it in the air.

"Oh no," I say. After a few drinks, the girl does love to show off her boobs. "You asked for it, Bryan," I say as Nance turns to me, a devilish twinkle in her eyes.

"Hold this." She puts her phone in my hand. I make a face at Bryan.

"No. Point it at me!" she shouts, so I turn the phone so the camera faces her. "The sun's going down soon and the girls need some sunshine." In a flash, she's undone her bikini top and tosses it down beside her.

I hear Bryan whoop and she flips her hair back, plucks my cooler from my hand, takes a sip, and wiggles around. The girl has great boobs, but God compensated by giving her no rhythm at all. That is for shizzle. I try to ignore her gigantic breasts bouncing up and down in the sun, though I should be used to her flashing them around.

I turn the phone toward me. "Okay, Bryan. You've had enough of a show. Bye." I click off her phone and Nance yells at me. "You're lucky he was too busy gawking to snap a photo of you. He'd post it everywhere. And that is *not* what you need to start your senior year. You have to stop doing that on the phone."

She laughs. "Yeah. Fair enough. Okay. No more phone flashing. But this is fun. Join me. Be free!"

"Me?" I laugh at the absurdity and put her phone down.

"Yes. Otherwise you'll have weird tan lines that will mess up your hot new dress."

I giggle and jump up and down, and in a sane part of my mind, I sense it's a little manic but don't even care. "I bought it!" I scream again. "Oh my God. I bought it."

"Come on, Jess. Show me your boobies!"

Can I do that? Can I? I suck in a breath as if I'm eight and have just been caught with chocolate stains all over my fingers after being told to stay out of the chocolate chip bag. "But what if your brother comes back?"

"He's at work," she says dismissively, lifts her hands, and twirls around on the deck. "It's so American to be repressed about topless sunbathing."

"Yeah. But we are American!" I shout.

"It's no big deal. I was half-naked the whole time I went to Saint Martin."

"Because you have great boobs," I say. I've hated my boobs since eighth grade when Johnny Ryan announced to everyone that my boobs were saggy. I've worn a padded bra ever since. Preferably a push-up one.

"Don't be ridiculous. Your boobs are fabulous," she says. "They don't have to be big to be beautiful." Nance twirls again. "Don't leave me topless all alone. It's more fun with someone else."

"You always do it," I remind her. "Last night, you were all party of one while you were flashing those boys."

"Boring," she says. "You are boring."

"Not boring," I tell her and sit up straighter. I take another swig of my cooler. What's the big deal? I mean besides baring my boobs to the entire world. Well. Nance's backyard.

"Jess-I-cup," she sings.

"No," I tell her.

"You're not scared, are you?"

Grr. Nance knows the buttons to push.

"Bock, bock, bock," she says, imitating a chicken.

"Not scared." I reach around my back, then I pull my fingers back away. "No. I can't!"

"Free yourself!" she chants. "Lose your inhibitions."

I shake my head. "I can't."

"You can! Free those boobies!"

I shake my hands. Breathe in and out, in and out quickly.

"You can do it!" she says. "Go, Jess!" she cheers. "Go!"

I can't. I have saggy boobs. But also, I'm kinda drunk.

"Free them!" she squeals.

It makes me laugh. I'm tired of myself. I don't want to be like the little girl next door, clutching my chalk and trying to hide my feelings. I squeeze my eyes closed, pump my fists in the air, and try hard to rock my inner *Girls Gone Wild* vibe. "Okay, okay!" I squeal as my fingers fumble over a knot. "Oh my God!" I say. "What is wrong with me?"

"Show me your boobies," Nance chants.

There's a weird humming noise coming from my throat as I struggle to undo the knot, and then it gives and I pull off my bathing suit top and fling it for good luck. It flies through the air, and I watch in horror as it lands way too far away, in the middle of the yard on the grass.

"Oops!" I say and stare at it, covering my boobs with my hands.

Nance is laughing so hard, tears drip from her eyes. "I can't believe you did it!" she yells.

Actually, neither can I.

"Girls?"

I blink. Holy crap.

"Nance," says Mrs. Green. "What the *hell* is going on here?"

As if she's got magical powers, Nance's mom is suddenly standing on the deck. She's wearing her real estate agent costume. Power suit. Tight short skirt, low-cut blouse, a fitted blazer, and mile-high heels. My mom used to wear the same thing. When she worked.

She's glaring at us, and my face heats up. I wrap my arms tighter in front of myself and stumble. I have had way too much to drink to deal with this right now.

"Jesus, girls," Nance's mom sputters, glancing around at the coolers and cigarettes, her mouth open, her eyes shooting sparks. "This isn't a nude beach. The neighbors can see you. Put your clothes back on." She looks around, horrified someone might be peering over the fence, witnessing the debauchery in her backyard.

"What will the neighbors think?" I shout with glee, but my giggle dies quickly in my throat when I see the look from Nance's mom.

Nance nonchalantly grabs her top and slides it over her head and hooks the back together with one hand. She rolls her eyes and inhales her cigarette and exhales smoke that travels toward her mom's face.

I'm frozen to the spot, my arms wrapped over my boobs, watching Nance's mom cough and wave her hands in the air. Her eyes are bulging, which is kind of a feat with the amount of Botox she's got injected in her face. Her eyes get even wider and her lips turn down. "Put that cigarette out. Now." She turns her attention to me. "Jess! Put your top back on!" She looks about to commit murder. "Right now."

I'm too shocked and kind of looped to do anything but stand there staring at her, my hands over my boobs. I glance at my bathing suit top in the grass about thirty feet away, but I can't make myself move to get it.

"We didn't expect you for a while," Nance says and then glances at my face and bursts into laughter.

"Jess." Her mom's voice is pitchy and high. "What's wrong with you? Put your top back on. Immediately."

My face burns brighter, and with my arms still crossed in front, I run off the deck like a spaz and trip on the stairs. Nance laughs even harder as I scramble up and over to the spot on the grass where I threw my suit. I bend, trying to pick it up and keep myself covered. I finally manage to pull the top on and then clumsily tie up the strings in the back. Oh God. Nance's mom saw my boobs. My mom hasn't even seen my bare boobs in years.

"I thought you girls had more sense," Nance's mom says.

"So did I," I tell her as honestly as I can, digging my toes into the grass, looking around the yard and not at her.

Nance snorts though, and the absurdity and the heat get to me. A laugh starts to build. It's so ridiculous. And inappropriate and disrespectful. The more I try to stop the gigantic giggle that's building, the worse it gets. I cover my mouth, but I can't stop the laughter from spilling out of me. For a moment, I kind of lose my shit.

When I can finally breathe again, I inhale gulps of air and stand straighter. They're both staring at me. Even Nance has a look that could almost pass for concern.

"Jess!" Nance's mom says. "You need to go home. Are you okay to drive?"

I don't think I am. But I don't want to admit it. I bite my lip and stare at the grass, wiggling my toes around.

"For God's sake, get dressed. I'll take you home."

Nance's mom starts digging around her purse.

"Martin," she says into her phone after she's found it and dialed. "It's Carol. Jess is here. She and Nance have been drinking. I'll bring her home. No. She can't drive herself. She's had too much."

She turns her back on me, and I can only imagine what my dad is saying in the silence that follows. "No. It's fine. I don't mind. Yes. I'm sure. I'll take her straightaway." She listens for another moment and then hangs up.

"Get dressed, Jess," she commands. "Nance. You go and wait for me in your room."

I silently find my shorts and shirt and pull them on. My face is hot and it's not only from the time in the sun. Nance is gone by the time I go to the front door to find my shoes.

Mrs. Green drives me home in silence. When we pull up to my house, she turns to look at me.

"You're not to wake your mom," she says. "Your dad asked you not to. You're supposed to wait up for him."

I nod, my head down, concentrating on my hands in my lap.

"Jess?" I hear concern in her voice. "Are you okay? Is there anything you'd like to talk about?"

"No. I'm fine. I'm very sorry," I say. I can't look at her or I'll cry. Tears bunch up in the corners of my eyes. Nance and I were stupid. So stupid. I move my head so my hair falls in front of my face, hiding me.

"I hope so," she says with a sigh.

I open the door. "I am sorry," I say again.

"Good-bye, Jess," she says right before I close the door behind me.

The house is quiet. There's no movement from Mom's room. Allie isn't home. I sit on the couch and stare at the floor. I don't have to wait long before my dad arrives.

He closes the door quietly behind him, but his face is white he's so angry. "I don't understand you, Jess," he says.

I expect him to yell, but he doesn't.

"Not only were you drinking and sunbathing topless. MasterCard called me," he says in a quiet voice. "You charged over ten thousand dollars to our account? For a dress?"

"It had ostrich feathers," I tell him and close my eyes. It doesn't seem hilarious anymore. Or like the perfect prom dress. I don't tell him Mom gave me permission to buy a dress. I'm stupid but not that stupid.

I wait. But there's no yelling. Nothing.

Finally I open my eyes and what I see shocks me more than anything.

He's sitting on his leather chair. His favorite chair. Across the room. His head is in his hands. His shoulders are shaking.

He's crying?

I've never seen him cry in my life.

I feel even worse.

chapter **four**

She'll work here for the whole summer," Dad says to the woman on the other side of the table. Stella is the volunteer coordinator at New Beginnings, the missionary shelter on Broad Street. For years I've been warned to stay away from Broad Street by the very man who dragged me here this morning.

Dad clears his throat, and I keep my head down since he's acting like I'm not there anyway. "Every day you need her, she's available," he says to Stella.

His arms are crossed, and he's leaning back in his chair. His hair is slicked back, as if he's in a competition to keep every piece perfectly in place. He's ignoring me, his body tilted slightly away, his chin up. The problem is he's my dad, and I'm biologically programmed to want his approval. No matter how huge an asshole he is. Truthfully, I've been an asshole too. I think of what I did, and I'm hit by another tsunami of guilt. But this? He's taking the punishment a little bit overboard.

"We'll work her shifts out," says Stella, watching me. She has potted plants on a ledge of wood by the tiny window in her office. Green leaves reach down to the floor like they're bowing to Stella. It's the only thing I like about the place.

"Well. Whenever you need her. She's available," my dad tells her.

Stella tilts her head slightly, chewing a pen, studying me like I don't belong. I agree, but she looks out of place in the stale room too. She's colorful and vibrant. Everything in this multistoried building looks old and run-down. I pretended not to notice the people hanging around the building when we came inside. The tired-looking men with bad teeth and dirty backpacks. The weathered women with cynical slants to their bodies made me want to run. One lugged a suitcase behind her on wheels, probably with everything she owned in the world inside it. They robbed me of my voice and scared me a little.

"Don't hesitate to work her hard. She needs the discipline," Dad says.

"All teenagers need discipline," Stella says.

I squirm on my chair, the epitome of the privileged white girl. He's making sure it shows, but maybe he doesn't realize it exposes him for what he is too. He's intent on pretending he's not spoiling me and that he's in charge. In addition to working at New Beginnings for the rest of the summer, an idea I have no clue how he came up with, he also confiscated my phone. It's a toss-up which is worse, but he won't give it back. Not until the end of the summer. I feel almost violated. Sick to my stomach. I'm completely out of touch with everyone and everything. The loss makes me even more alone, if that's even possible at this point.

"We're short on servers right now. Or kitchen helpers." Stella says it like it's a question.

"Server," I immediately say.

"You'll work wherever they need you," my dad snaps and then glances at his watch. "Speaking of, I have to get back to work soon."

"Please. Go ahead," Stella says. "I'll get the child started. Show her around."

She says "child" and it makes me want to act like one. I want to yell and stomp my feet and have a temper tantrum. I've got so much anger inside and nowhere to put it, and I shiver, even though the office is warm and it's hotter than normal outside. A small fan whirrs on Stella's desk, but it barely stirs up the air.

My dad stands, pulls his fancy car keys from his pocket, and jangles them on his finger. "I'm heading to Houston today, but I'll see if Allie will pick you up." He glances at Stella. "She'll be done around six?"

Stella raises an eyebrow. "Day staff and volunteers usually clock out at two or three. She won't be needed for the dinner service."

I breathe out a sigh of relief.

"You're sure? That's not even a full day."

"We don't want to burn our volunteers out," she tells him. "She can stay late some days if she wants to, but it's not an obligation."

He makes a sound in his throat. It's not directed at her, but she sits up a little straighter in her seat. "Allie can't make it at that time," he says to me. "She's working." My sister has a summer job with an engineering firm. She needs work experience to go along with her university degree, but she doesn't have to do her work for free.

"I'll take the bus," I tell him and lift my chin. Pretend it doesn't make me nervous to be taking a bus from this part of town. I can't even remember the last time I used public transportation.

He jangles his keys and glances at Stella, and I can almost read his thoughts. He doesn't want me taking a bus from this neighborhood either, but he doesn't want to tell her that.

"She'll be fine," Stella says. "We can have someone walk her to the bus stop if you want."

That might be even worse. Dad nods and presses his lips tight. He stares out the door and briefly squeezes my shoulder. I pull away, and he frowns and spins, walking out of the room without a good-bye.

The air in the office lightens. Some of the chill leaves my skin, and the warmth of the building seeps in. I wrinkle my nose. It smells moldy. Stale. I imagine Nance. At home. Still asleep. With nothing pressing planned for her day except maybe shopping. For clothes and boys. I frown. Angry to be stuck here. Knowing I don't belong.

Stella leans back in her chair. "So," she says. "You're here because you're dad's making you work?"

I shrug instead of answering.

She laughs as if this pleases her. "Maybe we'll grow on you, sour-puss. Come on. I'll give you the tour," she says.

* * *

Stella takes me from her office into a room with three exits. "Lockers are right there," she says, gesturing, and then she points at a basket of locks. "Use one of those to put away any valuables you bring." A tiny ripple of fear sticks in my gut. Locks mean people steal. What else do they do?

Signs are posted on a billboard over the basket. *Thanks for volunteering.*

Women's Outreach Program, Wednesday Nights at 7 p.m. in the Arts and Crafts Room.

Stella shows me where to sign in and out and points to the kitchen, which goes off in the direction ahead. "We'll go there last. That's where you'll be working."

I follow her slowly, my shoulders scrunched up tight, trying not to touch anything or breathe too deeply because of the musty smell. She leads me down another narrow hallway. "Volunteers sort donations over there," she says. I see piles of T-shirts and plastic containers full of socks.

"Our guests can get clothes and necessities here once a week. We serve lunch and dinner every day of the week, and we offer overnight shelter in emergency situations."

We walk past bins of deodorant and soap and a room filled with racks of boots and jackets. They're out of style. "They pay for this stuff?" I ask, my eyes wide.

"No." She turns to me. "It's a shelter, hon. It's free. They're donations. You'll learn. Anyway, serving in the dining room is where we need your help, so don't worry too much right now."

At the back of the building there's a loading dock. "This was a warehouse?" I ask.

Stella nods, but my gaze goes to someone walking toward us, pushing a cart. The cart is loaded up with potted plants. I perk up as I recognize them. The dock door opens, and the cart is pushed outside into the sunny midmorning air.

"What are they doing with those plants?" I ask.

Stella points to a building outside. "That's our greenhouse over there. Donated by a longtime patron. Wilf MacDonald. He paid for the greenhouse in his wife's name. She volunteered here for years, but she passed on a while ago. He's with us now."

"There's a greenhouse?"

"You like plants?" Stella asks, staring at me, her hands on her hips. Noticing too many things.

I shrug again.

"You can check the place out on your own after the lunch service if you like. Wilf will be around somewhere. He locks the place up. You'll need to talk to him if you want to help out."

"They're just plants," I say and bite my lip.

Stella starts walking again, explaining a couple of other rooms and what happens in them, and then we find ourselves back on the main floor, in the volunteer center.

"Okay," she says, leading me through the kitchen to the dining room. "I'll introduce you to Sunny. She's in charge of the servers. Where's Sunny?" Stella asks a white-haired man when we walk into the dining room. He's got a stack of place mats draped over an arm. "Wilf, this is Jess. She's a new server. She's going to be here all summer."

"Lucky you," he says. "Sunny's in the supply room. A huge shipment of plastic cutlery came in, and she's not happy about it." He glances at me. "We have our own cutlery, and Sunny hates environmental irresponsibility. Here." He divides a stack of place mats and hands half to me. "Put these out on the tables. Four per table."

I glance down at the stack in my hands. The place mats look

homemade. Stamped with a company logo. Stade Golf Course Valentine Classic.

I frown at them.

"What are you frowning about?" Wilf asks.

"It's July. These are Valentine's place mats."

"This ain't the Ritz, Chickadee," Wilf says.

"Some of them are wrinkly and torn." I hold them up to show him.

"They're clean. Suck it up," he says.

I swallow a retort. I wasn't brought up to get snarky with old men. Of course, I wasn't brought up to do a lot of the things I've been doing lately.

"Be nice," Stella says to him. "This is her first day. She's never been in a place like this before. I don't think you have much choice, being here? Punishment for your sins?" she asks.

I bite my lip harder and feel their judgment. The poor little rich girl.

The old guy stares at me. "She looks too young and fancy to get into trouble. What were your sins?" he asks.

I straighten my shoulders and stand taller. No way I'm going to tell this guy I got drunk, bought a ten-thousand-dollar dress, and flashed my boobs. "What are yours?" I ask instead.

Stella chuckles. "I'll leave you two to work this out. Wilf, introduce her to Sunny. She'll show you the ropes," she adds for me. She shows me a long enough rope and I might try to hang myself with it.

"Not worth it, Mess," the old guy says as if he read my mind. He winks.

"Jess," I tell him.

"That's what I said." He points at his ear and smiles a crooked old-man smile and starts to whistle. "Go on then. Start putting out those fancy place mats."

Stella laughs and turns and flows back to the kitchen. For a big woman, she moves with lightness and grace.

Wilf and I work silently, putting down place mats, and then he grunts out instructions for setting out the plates and glasses. We set those out, and when we're done, a tall black girl walks through the kitchen into the dining room. She's not too much older than me, and she's skinny. She actually makes me look big.

She's holding a bin. "Damn plastic stuff," she mumbles. She walks by, and I peer inside the bin and see rows of plastic cutlery wrapped in napkins and tied with ribbons. "You must be Jess?"

I nod.

"Sunny," she says. "You ever served before?"

I shake my head. "Not really. No."

She looks me up and down. My pants are expensive and my top is designer. I definitely don't shop at Target for clothes. "Yeah. You've never needed a part-time job, I'm guessing."

I stand straighter and lift my chin. "I'm here and I'm working. So. Yeah. I guess I do."

"Not the paid kind though."

I don't have a ready argument, and Sunny mumbles something under her breath. I don't hear her and decide it's for the best. We obviously have an understanding. We don't like each other.

"You want us to put out this plastic cutlery?" Wilf interrupts.

"We have to use it sometime. Did you explain to her how this works?" She nods her head to me, as if she can't be bothered to remember or say my name out loud.

"I did. Why? Are you mad because I'm stepping on your toes?" Wilf asks.

"My feet are bigger than yours, Wilf. Worry about your own toes," she tells him.

"I'm too much of a gentleman to point out your flaws," he says. "Big feet being only one of them."

I decide then that I might like the old guy better than I thought. Wilf and Sunny argue for a moment, and I look around, swallow, and take deep breaths.

"I have a million pages of paperwork to catch up on," Sunny finally says and glances at the clock on the wall and then back at me. "Please try to get up to speed quickly."

I want to point out that, in theory, I'm a volunteer. No one even seems to want me here. Not even me.

"Don't worry. She hates everybody, not just you," Wilf says when she leaves the dining room. I hide a smile as we lay out plastic cutlery packages and he explains more about how the lunch service works. Go to the doorman, escort guests to a table. Repeat until the section is full. Pick up their meals, deliver them to tables. Clean up when they're done, set up new place settings, return to door for new guests.

"Most days in summer, we don't get huge crowds for lunch. The two of us can handle it. Dinner is another story." He frowns at me. "We're done setting up, and our guests won't be here for another hour." He glances around, as if he's looking for something for me to do. I feel kind of stupid and useless and wish I could go home. Even home is more comfortable than this place.

I lean against the table I finished setting. "I saw the marigolds and geraniums," I say to fill up the awkward silence.

He cocks his head to the side. "The what?"

"Plants. Going to the greenhouse." I wonder if he's always so grouchy.

"How do you know what plants are going to the greenhouse?" he asks.

"I saw them on the cart. When I was in the warehouse with Stella, she said they were going to the greenhouse. I recognized them. I used to like plants, okay?" I tell him.

"You mean the kind of plants you kids smoke these days," he grumbles.

"You growing something you don't want me to see?" I ask.

He glares at me. "Isn't it weird? A kid your age, interested in plants?"

"Probably not as weird as a guy your age."

He stares at me for a long moment and then he laughs.

It relaxes the knot in my stomach. I was kind of holding my breath, pretending to be cocky. This whole place makes me jumpy. And here I am, stuck in the middle of it, smack-talking an old man.

"I had a garden at home," I tell him, trying to be more polite. "My mom and I did. Well. We used to. We used to have vegetables and herbs. Flowers too."

"You lose your mom?" he asks gruffly but not unkindly. "That why you're here?"

I stare at him and then down at my feet. "Not really."

"You shoot somebody?" he asks.

I look up then but shake my head.

"Rob a bank?"

I try not to grin. "Nothing that exciting, trust me. Maybe I just wanted to volunteer."

"And maybe I'm Santa Claus."

For the first time all day, I laugh out loud.

He crosses his arms and studies me with narrowed eyes. "Fine. You can come to the greenhouse," he says as if I asked. "But don't knock anything over. And there's someone in there right now, working on my shelves. One collapsed and almost killed some azaleas. They were Rhea's. So be careful."

"Rhea was your wife?" I ask.

"Rhea was my everything." He turns and starts walking, and I follow. He's a slow plodder, but I stay behind him. We don't talk, but I wonder why this grumpy old guy has a greenhouse at a shelter. I'm not about to ask, but I wonder.

The greenhouse is sort of shaped like an old barn. It's opaque with plastic and steel siding. The door is open, and I follow Wilf inside and pause and then breathe it in. The smell nourishes me. Moist air fills my lungs. I've forgotten how much the scents of greenery soothe me. It reminds me of different times. Simpler times.

"Nice," I tell him, looking around at rows of plants on tabletops and plants stacked on the floor. I realize I've missed the satisfaction of nurturing plants.

There's a man on a ladder in the middle of the greenhouse, fixing a shelf, with his back to us. A little boy stands at the bottom of the ladder, watching. Wilf walks over and pats his head and kneels down to his level. "How are ya, big guy?"

The little boy stands taller and giggles and holds out his hand. He's got it wrapped tightly around a plastic blue train.

The man on the ladder turns and looks down at me. My heart stops.

It's not a man at all. It's him.

Flynn.

chapter **five**

My face burns.

"What are you doing here?" he asks.

Wilf frowns and then looks at me. "What's up with you kids these days? In my time, we treated nice-looking young ladies with respect," he says to Flynn gruffly. "Flynn, this is Jess. She volunteers here."

I say a silent thank-you to him for calling me nice-looking and glance back at Flynn.

"Since when?" he asks.

"Since now. How about, 'hello, nice to meet you'?" Wilf says to prompt both of us. "Is that so hard?"

"We've already met," Flynn says.

My cheeks stay on fire as he climbs down the ladder.

"The shelf is fixed," he says to Wilf. "Slumming?" he adds to me as he jumps to the floor. He folds up the ladder and then leans it against a counter lined with plants.

The little boy stares back and forth.

I try to think of something light and witty to save the moment, but my mind is blank. Instead, I panic. "What'd *you* do to get stuck working at this place?" I say, channeling my inner Nance.

"What'd I do?" He stares at me and then his lips turn up. "I didn't have the right daddy, I guess. I'm here to have lunch. With my little brother. I'm not a volunteer."

My stomach drops. Fail. Epic fail. But he's working?

"You're having lunch here?" I ask as he ruffles the hair on his brother's head.

"Yup. We do a few times a week."

"Excuse me, when did you two meet?" Wilf interrupts.

Flynn turns his back on me. "My friend gave her a ride home the other night. She lives in Tuxedo. We're a little far from her homeland."

I bite my lip and frown, hoping he doesn't tell Wilf the whole story.

"We don't judge around here," Wilf says to him as he sticks his finger in the dirt of a nearby pot. "And we don't make assumptions because of where people live." He narrows his eyes at Flynn. "You should know that."

"Yeah, well, Tuxedo's not really my hood." He looks back at me and then reaches his hand out, and the little boy takes it and looks up at him and then at me.

"My name's Kyle. I'm Flynn's brother," the little boy announces, clearly not big on being left out of this conversation. He's watching me with wide eyes. "This is Thomas." He holds his blue train up. "My train."

"Hi, Kyle," I say softly. "Nice train."

Flynn pulls him closer with a hand protectively on his shoulder as if I'm going to corrupt the little kid or something. I notice a silver bracelet on Flynn's wrist. It looks like one of those medic alerts, but I can't make out what it says.

"Thomas is my favorite engine," Kyle announces to me.

I smile at him, thankful for the diversion. Little kids have always cracked me up. There are lots of them in our neighborhood. I like talking to them.

"Who's your favorite engine?" Kyle asks me.

"There you go, getting to the point of what's important," Flynn says to his brother. "But girls like her don't know about Thomas the Tank Engine," he tells him.

Girls like me?

"Just so happens I like Mavis the best," I tell the little boy and narrow my eyes at his big brother. "I loved Thomas the Tank Engine when I was a kid too. And the Teenage Mutant Ninja Turtles. I wasn't a doll kind of girl."

"See," Wilf says as picks up a bottle and sprays a plant with water. "No judging." He wipes down the leaf with a cloth.

"Exactly," I say and reach out to the nearest plant and stroke the leaf.

Kyle rolls his eyes. "Girl engines aren't nearly as good as boys."

"Not so sure about that," I tell him.

"Boys rule. Girls drool."

I laugh. "That's what you think now. But wait." I take a big breath and look at his brother, still having a hard time believing he's here to eat. As a guest. I don't know what to say.

Flynn drags his hand through his hair, moving his long bangs from his eyes. "So, what'd you do to get 'sentenced' to this place?" He throws the question back at me.

Kyle stares up at me with his big eyes. "Were you bad?" he asks.

"Well. Sort of," I tell Kyle. All three of them stare at me, waiting to hear more, but I won't say anything else about it. I'm humiliated already. I don't need to overshare.

"Well. Tough break for you," Flynn says after a pause. "Being punished by working here." He rubs the back of his neck without looking at me and turns away. "You see Stella around?" he says to Wilf. "She wants me to fix something in her office."

I watch him dismiss me. It bothers me, what he thinks about me. Even if it might be kind of true. I can't explain it, but I want him to like me. "But you do volunteer here too?" I ask, trying to sound polite, glancing at the ladder he folded up.

His eyes flash when he turns back. Anger sparks from them. "No. I help out. Big difference."

Wilf clears his throat and coughs. "Okay, Flynn. Stella's probably in her office. You want to leave Kyle here so you can get your work done?"

Flynn shakes his head. "Kyle can come with me, right, buddy?"

"I'll stay," he says. He steps closer to me and reaches for my hand. His is small and trusting inside mine. "Sometimes I'm bad too," he whispers. I'm like a stick of butter in the heat the way my heart melts for the little guy. I want to hug Kyle and take him home. I think I've just fallen in love.

"You sure?" Flynn says to him. "You can help me. Maybe even use the hammer?"

"No." Kyle uses his whole body to shake his head. "Want to stay here."

"He'll be fine," Wilf tells him.

Flynn runs his hand through his hair and stares at me. I can't look away, but he doesn't have the same problem. He turns to leave. "I'll come and get you when it's lunchtime, dude. Behave, okay?" he says to his brother.

Kyle ignores him and tugs on my hand. "You're pretty," he says to me, and my cheeks warm. Flynn mumbles under his breath as he frowns and marches out of the greenhouse.

"Well, that was painful to watch," Wilf grumbles as he puts the water bottle and towel down. "Awkward as hell. I'd never go back to my teen years."

I want to stomp on his foot. "Oh my God," I say to him. "Please don't speak."

"You shouldn't say the Lord's name in vain," Kyle tells me. He's frowning. "It's a commandment." He points at Wilf. "And you swore." He looks back to me. "He swears a lot. My mom says he should have soap in his mouth."

"You're right," I say to Kyle. "He should. You're pretty smart for a little guy."

"Not little. I'm five," he tells me.

"Big," I say. "Like totally huge."

He grins at me, and he's so adorable, my heart swells some more. I look back to Wilf. He's staring at us.

"You're good with kids?" he asks.

I frown at him. "Shouldn't I be?"

"Maybe it changes my opinion of you a little, that's all." He reaches his hand out to poke his finger in another pot.

"Which was what?" I ask.

He chuckles but ignores me.

"He thinks you're pretty," Kyle offers.

"Ha! You're paying attention," Wilf tells Kyle and walks closer. "A girl who likes plants and children can't be as bad as she seems," he tells him.

That's definitely a backhanded compliment if I've ever heard one, but I lift my chin a little.

"And so you know, Flynn hates feeling like a charity case," he tells me. "It's kind of a sore spot. That's why he helps out. He's a hard worker. He'll do better things one day."

"Ugh" is all I can say, thinking of Flynn and the way he looked at me.

"My dad took all our money and left us. My mom works a lot," Kyle tells me solemnly.

I look down at him. "Yeah? My dad has stinky farts," I tell him. "And my mom sleeps a lot."

Kyle stares at me and then starts to laugh and laugh.

Wilf raises an eyebrow. "Kyle," he says to the little boy and points at a table across the room. "You run over there and get me a water pitcher. The yellow one. It's heavy, so be careful," he grumbles.

Kyle scoots off.

"You have a thing for him?" Wilf asks. "And I mean the older one."

"No!" I stand straighter. "I barely know him." There's a tingling in my stomach though, and when I look up, Wilf is staring at me.

"Rhea always said I had a sixth sense for stuff like that. It's what made me such a good lawyer."

I glare at him, almost telling him my dad is a lawyer and a jerk too but say nothing instead.

"Flynn and his family are good people," Wilf says. He bends down and picks at the leaves of a plant growing up from a pot on the ground. "Kyle's dad gambled. Spent everything and then some and took off and left her with his debt. Her house foreclosed, and they moved into a grubby old rental in town. She works at a bakery and struggles to keep up with bills and the rent. They come for meals so that the boys eat properly. Especially Kyle."

I swallow and nod and stare down at my feet, which seem to be shuffling around on their own.

"The people here all have stories. Remember that. Flynn's not a charity case."

I look up and nod again.

"Probably won't hurt a girl like you, seeing life on the other side."

I shift my feet again, wanting to argue about what kind of girl I am, but it's kind of pointless.

"Good job, kiddo," he says to Kyle, who has returned with a jug of water that's slopping over the sides. "I have some things to look after," he says to me. "Would you be okay looking after Kyle?" he asks. I glance around as if he might be talking to someone else.

"Uh, sure," I manage.

"You can take him to help in the kitchen," Wilf says. "His mom works in a bakery, and Kyle can help cut pies as long as he uses a butter knife."

"Yeah, sure," I tell him, even though I don't want to leave the safety of the greenhouse.

Wilf glances down at Kyle. "You look after this one," he says, gesturing his head at me. "She's new around here. She doesn't know the rules."

Kyle's eyes open wider and he nods his head up and down.

"You want me to look after your train?" Wilf asks. "So you don't lose it while you're working?"

Kyle stares at him and then down at Thomas. "Promise you won't lose him?"

"Promise," Wilf says. "I'll bring him back to you at lunchtime."

Kyle hands the train over and then slips his little hand inside mine. "Come on," he says. "I'll take you to the kitchen." We walk hand in hand out into the sunshine and then up the steps to the main building.

"My favorite five-year-old came to help in the kitchen?" Sunny asks when we reach the kitchen. She's at a counter, cutting up cakes. She barely looks at me.

"Can I cut cakes?" He stares up at her with big, worshipful eyes.

Something like jealousy roams around in my belly. I'm selfish and kind of want this little guy's worshipping all to myself.

"Go wash up," Sunny says. Kyle drops my hand and runs toward the dishwashing sink. My empty hand feels cold. "You'll wanna do something too, I suppose?" she says to me.

She doesn't like me much, that's for sure. I don't like her either, and I don't really want to help, but there isn't much choice. That's why I'm here. "I'll help Kyle?" I ask.

She sighs, long and heavy, and I fiddle with the bottom of my shirt.

"Go wash up."

When I get back, Kyle is beside her, watching her finish cutting up a pie.

"Where'd you get all the baked stuff?" I ask.

"Day-olds. Grocery stores donate the stuff that doesn't sell before the best-before dates." She laughs to herself when she sees the look on my face. "Don't turn your nose up, missy. There's nothing wrong with them. Nothing wrong with the people who come here either. They all have stories," she says, echoing Wilf.

Kyle nods. "I have stories too. Like the one where Thomas the Tank Engine wanted to be a bigger engine."

I can't help but smile. Sunny scowls at me but gently puts Kyle up on a stool, hands him a butter knife, and a pushes an old chocolate cake toward him with a stack of plates. He slowly digs his knife into the top and she shows him how thick to make each piece. Then she goes off and fetches me an apron and a hair net, and I swallow my pride and put it on my head. She fires out instructions to me, explaining the proper way to cut and which plates to put pies on and which plates to put cakes on.

"Can you two finish these up?" she asks. There's about a dozen or so cakes and pies left on a cart.

I nod.

"Good. I'll go and make myself useful somewhere else." She ruffles Kyle's hair, frowns at me, and then leaves. While we work, Kyle chatters on, telling me all about Thomas the Tank Engine and his friends. It's easier than I thought to slice up the desserts, and I've done them all by the time Kyle finishes off his first one.

"Awesome job, dude," I tell him. His hands are covered in chocolate. He licks his fingers, and then we clean up at the sink. We take off our aprons and throw them in the laundry basket, and I throw out my hairnet. I'm not sure what to do next, so I take Kyle's hand, and we find our way back to Stella's office. She's not in there, and neither is Flynn.

I have to use the washroom, so I tell Kyle to stay in the office and walk out, trying to retrace my steps and find it. A toddler runs past me as an older woman yells at her to stop. I dart after her and catch the little girl, leaning down and grabbing her gently under her arms. She screams and fusses, but I calmly hold her and wait for the older lady to reach us and hand her over.

"My grandchild," she says.

I smile and go off to find the washroom. I take a wrong turn on the way back to the office and have to double back again to find Stella's office. When I open the office door, my eyebrows arch up.

It's empty.

"Kyle?" I call.

There's no answer. My heart pounds a little quicker. "Kyle?" I call again. I bend down and look under the desk, but he's not there. The most logical explanation is that Stella came to the office and took him, but I pace, tapping my fingers on my chin, and then hurry out of the office to look around the main room. I head back to the kitchen. No sign of him. Or Stella.

"You seen Stella?" I call to Sunny.

"I saw her in the basement," she says. "Where's Kyle?"

I ignore her, but my worry begins to fester as I walk down the dingy halls to the basement. Stella's in the sorting room. She's talking to a gray-haired woman about the shortage of underwear for men. Kyle isn't with her.

"Stella?" I say, not wanting to be rude, but I'm getting kind of panicky. "Do you have Kyle?"

Her gaze snaps over to me, and she glances down at my empty hands. "What do you mean, do I have Kyle? Flynn said he left him with you in the greenhouse."

My face flushes at the mention of Flynn. And the possibility that I have lost his little brother. "Where's Flynn?" I ask.

"He went outside to fix a picnic bench. He said Kyle was with you."

"Wilf sent us to cut cakes. And we did, but then I had to go to the washroom. So I left him in your office. I got kind of sidetracked by a little girl, and then I got slightly lost." I glance around, as if he's going to pop up somewhere in the room. "When I got back to the office, he was gone."

"Dear mother of God," Stella mumbles and darts past me, out of the sorting area. "It took you less than an hour to lose a five-year-old boy?"

My face burns, and I swallow an insta-lump in my throat.

"Where would he go?" I ask as I hurry behind her.

"We have to find him immediately," she says. "The lunch crowd will be arriving soon."

I close my eyes and struggle to take a deep breath. My heart is pounding, and there's a strip of sweat on my upper lip. She moves surprisingly fast for a woman of her size, and I hurry up the stairs behind her. She opens the door that leads outside to the back of the building. "Flynn was over there," she says and points.

There's no sign of him.

We hurry back toward the office but he's not there, and we move to the dining area. Flynn's inside, carrying a bench. I sprint past Stella to reach him. "Flynn," I say, breathing fast and hard. "I can't find Kyle." I swallow a lump and hold in tears. Each one represents something different. Fear. Worry. Guilt.

He blinks, puts the bench down, and scratches his head as he registers my words. "What?"

"He was in Stella's office. I went to the bathroom..." The reality of the situation kicks in, and my eyes burn with the fluids trying to escape.

"Where have you looked?"

I tell him, and Flynn takes off running. I follow behind him.

"I'll get everyone looking," Stella calls as we race out of the dining room.

Kyle is nowhere in sight.

chapter **six**

How can this be happening? I can't catch my breath.

"You look in the kitchen. I'll look in the art room," Flynn calls.

I race to the kitchen. More volunteers are around now. There's a man stirring a huge pot of soup and lining bowls on a table in front of him. People wander around, each doing a task. Some are tossing big bowls of salad, and others are putting sandwiches on a platter. A few older women are filling pitchers up with orange juice.

"Has anyone seen a little boy?" I yell and hold my hand in the air where his head would come to. "Kyle?" I realize I don't even know his last name. "He has black hair. He's wearing jeans and a blue Thomas the Tank Engine shirt."

A few people look over, but they all shake their heads. I keep moving, my eyes scanning. I go through the kitchen back to the dining room, where the tables await guests who will be arriving soon. I scan the room from left to right, but there's no sign of him.

I run toward the entrance of the building, past a security guard who's manning the door. Guests are already beginning to line up in the hallway and out into the street. I run back inside to the women's washroom and peer below the door in each stall. Nothing. I rush back out and run into the men's room and do the same thing.

"Kyle?" I call. My voice is shrill and high. My hands are shaking. I run to the other side of the dining room where there's a stage. On it, there's a microphone on a stand. A couple of men are standing behind it, talking. I speed toward the stage and run up the stairs.

"We have a lost boy!" I shout at the men. "Kyle. I was watching him for Flynn." My face burns. My heart is ready to explode right from my chest. I should have found someone to look after him while I went to the washroom. I didn't know kids could slip out and disappear so quickly, even when you told them not to.

One of the men nods and steps up to the microphone. "Attention, please. We have a lost little boy. Kyle Carson. He's five. Brown hair."

I glance around the room and see Flynn. The panic on his face as he runs toward the stage makes me want to pass out.

"Everyone in the building, please search the area around you," the man says over the mike.

"What the hell?" Flynn says to me when he reaches the foot of the stage. "Where the hell did he go?" He runs up the stairs and grabs a hold of my arm. Hard. "Where did he go?"

My heart freezes, yet somehow a hot tear drips down my cheek. I shake my head, my lips tight. I have no answer. What were we all thinking, leaving me in charge? I'm not cut out for caring for myself properly, never mind a child.

A buzz travels through the crowd outside the building as the guests discuss what's going on inside, and someone asks if lunch is going to be late. I close my eyes and try to breathe. We have to find him. I have to find him. There're bad people in this world. I know that for a fact.

"For God's sake," Flynn says to no one in particular. "Where the hell is he?"

I'm ready to throw up or run away myself. What can I do? I think of my dad's words. "You can't always hide away from your trouble," he says. Not even ironically, as if he doesn't notice that everyone in my family has gone into hiding.

Hiding.

I remember the story my mom used to tell. From when I was a kid. Hiding in closets. I run off the stage and hurry through the dining room and into the kitchen. I keep running and don't stop until I reach Stella's office. I pull open the first cupboard level with the ground. Nothing. I pull open the next. Nothing. I run to the closet and take a deep breath. And then I open that one.

chapter **seven**

Kyle's curled up in a ball on the floor. Sleeping.

The what-ifs I've been holding back rush into my brain, and I sink to my knees.

"Kyle?" I say. His eyes open and he smiles at me, his little face innocent and sweet.

"Are you crying, Jess?" he asks.

"Kyle Carson," a voice yells from behind me. Flynn races to the closet and stares down at the two of us on the ground. "You scared the living *shit* out of us," he says.

Kyle looks up at him with huge eyes. "Flynn, you *swore*," he says.

I can't stop. It's as if a dam has been opened in my head, and I can't shut it off. I sniffle and sit on the floor, crying like a big old baby. I'm not sure it's even about Kyle after a while.

Flynn kneels down beside me and puts a hand on my shoulder. "Hey," he says softly. "It's okay. He's okay."

I shake my head, but my face and my nose are running and gushing gross liquids all over the place. What if he hadn't been there? I feel like a complete and utter failure.

Flynn's hand stays on my shoulder. "It's okay," he mumbles, like I'm the little kid.

Kyle sits up and crawls into my lap and wraps his arms around me. It shocks the snot out of me.

"What were you doing, buddy?" I ask him and hiccup and sniffle.

"I was really tired, Jess." He yawns and puts his head on my shoulder. The warmth of his hug quiets all the noise that's warring inside of me, and I'm filled with a gooey kind of calm.

"Kyle," Flynn says, and Kyle lifts his head.

"You scared Jess. You shouldn't have hidden on her. You're not supposed to wander off. You scared us."

Kyle blinks at me. "You were scared?"

I nod. "Yeah. Really scared."

Stella walks toward us. I didn't even hear her come in. She kneels down beside us. "We were all scared. You have to be careful, Kyle. No hiding." She stands, walks to her desk, and leans against it, her arms crossed.

"Not even when we play hide-and-seek? I wanted to play hide-and-seek with Jess when she went to the bathroom. But I got tired of waiting, and I lay down and fell asleep."

"I'm sorry," I interrupt. "I didn't mean to leave him alone for long."

"No," Flynn snaps.

I cringe, waiting for him to berate me, tell me what I already know. I'm irresponsible and stupid. I've got a bad track record.

"It's not your fault." He stands up. "Not cool, little dude. You don't start a game of hide-and-seek without telling anyone. Especially not when you are being babysat."

"I'm not a baby," he says. Kyle wiggles his head back and forth.

"Then don't act like one," Flynn tells him.

He looks up at his big brother and blinks. "Am I in trouble?"

He's so friggin' adorable, but fear and attention get to Kyle, because he starts to cry too.

Flynn leans down and takes him from my lap and stands him on the floor. "Apologize to Jess," he says.

I shake my head, but Flynn glares at me, so I stop.

"I'm sorry, Miss Jess," Kyle says, his little lip jutting out and quivering.

I think before I say anything. "Um. It was a mistake. And we learn from those." I wipe under my eyes and sniffle, and Flynn holds out his free hand and helps pull me to my feet. He flicks his hair back, and I have a brief desire to spin around and flee, because even now with all this drama, I still can't help appreciating that he's stupid hot. And I don't know how I'm going to see him every day when he thinks I'm such an idiot. His lashes are longer than most girls who spend their money on Latisse.

He smiles at me though, and my insides freak the hell out.

"Sorry for being a dick," he says and glances at Stella. "I mean jerk. Kyle is my responsibility. I shouldn't have put that on you."

"No. I mean, you'd think I'd be able to keep track of a five-year-old for a little longer."

"It wasn't your fault," Flynn says. "Anyhow, you found him."

"I used to have naps in the closet when I was a kid," I tell him. I walk to the front of Stella's desk, plunk down in a chair, and let out a big sigh.

Flynn follows me to the other chair, and all at once, he's staring into my eyes. It feels like he's seeing things I don't even know are there.

There's this huge swoop. It starts in my belly, and my whole body goes on its own roller-coaster ride. It leaves me with goose bumps. I stare down at my shoes, wondering if he can tell what I'm feeling.

Stella clears her throat.

"Is Jess your new girlfriend?" Kyle asks. I look up, and he's standing beside Stella, watching us, his head barely visible over the top of the desk. He blinks at me. "He has a *lot* of girlfriends."

"Dude," Flynn says. "We've talked about that."

I can't help laughing out loud, and Kyle giggles. Even Stella laughs. "You want me to clean this handsome boy up?" she asks Flynn.

"Yeah. One second though. Come here, big guy." Kyle scoots around the desk, and Flynn bends down so he's at the same level as him. "No more running off?" Flynn says.

Kyle's eyes fill with tears, and his lower lip goes in and out. "I promise," he says. It's about the cutest thing I've ever seen.

"Okay, handsome." Stella gets up and walks to Kyle, holding out her hand. "You come with me and we'll clean you up, and then Flynn can take you to lunch." She glances at me. "Good job finding him."

I lower my eyes as they leave the room, because really, if I hadn't *lost* him in the first place, I wouldn't have had to find him.

Flynn stands. "Well, I guess you need to get back to work," he says. His voice is slightly deeper, and Nance would say it's sexy. Who am I kidding? I'm the one who thinks it's sexy. The big brother thing, it works for him.

"Yeah." I sneak a look up. He's watching me. Neither one of us moves.

"It must be kind of cool to have someone little who looks up to you like that," I say. "My sister and I, we're nothing like that." I don't know why I admit that.

"No? I don't know. Sometimes I worry I'm a bad influence." He coughs and looks away. "I look after him when my mom works." He glances back and smiles. "Your mom probably doesn't work. Or does she do charity work instead of a real job? I hear lots of the moms in Tuxedo are into that." He doesn't say it with meanness, but it makes my stomach lurch.

I stare at him. "You honestly believe that?" I ask.

He hesitates. "Well, I saw your house, remember. I mean, it's pretty huge. I guess I assumed she doesn't have to work." He eyes the door Stella walked out of.

I cross my arms. "Maybe she's the one with all the money."

He purses his lips but glances at me. "She is?"

"Well. No. I mean, she did work. She had a good job." I inhale deeply through my nose, trying to calm myself. "Some women like to work, you know. This isn't the sixties."

"No. I know. I didn't mean it like that. Sorry. I just mean, she has a choice, right? She doesn't have to. Anyhow, you know what they say, all the stay-at-home moms live in Tuxedo. Sorry. It was stupid. Forget it."

I glare at him. He doesn't know how far from the truth he is about my mom. "You think my mom has an easy life because of where we live?" I ask. Hot anger licks at my brain because that is so far from the truth.

"Hey, wait. I mean…well, kind of. I thought…" Flynn sputters and stares longingly at the exit.

"She worked," I say through clenched teeth. "No. She had a career. And she loved it. But she doesn't anymore…" I take a breath, stopping myself before everything spills out. I won't do that just to prove my point. I uncross my arms. "She can't work. She *doesn't* have a choice."

"Hey. I'm sorry," he says after a moment of silence. "I didn't know."

I wrap my arms around my waist. My face is hot. "Whatever." I untangle myself a second later. "I have to work." I stand up. I want out, away from him. He's a lot less hot now. I don't care how cute he is, he doesn't get to judge my family. It's none of his business.

He lightly grabs my arm to stop me as I try to slip by, but I pull away. He immediately lets go, but it tingles where his fingers pressed into my flesh. Treacherous arm. I frown at it.

"I really am sorry," he repeats. He clears his throat again as if he's viewed inside my head and sorted through my thoughts. "You're not at all what you seem, are you, Jess?"

"Depends." I bite my lip. "What do I seem?"

He tilts his head, watching me, and then he smiles. "Entitled, reckless, and maybe a little spoiled." He laughs at the look on my face. He holds his fingers up to show me an inch. "A little?"

He grins then, full-on, and I try to be mad. But it's hard.

"But you're also good with my brother and maybe a little softer than you seem. Wilf likes you. That counts for something." He bends his head, but the blush is visible on his cheeks. "I don't know what happened to you or why you're here. Maybe someday you'll tell me." He smiles again, and it's lopsided, but his whole demeanor shifts. He's good-looking, but when he smiles…my heartbeat pounds.

"Maybe not," I say, even though I'm about ready to tell him anything he wants to know.

"Is she sick?" he asks. "Your mom?"

I lower my gaze. Blink. Blink. Blink. No one asks. No one talks about my mom. "Kind of," I say softly.

He watches me, his head tilted, his eyes soft. "That's rough," he says.

I blink some more, resisting the urge to cry all over again. Two words. Nice ones, but I don't cry in front of people. Well, I usually don't. I smile to keep myself from blurting out the whole story. He seems like a good listener. But I can't. We. Don't. Talk. About. It.

"My mom works like a dog. My stepdad made sure of that. Such. A. Jerk. " He shifts from foot to foot and attempts another smile, but it doesn't last.

I recognize the anger in his eyes. He sees me recognize it, understand it, and then he looks away. "Anyways, who does that?" He takes a deep breath and slowly lets it out.

"I don't know," I say honestly. "I don't know." The walls of Stella's office feel like they're getting smaller. The air is harder to breathe.

"We moved to Tadita. To start over." Flynn flicks his hair back with his hand. "Too much information. Sorry. I don't usually go on about it."

"No," I say quickly, and without thinking, I reach out and touch his hand. The hand that moved back his hair. I want to touch his hair. I drop my hand to my side before I do anything stupid with it.

I could tell him the truth. Right here. Somehow, I know I can trust him. How it makes me feel. Terrible. Lonely. But it's so ingrained in me not to say anything, to pretend everything is fine, that I swallow the words. And say nothing.

Flynn clears his throat. "Well, I guess we're here for different reasons."

"I guess."

"For sure we're both sorry asses," he says and raises both eyebrows, joking around.

"You have no idea," I admit, "what a sorry ass I am."

His expression changes. Gets serious again. "I worried for you the other night. When Braxton drove you home. Wandering around by yourself like that. Getting in the car. We could have been anybody. Guys who weren't so nice."

"Sometimes I do stupid things," I admit. I bend my head, remembering some of my other stupid human tricks. "It's like I'm testing myself or something," I say softly.

I think about the stupid dress I ordered. How much it cost and what the people around here could do with all that money. I think about drinking with Nance and stealing a T-shirt from Abercrombie a while ago, just for the rush, just to see if I'd get caught. I'd almost wanted to. But I didn't. All the bad decisions. And that's only covering the last couple of weeks.

He presses his lips together and takes a step closer to me. "Be careful, Jess. Okay?"

I can barely breathe. I have an urge to confess that sometimes I don't even know who I am anymore. That sometimes I'm so caught up in pretending to be someone else that I don't feel anything at all. And that's why I test myself. To see if I'm still alive.

"I wish I had a little brother," I say instead of blurting out the rest.

"I'll share him," he says. "As long as you don't lose him again."

I cover my smile with my hand. "Deal," I say.

We're staring at each other again. As if we're really seeing each other. My stomach is a mess. Hormone alert. I focus my gaze on his bracelet.

"You're allergic to something?" I ask, pointing at it, the red symbol.

He covers it with his other hand. "Nope." He looks at me.

The air around him is sparkling and sizzling with an invisible energy. I wonder if he knows.

"It was my dad's," he says softly. "He gave it to me before he died." He hesitates. "I don't usually tell people that."

"I'm glad you told me," I whisper back. My whole body tingles and I wonder what the hell I'm doing. Am I flirting? In Stella's office? But no, it's not even flirting. Not really. I'm being honest. We're connecting. And I realize with a flush that I want to kiss him more than I've ever wanted to kiss any other boy. My cheeks light up. I have a knack for the inappropriate.

"Jess?" Sunny pops her head into the office and crosses her arms when she sees the two of us standing together. "We need you in the kitchen."

I take a step away from Flynn.

"Stella wants you to go get Kyle," she tells Flynn. "It's lunch-time in minutes. Jess, come on. You need to get your scrawny butt out there."

Sunny waits, a hard gleam in her eyes, until I'm walking, and then she spins and leads me to the kitchen, grabs a black-and-green striped apron hanging from a hook, and shoves it in my stomach. I put it on and tie it around my waist. "The stripes are the serv-er's aprons." She pushes me to the other side of the kitchen. "You have tables one to six. The family section. Get the salads to their tables first. We already sat your first group at the tables. Don't be late again."

I hurry toward the dining room and rush around to get orders out, and when I hurry back to the kitchen, Kyle and Flynn are walking toward me. I step one way and Flynn steps the same way, and we do the awkward dance of stepping to the same side and then back. He laughs and then holds out his hand. "Go ahead."

I smile at both of them, lower my eyes, and slip past as they take a seat in my section.

"Jess," Sunny calls to me as I'm grabbing bowls of soup. "Don't mess with the people here," she blurts out. "You are not near good enough for that boy."

And then she's gone. A shiver goes up my spine.

chapter **eight**

After my shift, Stella asks Wilf to walk me to the bus stop.

"It's still daytime," I tell her. "I'll be fine."

She insists. "Don't want your dad complaining to me later," she says. "Wilf doesn't mind."

Wilf waits for me at the door while I get my stuff from my locker. "You really don't have to walk me," I tell him. "God."

"You don't have to call me God, love," he says. "But something tells me you might need a little assistance figuring out which bus to take."

I roll my eyes as we walk together through the kitchen, not wanting to admit he's right. He's kind of fragile-looking, but he opens the front door and waits for me to walk through. There's a group of men sitting on the stairs out front. I try not to cringe at the smell and then recognize one of them and strain for his name. Martin. Same name as my dad. I have lots of tricks to remember people's names.

"Bye, Martin," I call nervously when he grins at me with half a mouthful of teeth.

"Thanks for the extra sandwich," he calls and bows deeply. "I feel like I went to heaven today. 'Cause you're a real angel."

The old guys with him groan and make jokes. I smile to show I'm perfectly calm. I don't want to acknowledge my conviction that I don't belong here. That I feel uncomfortable because I live in a different world. A better one.

"That was nice," Wilf says when we're out of earshot. It takes a while. He moves pretty slowly.

"What?" I ask, watching a younger man leaving the building. He's carrying a construction hat under his arm and has on steel-toed boots.

"Remembering his name."

I lift a shoulder. "I'm good with names. Hey. Does that guy work?" I ask.

"Lots of people who come to New Beginnings work," he tells me.

"So why are they here then?" I wondered the same thing about Flynn's mom.

"You've haven't seen much of this world, have you, kiddo?" he asks.

"I've seen enough," I snap.

He doesn't say anything, but his expression changes. I feel kind of bad, but he doesn't know me. He's making as many assumptions about me as he thinks I'm making about others.

"How come you volunteer?" I ask.

"Not because my dad makes me, that's for sure," he grumbles. And then he looks over at me. "If not us, then who?"

I think about that as we walk the rest of the way in silence, and when we reach the bus stop, he sits on the bench as soon as he reaches it.

"You shouldn't be walking me all the way here," I tell him. "You're tired."

He frowns at me. "You think I'm too old?"

"Well, let's say in your day, I think rainbows were in black and white."

He chuckles. "I admit I'm at the age where I pick my cereal for the fiber content, but you're still at the age where you pick your cereal for the toys."

"Funny," I tell him. "As in not funny at all."

"You have sass," he says. "And I think you use sarcasm to keep people from looking too deep. You remind me of someone I used to know. In spite of yourself, I've decided to like you."

I turn my head and pretend to be watching for a bus so he doesn't see that his comment pleases me. "How do you know I'm not just mean?" I ask.

"Because your remember people's names."

A bus is pulling toward us, and he tells me it's the right one. He gives me instructions on transferring to Tuxedo as the door opens. "You have change?" he asks.

"I'm a spoiled rich girl, remember?"

"We all have burdens to overcome," he says.

The door closes behind me, but I see him watching me from the bench, and he's smiling.

• • •

Over the next while, Flynn brings Kyle in for lunch almost every day. He usually drops in before the lunch service to help out, and Kyle hangs out with me while Flynn works. My new best friends are a five-year-boy and a grouchy seventy-five-year-old man, and Flynn, well, I'm still figuring out what he is to me. The days he doesn't show up, my shift goes by a lot slower.

The air between us is easier now, almost like friends. New friends but real. Not the fake, party kind of friends I've chosen to be around since Penny and I stopped hanging out. And not the easy friendship of a five-year-old boy or my love/hate relationship with Wilf.

I suspect I may have a crush on Flynn but try not to think about it too much. It's not only because he's super easy on the eyes, but because when we talk, and he asks questions, I feel like he listens to the answers. And sees who I am. And thinks that maybe I'm not that bad after all.

I'm getting to know the other volunteers at the shelter. Most of them are older than me, way older, but they mostly treat me like an equal, not a bratty kid, and they don't question my reasons for being there, so I don't mind. I hear bits and pieces about why they work there. "We all have sins to atone for," Stella told me one day when she was in a rare talkative mood. It's nice to know I'm not the only one.

I recognize most of the regulars now too. They're polite and gracious, and I begin to realize they're just regular people who are a little down on their luck. I keep my fears and silent judgments buried as deep as possible. As I see the guests trying to have some dignity in tough circumstances, it's easier to chat with them with respect. I can call almost all of them by name. It's a secret source of pride, since Wilf pointed out it meant something.

Wilf keeps walking me to the bus stop because I refuse to bring the Audi to work. Mostly I enjoy that taking the bus makes my dad nervous. But also, it's an Audi. That's begun to embarrass me a little. For a lot of different reasons.

Dad comes and goes, but he's mostly away. I've seen my mom and we exchange small talk, but she still spends most of her time in her room. Allie is like a ghost whose memory lingers in the house but who I never see anymore. She's either working or at "Dana's."

I actually start looking forward to work, because without a phone I have no social life, and no one even tries to get a hold of me. I use the computer in Dad's office to go online, and most of the time end up googling things like poverty. My eyes are open to a lot of things I didn't know about being poor. I always knew my family had money, but it always seemed like everyone else did too.

By the middle of my third week, I'm staying at work later and even sneak into the greenhouse before my shifts start up. One morning, Wilf surprises me when he comes up behind me.

"Hey, Chickadee," he says, and I drop the cloth I'm using to clean leaves on an ivy plant.

"You trying to kill me?" I ask as I bend to pick it up, and he smiles.

"If I were trying to kill you, you'd already be gone. I'm a retired lawyer, remember? We have ways of making things happen." He doesn't crack a smile, but it's his teasing voice.

I roll my eyes at him.

"You keep rolling those, they're going to roll right out of your head."

I laugh out loud.

"Listen, I can't walk you to the bus today. But I asked Flynn to do it for me. That's not going to be a problem, is it?"

There's a fluttering in my stomach, and then a rush of adrenaline shoots through me. My flight response? Am I afraid of Flynn? I shake my head. Of course not.

"I didn't think so." Wilf walks toward the shelf where he keeps his gardening tools and starts whistling Johnny Cash's "Ring of Fire," which I recognize, thank you very much, but choose not to believe is aimed at me and my crush that Wilf seems to notice.

I'm nervous all through the lunch service and make Wilf serve Flynn and Kyle. While trying not to notice them, I spill most of a bowl of soup on Martha, an old regular who always wears layers and layers of clothes despite the summer weather. Her trench coat is wet, but she pulls it off and pats my arm and tells me not to worry. "You remind me so much of my daughter," she says, like she says every time I talk to her. I wonder where her daughter is and why she's alone on the streets now.

Finally lunch is over and I'm cleaned up, and Flynn slides up to me after I come out of the staff room.

"I left Kyle with Stella so I could take you myself," he says. My stomach swoops with happiness, and in my head I give myself a talking to. It doesn't mean anything. Does it?

I'm quiet as we walk out of the building and trek toward the bus stop.

"What's wrong?" he asks as we stroll. "You're quiet today. Is everything okay?" The air between our arms dangling at our sides seems charged, but I'm pretty sure it's only on my part. I wish there was an easy way to tell if a guy likes you just as a friend or as more.

I tell him about Martha, which is still bothering me, but not as much as worrying about what to say to him. He tilts his head, watching me. "It was an accident, right?"

I nod. "Yeah. But I mean, I spilled on her coat. And she can't get it dry-cleaned or even take it to a Laundromat or anything. I feel so bad."

A bus whizzes by, but I glance up and it's not the Tuxedo bus.

"Don't worry about it, Jess. I mean, she likes you. I've watched her with you. She lights up when you make a point of going to talk to her. People who live like us"—he points to himself—"we don't get as attached to material things. Especially when they're coming from donations."

"You don't live like Martha," I'm quick to say. Defending him.

He stares at me as we walk. "Well, I may not live on the street. But we have a lot in common."

I like Martha. I'm not trying to insult her. But still. "No," I blurt out. "You're different." We reach the bus stop. "You won't need New Beginnings forever." And then I duck my head, not wanting to insult the people who will. "What I mean is, what you have doesn't matter. I mean, it matters. But it's not who you are, not what you have. You're more."

He stops beside me. My words hang in the air. Have I stuck my big fat foot right in my mouth? Something tickles my hand, and I glance down. He's squeezing my hand and staring into my eyes.

I stop breathing and stare back. I hope the bus is late so I can stay with him longer. He grins. "I like you for who you are, not what you have too," he says softly and laughs. "Maybe you convinced me not to judge a book by its cover." He lets my hand go, and I try not to whimper.

"You don't like my cover?" I ask, trying to keep my voice light. But it sounds husky in my ears, husky and slightly desperate.

"I don't have to tell you you're beautiful," he says.

You don't? I think. *Yes, yes, you do.*

"Because you are. But you're good people too, Jess. Even if you don't know it yet. I can be completely honest with you. I can be myself. And I really like that. I don't have that with many people."

It's nice, to be seen with fresh eyes that don't have all sorts of preconceived notions about me. In some ways, I feel like he's looking inside. At the real me. And amazingly, he seems to think I'm okay.

I almost cry when a bus rumbles up behind us. I want him to stay and talk and listen, but I turn and of course, it's the Tuxedo bus. It takes me away from his world and back into my own.

chapter **nine**

The house is quiet when I get home. I'm floating on air, still reliving every second and every word I exchanged with Flynn. I slide off my shoes and walk through the living room, noticing everything's neat and tidy now, the way Dad likes it. I left the place in kind of a mess this morning, so it's a good thing.

Thank God for Isabella. Mom hired her for once-a-week clean-ups a few years back, when she started doing well in real estate. Then Dad asked her to come in every other day when Mom started spending so much time resting.

I'm dying to talk to someone even if I can't talk about Flynn. I walk to the kitchen, grab the house phone, and dial Nance's number. It goes straight to voice mail. I hang up without leaving a message, because I've already left dozens she hasn't bothered to return.

I head upstairs and stop outside Mom's bedroom, listening at the door and opening it as quietly as possible. She's lying on her side in bed, her face covered by blankets, so I close the door quietly. There's a sound behind me, and someone touches my shoulder. I jump and bump into a framed picture on the wall.

"Looks like Mom's having a bad day," Allie says quietly. She's behind me, her backpack over her shoulder.

I straighten out the picture. Ironically it's one of me and her when we were about three and five years old. We have on matching pink jeans and long-sleeved T-shirts. Hers says "big sister" and mine says "li'l sister." She's smiling at the camera, but I'm staring up at her with total awe and love.

"I didn't know you still lived here," I say.

Between work and her boyfriend, she might as well not. I hate her a little for being able to escape. I walk quickly toward my bedroom, but Allie follows me.

"You smell like Caesar salad," she tells me. "And garlic."

"Because I served lasagna and Caesar salad for lunch." I wonder if Flynn thought I smelled funny too. My hand tingles where he held it. I have an urge to tell Allie about Flynn.

"Dad's really making you work at that place all summer?" She scrunches up her nose, and I press my lips tight.

"Yup."

When I open my bedroom door, she follows me as far as the entrance and stops. Allie glances around at the heaps of clothes lying on the floor and makes another face. She doesn't say anything about it, even though Allie hates mess. She's like Dad that way.

"Pretty harsh."

"It's not so bad."

"Really?" She ponders that. "What'd you do to piss him off so badly? He didn't tell me. I'm guessing it must have involved Nance."

Allie and Nance have never gotten along, so her assumption doesn't surprise me. I shrug again and flop down on my bed. "He took my cell phone for the whole summer," I tell her instead of admitting what I did.

"Whoa," she says. "You must have *really* pissed him off."

I roll to my side and sit up. "I've never been the perfect child in the family." I look knowingly at her.

"Trust me, Jess, neither am I. I'm just better at not getting caught when I do things." She pushes off the doorframe she's leaning on. "Anyway, I'm staying at Dana's tonight. I'll see you later."

"You mean Doug's?"

She stops and turns back, narrowing her eyes. "No. I mean Dana's."

"Whatever." I flop on my back. "It's not like I care, but I'm not stupid. Everyone knows you've practically moved into Doug's house." The only people who don't know, or who pretend not to know, are our parents. "Has his mom kind of adopted you, or is she grooming you for future daughter-in-law status?" I glance over, and her hands are on her hips and she's glaring at me.

"Shut up, Jess," she says. She looks behind her, as if Mom might be listening. Fat chance.

I shrug again. "I'm not going to say anything. But just so you know, it's not a big secret." I pick at a loose string on my comforter. It's getting raggedy and it's juvenile. It needs to be replaced.

"God knows this family loves secrets." She stares at me, her eyes narrowed. "I sleep in the spare room." Her face is all tight.

"Whatever."

"No. I really do. His mom isn't that cool."

"Yeah. I can imagine." I don't really blame Allie for staying away, but I miss her.

She sighs. Her shoulders fold in. She looks tired. The same way I feel. "You sure you're doing okay?" she asks softly. "I mean, working there is okay?"

I hesitate. I have an urge to tell her about Flynn. Ask her advice. I want to ask if my crush is inappropriate. But what if she says it is? What if she disapproves? Her boyfriend lives in the right neighborhood and goes to Washington University. He wants to be a doctor. Dad loves telling his work friends about Doug. The only kind of friends he has. Work friends.

"I'm fine." My words are tainted with bitterness.

"Okay. Stay out of trouble." Allie is already disappearing.

I stare at the back of her head as she leaves and swallow a sudden lump. I hear her feet stomp as she goes down the stairs. A moment later, there's a muffled voice calling my name.

Mom?

She's awake.

I want to pull the covers over my head but get up and walk down the hallway to her room, take a deep breath, and open the door. "Hey," I say. "You okay?"

She's sitting up on the edge of the bed, her feet on the floor. "Jess?" She smiles softly when she sees me. "I'm glad you're home." The smile doesn't reach her eyes. It never reaches her eyes. "I was having a rest. But I'm up. Your dad's gone to Houston. What about Allie?"

"She's gone to Dana's," I tell her.

She pushes herself up. "I'm hungry. Want to get something to eat?"

I don't. I want to go to my room and listen to music on my head-phones and think about Flynn.

"Sure," I tell her.

"How about some soup?"

"Sure." I follow her as she slowly makes her way downstairs to the kitchen.

• • •

Mom stands in front of the stove, stirring the can of soup. I lean against the counter, watching her.

"I miss the fresh soup we used to make with vegetables and herbs from the garden," she says.

I turn and open the cupboard and take out a couple of bowls. I'm not sure if she's blaming me or herself for that. We had a great garden once. When I was a kid, we searched and searched "for Jess's thing." She assured me we would find it. We tried dance and piano lessons. We signed up for Judo. When I was about eleven, she encouraged me to grow some things in her garden to enter into the Lavender Festival. I took it way too seriously and spent the spring testing soil types and googling plants. Later that year, I grew my first herbs. My thing turned out to be a green thumb. Not anymore. When she gave it up, so did I.

But then I imagine Wilf's greenhouse and hide a smile. Maybe it's growing back.

I grab a couple of spoons and then put the dishes on the table and sit down, watching her. Her hair is in a ponytail, and she looks pretty even without makeup, but her glow has dimmed. Compared to Nance's mom, she's starting to look weathered. Of course, Nance's mom has regular appointments with filler needles.

"So how's it going at New Beginnings?" she asks as she stirs the pot.

"Fine," I tell her. "I'm actually starting to like it, but don't tell Dad or he might make me quit. He hates to see me happy."

She shakes her head. "That's not true"

How do you know? I'm tempted to ask.

She sighs. "Maybe working at New Beginnings is a good thing. I mean, your dad has good intentions. He wanted you to realize how much we have."

"Yeah," I say, thinking of Flynn.

"You feel safe there, on your own?"

I glance up quickly.

"I mean, the people are...okay?" she asks.

"Most are really nice actually."

"Yeah?"

"Yeah. Some of them are going through a hard time." I pick up my spoon and study it as if it holds answer. "Some have addictions, but the staff is strict. People who are drunk or high can't come in. They have to go to another shelter in town. Anyhow, I usually get the family tables."

"Kids?" she asks.

"Yup." I think of Kyle and his trains.

"That's sad."

"Yeah. Some of them have jobs, you know. Parents. Single people too. And they still can't make enough to cover food." I think of

Flynn again. "I've been doing research on poverty. It's crazy how many Americans live in poverty."

"Bring the bowls over here," she says. I pick them up and walk to the stove. She has a thoughtful expression on her face. "For sure, not everyone is as lucky as we are." She must see my surprise, because she actually laughs. "I mean, not everyone has money and everything they need. We have so much more than enough." She ladles soup into each bowl. "Things would be worse if we didn't have your dad and his security."

I don't say anything but take the bowls to the table.

She follows me. "I could be there. On the streets. If it wasn't for your dad." She sits, and I put a bowl in front of her and frown.

"Mom, that's not remotely possible."

"No, really. I'm a mess. Not working. Not coping. I've been thinking about it lately. The people you're working with. I should be ashamed of myself for my behavior. When other people have to deal with so much more. If it were just me, well, I might be there too."

I push my bowl away, my appetite gone. "It's not just you," I tell her softly. "And you have a lot to deal with."

"Yeah, well, probably no worse than some of those people you're helping," she says.

I tug on my earring, turning it around and around with my fingers, trying to think of the right thing to say. Or at least not the wrong thing.

She eats her soup in silence and, after a few bites, pushes her own bowl away.

"You want to go for a walk, Mom?" I say. "Around the block? Get out, get some fresh air?"

She stares at me, her lips pressed tight, then slowly, she nods her head.

I hold my breath. This small thing. It's big. I can't remember the last time she's gone outside the house without Dad at her side.

"Really? I mean, great!" I try to act natural, not overreact. I wish Allie were still here so she could help me deal.

"You don't mind if I go like this?" She points down to at her yoga pants. They kind of hang on her, but they're clean. She's wearing a "Life is Good" T-shirt. It's old.

"Not if you don't mind if I go like this." I'm still in my work clothes that apparently smell like Caesar salad and garlic. I wouldn't mind putting on something else, but I don't want to risk her changing her mind.

"You look perfect." She stands and reaches for my hand. "Leave the mess. We'll clean it up when we get back."

She pulls me up from my seat and squeezes my hand. Hers is smaller than mine. Fragile. She lets go, and we walk to the hall closet. She pulls out sneakers, and I slip on my shoes.

When we walk into cool evening air, we both see the little girl next door sitting on her driveway. She glances up and smiles. I walk over and Mom follows me.

"Hello, Carly," Mom says. I'm surprised she knows the little girl's name. Her family only moved in about a year and a half ago.

"Hey! How are you?" I ask. Carly's drawing a lopsided hopscotch game with blue chalk.

"Good." She glances at my mom with suspicion and doesn't say anything but looks back at me. "It works," she whispers loudly.

I bend down to her level. "Brave Monkey?" I whisper back.

She nods.

"I told you so," I say. And then I wink at her. "I'm glad."

"I get to see my dad tomorrow," she tells me.

I nod and stand. "That's awesome."

We leave her and walk down the driveway to the street.

"How's Carol?" Mom asks. A safe topic.

Aging backward? In appearance and maturity level. The best I can do is shrug. *She's gone too*, I want to say. "She's okay. I haven't seen her for a couple of weeks."

"Yeah. What happened?" she asks. "I know about the dress, but there's more."

I lower my eyes. "I'm sorry about that. We returned it. I had to pay the shipping costs."

"I know," she says without a lecture. She's letting me off the hook a lot easier than she should. "What happened at Nance's? Your dad was furious, but he wouldn't say why."

I glance at her. Should I lie? To protect her? I'm tired of pretending, sinking under the pretenses. A good dose of the truth might not be bad for either of us. "Nance and I were drinking. And we got caught…um, sunbathing topless. On her deck. She always FaceTimes boys. Topless," I admit. To punish her? I'm not sure.

I hold my breath, pretending to find the house we're passing interesting. It looks like all the others though, oversized and overly manicured and kind of empty.

She doesn't say anything, and I'm afraid I've given her too much too soon, but then she puts her hand over her mouth, and I realize she's laughing. I stop walking, and she has to swallow and take a deep breath. "It's not funny. Not really. It's just that I saw that coming since Nance was little. She was always taking off her clothes at inappropriate times. She'd go to the coatroom at day care and strip down."

I smile, remembering, and she smiles back.

"Of course, back then you didn't join her," she adds and wipes off her grin. "And you really shouldn't be drinking." It freaks me out a little. This is not the mom I've been around lately. She looks straight in my eyes, so I lower my gaze to the sidewalk.

"That's not like you, Jess," she says.

The thing is, she doesn't know what I'm like anymore. My insides ache, remembering how we used to have open conversations about everything. She used to err on the side of too much information. She made me squirm, talking openly about sex and drugs and alcohol. But things changed.

"Carol must have had a fit," Mom finally says.

"She has a new boyfriend." My way of evading that question.

She frowns. "Nance has gone through some hard times," she says. "With the divorce. She went through some hard times when she was younger. Marking up her arms." She shakes her head.

Nance doesn't talk about it, but she doesn't hide the marks. Instead, she pretends they mean nothing and she has everything together. Of course, I do too. Then I remember Nance trying to open up a little and the way I evaded her. Maybe she's more upset than she lets on. Maybe that has something to do with why she's avoiding my calls. Maybe she's mad. For sure, it's the reason she likes vodka coolers. It's an easy way to forget her parents have checked out of her life too.

I'm surprised my heart aches for Nance, and I acknowledge that maybe I haven't been a very good friend to her. I haven't tried to listen. She has feelings too, and I should ask more questions. We should talk about things.

But she's not even calling me back.

"What happened with you and Penny?" Mom asks softly.

I inhale quickly. "Penny? I guess we grew apart." It's not the right time to talk about it. I don't want to push too far. Things are still wobbly.

"It's too bad," Mom finally says. "She was a good friend. I miss my friends sometimes. I don't see them anymore."

I struggle to find something to say. We walk in silence. A row of apple trees stretches above the meridian almost like they're leaning over, waiting to hear more. A huge flock of birds flies out of a tree when we walk past. I watch them scatter, scrambling to find their place in the group.

"Your dad thinks everyone should be able to change things by sheer willpower. I used to think the same thing. But I can't seem to pull myself out of this."

I open my mouth, but she keeps going.

"He wants me fixed. Your dad. It's frustrating for him. I should be better by now."

I bite my bottom lip. I don't know what to say to make things better. "No," I say softly. "There's no timetable. You're doing okay."

She laughs. "Not so great, actually." She waves a hand in front of herself. "Look at me."

I stop and take a deep breath, studying her face, remembering how many colors it was when she was in the hospital. Purple swollen-shut slits for eyes. Bright red puffer-fish lips. Green and yellow bruises.

"I hate what happened to you," I tell her and then feel terrible. "I'm sorry. I don't mean to bring up bad memories." Dad would kill me for saying this. I'm not supposed to say anything.

"It's okay. We tiptoe around what happened so much. Like if we don't talk about it, it will go away. It can't be healthy." She tries to pass it off as a light comment, but then she closes her eyes and stops walking. She wraps her arms around herself as if she's suddenly cold.

I reach for her hand and squeeze it. She'd been the strongest person I knew. Eating challenges for breakfast. Then she was lying in the hospital bed. Tiny. Breakable. She had a concussion. They had to keep her jaw shut so it could heal. She stayed in the hospital for weeks. When she came home, she seemed to have shrunk. Gotten smaller. Even after the scars were gone, the damage didn't disappear. She changed. Of course she did. It makes me sick and afraid, scared to imagine anyone hitting me so hard that my skin bruised. Never mind three men hitting me over and over and over.

I wonder what she was thinking while the attack was happening. If she thought she was going to die. If she wanted to. To make it stop.

She breathes out deeply.

"I'm sorry," I tell her.

"I know. Me too." She lets my hand go. There's so much I want to ask her. What does she think about when she's locked away in her room? Do the drugs the doctors gave her make her forget? Does she take a little bit too much on purpose so they'll knock her out like that?

Her whole body deflates as if someone let the air out of her. "I should get home," she says.

I hold in new tears and watch as the birds return to their tree. A dog barks as we walk by Dayton Denton's house. Penny, Allie, and I used to play with him when were little. His black Scottish terrier is lying at the end of the lawn. I remember bringing him treats so we could hide on their lawn during hide-and-seek without him giving us away.

"I'm sorry," she says, watching the little dog bark at us. "That you don't have Penny anymore."

I nod. I suppose we're both sorry about lots of things.

chapter **ten**

Mom is in bed when I'm ready to go to work the next day, and I check in on her before I go. I stand at the door, my heart swelling, hoping I didn't push too hard. I hate whoever did this to her. I hate that they've never been caught. I'd like to make them pay. I imagine it must be how my dad feels. All the time. Sympathy for him surprises me. I tiptoe over to her side, kiss her on the forehead, tell her good-bye, and leave.

At work, I watch the clock, waiting for Flynn to come in, but soon lunch is over and it's another no-show day. I'm bummed and take my anger out on the tables I'm wiping down, scrubbing as hard as I can.

"Did you hear the joke about the roof?"

I glance up from the table. Wilf stands in front of me.

"What?"

"Never mind," he continues. "It's over your head."

I stand straight as I get the joke.

"Eyes rolling," I tell him. "Mine."

He grins. "They'll fall out. I warned you." He glances around the dining room. It's cleaned up, and the volunteer who took his place during the lunch service has gone somewhere else.

"Did you miss me today?" he asks.

"You look tired," I say instead of *yes*, because it's true. He does look tired. I throw my cloth toward a bucket of sudsy water at the work station beside me and miss it.

"Yeah? Well, you throw like a girl," Wilf says.

"Tell that to Anne Donovan."

"Who?"

With hands on my hips, I glare at him. "Only the best former female basketball player and U.S. Olympic coach."

He shrugs. "I only pay attention to hockey and football."

"That explains a lot," I tell him and then smile. "I only know her name because my sister played basketball all through high school." I walk over to the wash cloth, pick it up from the floor, and drop it in the soapy bucket. "I'm not a big sports fan."

"I will forgive you," Wilf says. "But admit it, you missed me today."

"I'm ashamed," I tell him. "I may have. You've crawled under my skin. Like a tick."

His grin is contagious. My bad mood fades.

"I'm not nearly as irritating as a tick. Compare me to something nicer next time." He spins on his heels and starts to walk away. Then he glances at me over his shoulder. "You coming to the green-house or not?"

I catch up to him, and we walk through the kitchen together. "Where were you?" I ask.

"Damn doctor's appointment. Doctor was running behind. Over an hour." He shakes his head. "And of course I'm tired. There's a reason old men get grouchy and not being able to sleep is one of them."

"I heard there's Viagra for the other reason," I tell him.

Sunny is putting away dishes, and she shakes her head as we walk by.

Wilf nods at her and turns to me with a scowl. "Disrespectful. That's what you are." He glares at me. "Aren't you about thirteen? You talk like a trucker."

"Seventeen," I say. Thirteen. Funny. Not. He holds the door outside open for me.

"Young enough not to talk to your elders like that." He doesn't crack a smile, but I'm learning when he's grouchy for show or grouchy for real. So far so good.

"It's okay to like the ladies," I tell him. "You're still kind of handsome, for an old guy. You've got some hair. And great glasses. A catch."

"You never met my Rhea," he says. "Or else you wouldn't even suggest that."

We walk outside, and I close my mouth. Now he's serious. "Sorry. Teasing. I would have loved to have known her." I reach out and touch his hand. The skin on his wrist is thin and spotted. "I didn't mean to offend you."

"Humph," he says as we walk toward the greenhouse. He clears his throat and side glances, as if deciding whether to forgive me or not. "I brought in some new azaleas of Rhea's. I put them inside the greenhouse yesterday. I want to see what you think. Maybe you can clean them up a little. You're good at that."

"I'd love to," I tell him and realize it's true. Besides, over the last while, I've learned he's not a natural gardener. He admitted he does it because it makes him feel closer to Rhea.

When we get inside the greenhouse, Wilf walks slowly down the middle row. His back is stooped. I wonder what he was like when he was young. It's hard to imagine him young.

"Here. These ones." He points out the plants he wants me to look at. I walk closer and lean in and see a little bit of azalea gall. The leaves are curled and pale. I listen while Wilf tells me a story about Rhea and the azaleas while I inspect the leaves. Some have to come off. I start pulling and check the soil for moistness.

"You need to go easier on the watering for these," I tell him. "They need to dry out a bit." His azaleas would do better outdoors, but I don't tell him that, understanding why he'd want them in the greenhouse.

While I'm working on the plants, Wilf gets out a spray bottle from the supply cupboard and squirts a nearby plant. I take a better look at him. He seems a little paler than normal, a bit under the weather.

"You feeling okay?"

"Fine," he grumbles, leaving no room for chitchat about that. He sprays another plant with gusto.

We work in silence, but a seed of worry has sprouted in my belly. "Do you have any kids?" I ask. It's more personal than I usually ask, but as his self-designated new best friend, I decide it's okay that we learn more about each other.

"We never had children," he tells me. "We wanted to, but it wasn't in the plans." He shrugs and sprays another leaf.

"I don't think I want to have kids," I tell him, thinking of my mom and dad.

"You're too young to decide that now," he tells me. "And far too young to have them now."

I wrinkle up my nose and check under another leaf for mold. "Um, yes."

No mold. At least that's a good sign. "I never got to have grandparents. I mean, I guess I did, but they both died before I was born."

"I'm old enough for the job," he says.

"Yeah?" I ask. "You want to be my adopted grandfather?" I smile at him. "I'll expect butterscotch candies in your pockets."

"Okay, but I expect homemade cookies. And don't hit me up for a loan when your parents won't give you your allowance."

"I don't get an allowance," I tell him. I do get more than enough money for my needs, and my mom gives me her credit card whenever I want to. Or she used to.

"Maybe you should do more chores."

"Probably." Truthfully, Mom's never really expected Allie or I to do much around the house. In the past, she liked to be in control of things. She could barely let us load the dishwasher without rearranging the entire thing. She doesn't do that anymore. But that's what I grew up with. And now we have Isabella, our cleaner.

"Shoot," Wilf suddenly growls. I'm so startled, I drop the pruning scissors.

"What?" I ask, frowning at him.

"I was supposed to pick up day-old bagels from the bakery

downtown." He slaps his head with his palm. "My memory and a quarter won't even get me a phone call these days."

"We don't need quarters anymore," I remind him. "We have cell phones." I bend over to pick up the scissors. "Well, most people do. Mine was confiscated."

"For your bad behavior?"

I shrug. I haven't told him what I did to get here.

"I would be lost without my iPhone," he tells me. "I program in all the things Rhea used to remind me to do."

I smile. "You know, you're a little bit cool for an old guy."

"Old is an understatement. When I told my doctor I wanted to stop aging, you know what he told me?"

"What?"

"That I'll stop when I'm in my grave." He laughs.

"That's awful." I wrinkle up my nose.

"Awfully true."

I don't find it funny. "Want me to help you get the bagels?" I ask instead.

"No. There're only a few bags today. You stay here. Work on these plants. You're better at it than me."

I smile at him. "Thanks."

"Can you stay awhile?" he asks. "I don't want you to walk to the bus stop yourself."

"My dance card is empty," I tell him, hoping he doesn't tease me about Flynn. "I can handle walking alone now. But if you want, I'll be here when you get back."

He walks to me, touches my arm lightly, and puts down his spray bottle. "Rhea would have liked you," he says softly, and then he turns toward the door. He glances back over his shoulder as he starts to walk out. "She may have washed your mouth out with soap a few times, but she would have liked you."

I smile, watching him hobble off. "Program your iPhone so you don't forget to come back," I yell.

"I'll lock the doors behind me." He lifts his hand in the air and then disappears.

I take a deep breath when he closes the door quietly behind him, the moist air and floral scents lifting my energy. I finish up Rhea's azaleas and then reach in the cupboards above the sink and take out new gardening tools. Walking up the aisle, I stroke leaves and check soil. The next plant I need to attack is a croton. I tsk at the dust buildup and wipe it off with a towel, so it'll be better able to photosynthesize.

"A clean plant is a happy plant," I tell it.

I do my rounds, and I'm about to put my tools away when I spot an ivy I've never noticed before, tucked away in a corner. It's looks like a newer plant, but it's wilted and close to dying. I clip and wash the leaves, chattering to it the whole time. "Come on, little guy. Give it your all. You can do it," I tell it.

"You talk to plants?"

I jump and look behind me. Flynn is only a few feet away. His dark eyes watch me, sparkling with amusement. My heart pitter-patters, noticing how he wears the shit out of his jeans and a plain black T-shirt.

"I didn't hear you come in." Now that his presence is known, it overtakes the room.

He walks closer, and I inhale deeply to try and get my thumping heart under control.

"You were giving that plant shit." He walks up beside me and reaches out to touch the plant.

"No, I was giving the plant encouragement," I tell him. "Big difference." My skin tingles, and everything in the greenhouse seems more alive and brighter. I clip another leaf, smile at it, and start gathering the tools to put them back in the cupboard.

"How'd you get in here?" I ask, knowing Wilf locked the door.

Flynn dangles a key off his finger and lifts it to show me. "Stella keeps an extra key in her office. Wilf lets me come here alone sometimes. I like the air." He glances at me. "Weird?"

"Not weird. Green thumb." I hold my thumb up in the air and examine it. "At least it used to be."

"Wilf told me." He looks at the miniature hoe I'm holding. "You're pretty handy with a hoe?" Flynn asks.

"Kyle said you were too." I place my hand over my mouth and giggle at my own joke.

"Very funny." He pushes back his bangs. "I really hope Kyle has no idea what a ho is." Flynn helps me carry a few things back to the cupboard.

I smile. "Doubtful. Not yet." I stand on my tiptoes to place tools back in the cupboard. "I didn't see you at lunch today."

"You noticed?"

My cheeks warm. He obviously doesn't know my entire shift revolves around whether he shows up or not.

"My mom was off work today, so we ate at home."

"Cool," I say.

"I came by to do something for Stella, but she didn't need me. She told me you were back here. I wanted to say hi before I left."

I nod, thrilled he thought about me and wanted to check in.

He nods. "So. Hi."

"Hi." I smile and tuck the last tool in the cupboard, press my lips tight, and shut the doors. I have no idea what to say next. The silence gets louder, and I search for something that doesn't sound stupid. "I'm glad you came."

He tilts his head. The hair on my arms stands at attention. "Do I make you nervous?" he asks. And then he grins. Slowly.

"No," I lie, barely able to breathe.

"I don't know about that," he says. It sounds like a challenge.

"About what?" I can't focus. I don't know where to look or what to do with my hands.

"I make you nervous," he says. His voice is low, almost a whisper.

My cheeks burn and I stare at him, mesmerized. He licks his bottom lip. The air between us sparks.

My face gets hotter. I remember what Mom used to say about Dad before she retreated into her shell. *We don't always choose the ones we fall for. Sometimes the chemistry chooses us.*

Is that what this is? Chemistry? Because it feels wonderful. And also scares the shit out of me. It's more real than anything I've felt lately. And dangerous. I like it.

He steps closer. "My mom and Kyle are waiting. I have to go." He says it softly, and we stare at each other. "Remember my friend, Braxton?" he asks out of the blue.

"Yeah. Of course."

"You into him?"

I shake my head. "No."

He smiles. "Good, 'cause he's trying to find you. I haven't told him I've got you hidden away. See you." With a wave, he walks out of the greenhouse.

A few minutes later, Wilf returns. I'm still standing in one spot, not moving, reliving the entire conversation over and over in my head.

"What's the matter with you?" Wilf asks as he walks over to inspect the azaleas. "You look like the bird that got the worm." He touches the plant and then looks at me and coughs into his long-sleeved shirt. "These look much better. Thanks."

"You feeling okay, Wilf?" I ask and snap out of my spell.

"I'm not about to keel over, if that's what you're asking." His tone is gruff. "What about you?"

"Me? I'm fine. And you're too cranky to keel over." I grab a water spray bottle and mist him.

He wipes the water away and stares at me with a sour expression, but it quickly disappears into a grin. "Cheeky," he says. "You're cheeky. My Rhea was cheeky too." He pauses. "Your googly eyes have anything to do with Flynn?"

I don't answer him but instead overspray a nearby pot of flowers.

"Jess?"

Something in his voice makes me stop and look at him.

"Will you look after Rhea's azaleas? When I'm gone?" He coughs, and outside the greenhouse, a gust of wind rattles the cover.

I stop spraying. "You planning on going somewhere, Wilf?" I ask quietly. The cough concerns me.

"We're all going somewhere, Chickadee," he says.

It's quiet between us, and I walk over to the plant he's pretending to inspect. "I will look after Rhea's azaleas," I promise him.

He nods, and then his eyes twinkle as he looks at something behind me. "I see I'm not the only one with a crush on the new girl," he says.

I turn to look. Flynn is back. He's standing right behind me.

"I, uh…" Flynn glances at Wilf and then back at me. "My mom decided to take Kyle to the park and doesn't need me. I'm not doing anything, so I thought I'd come back and see when you're done here, if you could…hang out?"

"Is that really the proper way to ask young ladies for dates these days?" Wilf grumbles.

I shoot him a look meant to silence him.

Flynn smiles though, and then he winks at me and bows at the waist. "Pardon me, madam. Would you care to join me at a waltz convention? Or shall I ask your father's permission first?" He uses a fake accent that is nothing like English.

I snort. Wilf rolls his eyes. "Very funny. That's not even close."

"You have any suggestions?"

Wilf reaches into his pants pocket and takes out a money clip. He pulls off a twenty-dollar bill and walks forward to hand it to Flynn. But Flynn puts both hands up in the air and steps away from it.

"For God's sake, take the money and the girl for an ice cream,"

Wilf says. "There's a parlor a couple of streets over. You can walk from here."

"I'm not taking your money, Wilf," Flynn says.

"It's not a crime, kid," he says. "I couldn't afford to take my Rhea anywhere when I started courting her. You've been working your butt off in this place. Take the money and take the girl. You're doing me a favor. She's always in my hair."

I giggle. They both look at me. "You said courting," I point out. "You have to admit, that's kind of funny."

"Go on," Wilf says. "See what I mean? She's cheeky. You really are doing me a favor. I need some peace and quiet already." He takes Flynn's hand and puts the money in it. "Ice cream," he says. "Go."

"So then you're paying him to get me out of your hair?" I ask Wilf.

He shrugs and turns his back on us. "Pretty much. Go on, you two. Git."

I shake my head at Flynn but smile. "Thanks, Wilf. I like ice cream."

"Everyone likes ice cream," he mumbles.

"Thanks." Flynn's cheeks are red, but he seems to know better than to try and give the money back. He holds out his hand. "After you."

"Wow," I say to Flynn when we're outside the greenhouse. "He just bribed you to make me go away."

Flynn smiles. "You know he's half in love with you. How come all the guys I know are half in love with you?"

I laugh. "I'm the granddaughter Wilf never wanted."

"What about my brother? Or Braxton."

I giggle like a lunatic, enjoying the attention, and wish we could slip out the side exit instead of going back to the New Beginnings building. I haven't signed out from my shift though, and it's not worth a tongue-lashing from Stella. Besides that, I have to grab my purse.

I check out while Flynn waits and swing my purse over my shoulder as we walk out the front of the building.

"Hey, Jess," a man calls. I glance over. It's John. He likes dessert, and I always make sure he gets the biggest slices.

"Hey, Chickadee," another man calls. Ian. He likes to talk and can barely sit still long enough to eat a meal. He gives me a thumbs-up.

"The ice cream place is this way," Flynn says. He's taller than me, and it makes me feel small and safe, walking beside him. We pass old brick buildings that look like offices.

"Wilf only pretends to be cranky," I say. "Inside, he's a marshmallow."

"I know. He's been at this place the whole time we've been coming," Flynn says. "I like him a lot."

We're both quiet. The shelter hangs between us.

"My granddad was like him," Flynn says. "Cranky on the outside. But he was pretty awesome to me. So is Wilf."

"You have any other grandparents?" I ask.

"No. My mom's parents were in China. I never met them. Only my dad's dad. He used to come and visit me. After my dad died. And then not so long after, he died too." He shrugs. "What about you?"

107

"No. I never met them. My mom's parents died when she was young. I never heard great things about my dad's parents."

I remember when I was younger and my dad called someone a racial slur. I got mad and he apologized, but later he sat me down and told me he was still fighting how he grew up, what his grandpa used to call people. Nasty stuff. It scared me that as much as he tried not to let it, some of the prejudices were passed down to him. I worried some slipped into me. Even now, some thoughts about people at the shelter slip inside my privileged head and shame me.

Flynn and I turn a corner, and the buildings get noticeably nicer. This part of town is trendier now with eclectic shops and restaurants. A lot of artists and creative people have moved into the area.

"How old were you?" I ask softly. "When your dad died?

"Five."

"Sorry," I say, but it sounds insignificant. There should be something better to say. "That's really sad. Do you remember him?"

"I have some good memories." He holds up his wrist and the bracelet dangles from it. "I wear this to remember him."

I look at it again. It's stainless steel. With the red medic alert symbol.

"He had diabetes. Went into shock. After he died, my mom was so sad. Lonely. He left her money, but my stepdad moved in fast." He frowns.

I gnaw my bottom lip. "He was really bad?"

"He never beat me up or anything. But he was just a jerk. He didn't work and totally screwed my mom over. I feel bad for Kyle, cause he's his dad, and there's nothing he can do to change that."

He shrugs. "At least for me, he isn't blood. The best thing for all of us is to never hear from him again. I'm sure he's hooked up with someone new to sponge off of. I hope for Kyle's sake he stays away."

"That's tough."

"Yeah. But we'll be okay. You know? It might take a while, but my mom works hard."

"I'm sorry," I say again.

"Don't be. That's life. Does it bother you? That my family has no money?"

I frown and shake my head back and forth. "No."

He watches me but says nothing, and then we reach a corner and he stops. He looks down the street. "Ice cream shop, this way." He looks back at me and brushes his finger against my cheek. "Dirt," he says. "From the greenhouse."

He holds out his hand for me, and a shiver scurries down my back. "This okay?" he asks.

Um, yes. I place my hand in his, and my whole body freaks out while I try to keep my face neutral.

"You really like it in there, hey?" He starts to walk again.

"Uh, where?" I ask. I have no idea what we're talking about anymore.

"The greenhouse."

I nod. "Yeah, I do. I used to have a garden at home. With my mom."

"Really? I used to work in the garden with my mom sometimes when I was a kid. I loved the worms and the slugs, but sometimes I liked flowers too. Not very manly, right?"

I'm not sure he isn't messing with me.

"Seriously?"

"Well, the flowers were mostly dandelions, but I was the master of blowing the fuzz off to spread their growth. Our neighbors probably hated me." He pauses. "I used to pick dandelions and give them to my mom, and she'd put them in her hair. As if they were beautiful flowers from Hawaii or something." He grins. "That asshole she married hated it and made me stop. Kyle never got to pick flowers."

He drops my hand and darts off to a patch of green grass in front of a store and picks up a dandelion. Then he walks back and presents it to me.

I laugh but take it and tuck it behind my ear.

"You look nice with weeds behind your ears." We tease each other until we reach the ice cream shop and walk inside.

There are rows of large white buckets with all kinds of ice cream on display, but I don't even have to look to make my decision. I have the same flavor every time.

"Mint chocolate chip," I tell Flynn.

"Mmm."

He picks strawberry. Not fancy. We smile at each other as he hands me my cone.

"You do know, if you agree to another date with me, I won't be able to give you things the guys from your neighborhood can," he tells me in mock seriousness as he pays.

"You mean lies, attitude, and trash talk?"

He laughs. "I meant expensive dates in expensive cars." He looks down at his feet and then up at me again, almost shy.

"I don't care about that stuff," I tell him. At least not anymore. I like him. Not what he has.

"Yeah?" He bites off a chunk of ice cream from his cone, watching me. "You sure?"

We walk outside the ice cream store and sit on the brick window ledge. I lick at my ice cream, and the minty flavor dances on my taste buds. "I like talking to you. I've never been able to…talk to a guy like this. Like with you."

He nods but he doesn't change his expression, just watches me thoughtfully while he devours his ice cream. "Me neither."

"You're never been able to talk to a guy like this?" I joke.

He smiles. "You're sure you're not embarrassed to be seen with me? A guy from the shelter?" He says it lightly, but it's obvious he means it.

"Not even a little."

He finishes off the last of his ice cream cone while I'm still licking mine fast to keep it from melting in the midday sun.

"I haven't been exactly perfect the last couple of years," I tell him. "You might hear some stuff about me. I mean, if we go out again." I duck my head.

"I don't listen to trash talk," he says and laughs. "Besides, I make my own opinions about people. And I'd like to. Go out again."

"Me too." The rest of my ice cream could melt on my cheeks they're so warm.

He smiles down at the ground. "I don't have a squeaky clean past either, Jess. And you know lots of people look down their noses at me. At my family."

"It doesn't matter," I tell him. "My family has problems of their own."

I frown though, thinking of Nance and her talk about summer flings. And the boys we're supposed to be dating next year.

No. It doesn't matter. Not if I don't let it.

chapter **eleven**

Later than night I run into my dad in the hallway. He follows me to my bedroom and doesn't come in, but his head almost touches the top of the doorframe. "How are things?" he asks, his voice gruff. "You're doing okay working at the shelter?"

"Fine," I tell him as I sit on my bed, not wanting to sound too enthusiastic in case he figures out something about Flynn. I used to believe he could read my thoughts. Of course, I grew up and learned he's human, just like everyone else.

"It's for your own good," he says. He's not good at this. This kind of thing was always Mom's job.

I pick up a pillow and hug it close. "Yeah," I say. I'm not going to make it any easier. Or admit that maybe he's right.

He waits for me to say more, but I've been able to match his silent treatment without cracking for a few years now.

"Okay," he finally says. "Well, I'm traveling a lot this month, so, you know, make sure you keep an eye on your mom too."

He walks away, and a flood of sadness brings unexpected tears to my eyes. The sadness curdles into anger though. It's just another dose of rejection, the way he always walks away from me. I blink, hating that I still hope for more.

I think about telling him about taking Mom for a walk. It would please him. It's news. But he doesn't turn around, so I let him go and don't say anything at all.

• • •

Flynn doesn't show up at New Beginnings the next day, and it makes me curse my dad again for cutting me off from the world by taking away my phone. There's no way to reach Flynn. No way to find out where he is. Talk to him.

Wilf isn't in either, and I miss him too. Thing only get worse when Sunny does her best to cloud my day, and then to top it off, when I ask Stella for help for the lunch service, she seems pissed with me, and I don't even know why. My chest is hollow as I serve my first tables lunch until I spot Martha. She stands and twirls around to show off a new overcoat. "I got it here," she tells me. "Do you like it?"

"I love it," I tell her. "You look beautiful."

She hides her toothless grin with her hand as she sits back down. "Did I ever tell you that you remind me of my daughter?" she asks, placing her napkin on her lap with shaky hands. I pat her arm.

"Thank you," I say. "I'll get you your tea before you eat."

I'm greeted by other regulars who seem happy to see me, and as I'm running to get salad and sandwiches to them, my heart slowly begins to fill up again. When I go to clock out, Stella is in her office on the phone. I overhear her telling someone she'll be staying late to help with the dinner service because a few volunteers can't show up.

"I'll help," I say.

She looks up from her phone.

"I can stay," I repeat.

Her expression changes. Her eyebrows go up.

I nod. "I have nothing going on."

She sits up straighter, watching me. "Never mind, sweetie," she says on the phone. "I'll be home after all."

She hangs up and pauses, letting out a breath. "Thank you," she says softly. "I appreciate it." She watches me for a moment and then points at her phone. "You need to check in at home?"

"I'll call."

After I leave a message, Stella stands. "Why don't you get something to eat and you can help out in the sorting area or in the greenhouse before the dinner service? It's going to be a faster pace. You're sure you're okay with it?"

I assure her I can handle it and go to the kitchen and, for the first time, grab a sandwich and soup and sit with a couple of volunteers at the staff table and eat. They're older women, but they welcome me and treat me like a cute grandchild. I even have a slice of day-old Black Forest cake with them. I'm not even surprised that it's delicious.

Later, after the dinner service, I'm exhausted but walk alone to the bus stop. I'm not afraid, even though it's much later than usual. The bus still drops me at the same spot, a block away from home. I walk along, not even noticing the familiar sights, thinking about Flynn and smiling to myself.

A car horn honks and startles me. My face burns bright when I spot the car.

"Hi, Jess," Braxton calls.

I peer inside his car and try not to show my disappointment that Flynn isn't with him.

"Hey!" he says and pulls his crappy car up beside me. It's noisy and smells like exhaust. "We keep meeting this way."

"Only once," I say. "It's been a while."

"I've wanted to text you. Or call, but I don't have your number," he says.

"Yeah." I shift from one foot to the other and glance around at my neighbor's houses. His car sticks out like a dead flower in a fresh rose bouquet. "My phone privileges are gone for the whole summer."

He turns his car off and opens his door.

"Whoa. That sucks. What'd you do?"

"I, uh, you know, pissed off my dad." Even I can hear the deflection. Not taking credit for my actions. My dad's voice is in my head again.

Braxton leans against his car, smiling at me. "That sucks. You grounded?"

"Not really. I mean. No." Not after my shifts are over anyhow. He never told me not to go out. Not that I've had any invitations.

"Cool."

I fake a smile and look around, ready to move along.

"So. There's a party not far from here. I don't want to seem like a stalker or anything, but I was about to pop by your house and see if you wanted to go. And here you are."

"Here I am."

He takes a breath. "I was kind of stressing about having to show up at your door, like a kid in first grade, you know, ding dong, can you come out and play?" He grins and babbles on, because apparently the boy has no filter.

"So the party," he finally says after a few topic changes. He glances at his car. "Do you want to come?" He looks back at me. "It'll be fun. Sounds like you could use some fun."

He reminds me of one of the boys from the Nickelodeon shows I used to watch with Penny. Wholesome and mischievous but trustworthy. I almost expect him to add an "aw-shucks."

"It's a few blocks over. On Setter Street," he tells me, nodding his head in the direction.

Our neighborhood. Actually the extremely executive end of the neighborhood. Brittney Mendes lives there. It has to be at her place. She's had a few wild parties this summer because her parents are out of town.

"I left a friend there," Braxton says. "The place was already hopping."

Flynn? Was he the friend? I stand straighter. I can't really imagine Flynn at a party at Brittney's, but I wouldn't put Braxton there either, and here he is.

I glance around, trying to play it cool, as if my stomach isn't doing a rain dance at the thought of seeing Flynn outside the shelter. "I should change," I tell him.

"You look fine to me." Braxton smiles. "Better than fine actually." His enthusiasm reminds me of a wagging tail on a dog again and makes me a little uncomfortable, but I choose to ignore it.

"Okay," I say and decide the chance of seeing Flynn is worth not putting on cooler clothes or touching up my long-gone makeup. Dad's out of town, but there's a chance Mom is up.

She'll have gotten the message I was working an extra shift and won't be expecting me. If I go home, she might want me to stay in.

If Flynn happens to be at the party, well, he already knows what I look like. He doesn't seem like the kind of guy who cares if a girl spends a ton of time getting ready. He's more of the jeans and tank top type. And I'm wearing my version of "dress up for work" clothes. Not jeans and a tank. Shoot.

A woman walking her little black dog steps around us so she can pass.

"I wonder if Nance is at the party," I say out loud and walk to the passenger side of his car. Braxton hurries over to open the door, surprising me. "I'm not sure how I feel about seeing her since she's totally abandoned me," I add under my breath. Braxton moves some fast food wrappers from the seat to the floor so I can sit.

"Nance?" Braxton asks, and then he goes to the driver side and climbs in.

"A friend," I tell him. "Or she was. I haven't heard from her since my phone was taken away." We talked once on my landline the day after the boob baring but not since.

Braxton's car smells like Christmas trees instead of hamburgers, and sure enough, there's a tree-shaped air freshener hanging from his rearview mirror. Music blasts from his speakers when he starts the car, but he reaches for the volume and turns it down. He revs his engine. I tug on my seat belt as Braxton throws the car into drive and squeals off.

"Confession," he blurts out with a guilty puppy-dog expression. "I saw the party posted on Twitter and drove to your hood, hoping to see you there. When you weren't, I left and headed over to see if you were at home."

"Oh," I manage and twirl my earring. I don't want to flirt with him, but I don't want to blurt out that we're only going to be friends right away. He might dump me on the street.

"These houses are fricking huge," he says as we pass the homes of people I've known since elementary school and drive toward Brittney's.

"Size matters in this neighborhood," I tell him.

He laughs out loud.

"Where do you live?" I turn to his profile.

He rolls up to a stop sign. "Clover Lawn," he says and narrows his eyes.

I nod noncommittally as if I don't know it's the seediest part of town. It does have beautiful trees though. Big trees.

"My whole house is probably smaller than your bedroom." He pulls out from the stop sign and takes the first right.

"Wasn't passing judgment," I tell him.

"No?" He whistles again as we get closer to Brittney's house.

I shrug. "Do you think it matters?"

"Shit, yeah," Braxton says as he pulls into the next street. "Whoa. It's gotten busier." Cars are lined up and down both sides of the street. He pulls his car into an empty spot, in front of a driveway.

"You're blocking them in," I can't help pointing out.

He laughs, so I shrug it off and climb out. Braxton's already on the street, jumping up and down, like a kid in a LEGO store. "This is going to rock," he yells with his "golden retriever fetching a stick" enthusiasm.

"You don't have a lot of inhibitions, do you, Braxton?" I ask.

He grins widely. "Not really."

"I only get remotely close to that when I drink," I admit as we walk side by side on the sidewalk.

"Well, let's go get you a drink!" he says and whoops again.

"That's not always very pretty," I say, trying to be honest and wondering if I'm giving him the wrong impression.

"Let me be the judge of that," he says.

This can't be a good idea.

chapter **twelve**

From the outside, the house is stupidly huge with a flawless yard. Not a weed in sight. There are no kids puking in bushes or throwing beer bottles at each other on the front lawn, which is a good sign, but a buzz of voices and laughter rise up from the back. There's a fence high enough to keep an illusion of privacy around the side and back, and there's enough distance between houses on the street that the neighbors probably won't complain unless things get really out of hand. It's summer, after all. Most of the neighbors are probably gone too.

"Her parents are in Europe on 'holiday.'" He says holiday with a fake accent.

"You know Brittney?" I ask.

"Saw the party on Twitter," he reminds me.

I do know Brittney, but he doesn't ask so I don't tell. Braxton walks ahead of me, bouncing up to the front door about to ring the bell, but I reach across him and turn the knob.

The front hallway is packed with bodies.

He grins. "*Now* it's a party." He goes off on another riff about great parties of the past, and I kind of want him to be quiet. While nonstop chatter is endearing in some ways, it's also exhausting in others.

The air in the house is stale. Fresh oxygen is being consumed and used up by the kids jammed into the main floor. I look around, contemplating the fake plants in expensive pots in the entrance-way. Beauty without commitment.

"Where's your friend?" I ask.

Braxton puts a hand on his ear. "I can't hear you."

I point ahead, and we walk past couples in an office off the entrance, pawing at each other on cream-colored couches. I make a face on the furniture's behalf. They'll need a good cleaning after the party or maybe a note for Brittney's parents to burn them. We keep walking into the living room, but instead of giving me energy, the lively atmosphere sucks it out of me. My trying to muster up some enthusiasm fails as we press deeper into the hub of the party, and my heart sinks. I should have gone home. Pulling out the fake bubbly party personality is too tiring. Too contrived. Almost everyone is fueled by mind-altering substances, but I'm as sober as a funeral floral arrangement.

"JESS!" a voice screeches, and suddenly Nance is throwing her-self at my side, hugging me tight, almost knocking me over. She stumbles and giggles as we both lose our footing in the attack.

"Whoo-hoo! You got a 'Get out of jail for *free* card'!" she yells right in my ear, and the vibration hurts.

I force a smile and step back to give my ear some distance. Nance throws her head back and laughs and then spots Braxton. "Who is this *boy*?" She emphasizes the word *boy* and squints to look closer at him.

"Braxton, Nance; Nance, Braxton," I say. Ugh. I want to be mad at her, but she's in no condition to even notice.

She grabs Braxton by the shoulder and spins him around.

"A little young. But nice butt," she tells him.

He grabs her by the hand and spins her around. "You too."

Nance giggles. "Sassy," she shouts. "Is this your summer fling?" she yells at me.

I frown and shake my head, but she's grinding up against me. I try to laugh and dance with her, but my body's as flexible and fun as a corpse. I want to ask why she hasn't called or tried to get hold of me some other way, but there's no use in her state.

Jennifer Deering slinks up to us then. She fake-smiles at me and I fake-smile back. "Hey, Jess," she says, but it sounds like "Get lost, loser. This is *my* best friend." We've known each other for years, but every time I see her, it feels like we're meeting for the first time. She makes me feel like that annoying friend no one really wants to talk to, but really, right about now, Jennifer should thank me because she's inherited the role of Nance's best friend. Which she's made no secret of wanting to be.

Jennifer throws an arm around Nance's shoulder and laughs at something Braxton said. She doesn't take her eyes off me though, silently judging me as she does so well.

I should have gone home to change. My outfit is lame and smells like leftover Taco Bell. "I just got off work," I tell her.

"You're working?" Jennifer arches a thin eyebrow.

I swallow an urge to physically push her away from me. "Kind of." I don't say more, because we both know she knows about New Beginnings. Nance talks, and Jennifer definitely heard.

"Oh. That's right. You're doing that charity thing." She makes a face and takes a sip of her cooler and spins away, cutting me off.

I glance to see if Braxton heard her, but he's too busy staring at her chest to register words.

"Who's this?" Jennifer smiles at Braxton, who is grinning at her, totally suckered in. There's a definite gleam in her eye too, like she wants to steal him away to show me she can.

"I'm Jennifer," she tells him and kind of wiggles around to give him a better eyeful of her low-cut top and boobs, which are almost as big as Nance's and I suspect one of the reasons Nance chose me as her number one. My smaller cup size.

"I'm Braxton." He grins at Jennifer, clearly charmed by her packaging. Then he keeps talking.

I shuffle my feet, wanting to escape the three of them and all the flirting and giggling. My party persona fails me as I glance around at the drinking and drugging.

"What's wrong with your face?" Nance says and pinches my cheek. "We don't do grouchy face at parties." She lifts her hands in the air to "raise the roof."

I paw my hand through my hair and bump Nance's hip with mine, trying to shake off my mood. "So what's new?" I ask, glancing at Jennifer, pretending to include her in the question. *I know how to do this*, I remind myself. *This is my world.*

"Whoa," Nance says. "You're way too sober and boring. Where is your alcohol, girl?"

My cheeks burn. Nance sees through me. She sees how self-conscious and ridiculous I am without alcohol. I always have a few drinks before we go out. To get me in the mood. I snatch her bottle from her hand and guzzle from it.

"We forgot to pick up booze," Braxton says to Nance.

I glance over. More like he couldn't afford to pick some up. Nance grabs Braxton's chin and smooshes up his face. "Well, Jess needs a drink! Brittney has plenty of booze. Go." She points to the deck. "Find this girl a drink. There's beer and stuff in the coolers on the deck." She looks him up and down. "Help yourself." She pushes on his back. "Get Jess a vodka cooler," she calls as he stumbles off. "Those are her favorite."

Braxton grins over his shoulder as he heads toward the deck.

Nance grabs her drink back from me. "So, where'd you find him? The bargain basement?"

"Nance!"

She boogies to the music pounding out from speakers in the ceiling. "What? He's cute. I'm just guessing he's financially challenged."

"Based on what?"

Nance stops dancing. "Um. His shoes. His jeans. The way he talks." She laughs like it's hysterical.

Jennifer laughs with her. "His style is kind of Grandpa's hand-me-downs. But he is yummy. Definite summer fling material."

Great. Jennifer is in on that too. So stupid. They giggle together, and I shake my head, trying not to show how pissed off they're making me. "No. It's not like that."

"Did you meet him at that place?" Nance squishes up her nose. "I mean, don't get me wrong; he's kind of adorable with his…" She makes a talking motion with her hand. "And he's nice to look at, but I'm guessing you'll be paying for your own liquor."

"Is he your new 'boyfriend'?" Jennifer makes air quotes around the word *boyfriend*. I have an urge to push her hard so she splats on the ground.

"Friend," I yell. "And I didn't meet him there." My face smolders, thinking of Flynn. What are they going to say about Flynn?

"He lives on the other side of town," I add with an eye roll and instantly hate myself. Like I'm admitting he isn't one of us. What does it matter where he lives?

"The bad side?" Nance asks.

"Clover Lawn?" Jennifer asks and flicks her hair back.

I press my lips tight together and pretend to look for someone across the room.

"Forget boyfriend, summer fling!" Nance yells.

"Friend," I say again but think of Flynn.

Nance rolls her eyes. "So where did you find him?" She drinks her cooler and eyeballs me.

"I met him through someone." I shrug and glance over her shoulder, hoping she won't ask who. We know the same people.

"Penny?" Nance asks and wrinkles up her nose. "She's here, you know. At an actual party. Did you see her yet?"

My heart almost stops. *Penny is here?* I shake my head and resist the temptation to scan the room until I find her. "She's probably outside." Nance contemplates me over her bottle. "But she's a bitch, right? Remember who your real friends are."

Someone turns up the music, and an old rock-and-roll song comes on. Nance wiggles her hips and pumps her fists in the air. She waves at someone across the room. "My brother's here," she tells me. "You should say hey to him. The way he's asking about you, I think he misses you more than I do."

That thought grosses me out. Jennifer moves in closer. "Yesterday when we were suntanning, Scott tried to convince me to suntan topless so he could take pictures of me to show to his friends. What an ass!" Jennifer laughs, but her eyes gleam, letting me know she's the one spending time with Nance during the day now.

What she doesn't know is instead of feeling bad, she's making me miss the cranky seventy-five-year-old man I spend time with. I'd rather be in the greenhouse listening to him complain about his bowel movements than where I am right now.

Nance throws her head back and laughs. "You should have seen Jess's face when my mom caught her topless." She imitates me by opening her eyes wide and wrapping her arms around her boobs, then laughs some more and throws her arm around my neck. "I miss you!"

A senior who graduated in June spots Nance and grabs her around the waist, pulling her away from me. She squeals and throws both arms around him, and he lifts her in the air. Jennifer fake squeals and then jumps at him when he puts Nance down.

With an arm around each of them, he leads them away without even a glance at me. Loneliness burns a little hole in my stomach as I watch them laugh and dance their way through the living room to the patio door. Jennifer turns for a split second before they disappear, a smug smile on her face.

I feel alone, but watching myself being replaced doesn't bother me as much as it would have a couple of weeks ago. I glance around for familiar faces, and my eyes open wider and my body temperature drops. I spot Penny. She's walking inside from the deck. Even from the distance, she looks slightly different. She's wearing eyeliner. Her reddish-brown hair is longer and curled. Her jeans are tighter than she used to wear them. They look awesome on her.

She must sense me staring at her, because she glances over and our eyes meet. A familiar look crosses her face. Sympathy. She knows I'm alone and uncomfortable. I remember the way we always understood each other across a crowded room. The music and noise disappear, and for a moment, it's only me and her in that room. I can hear her ask me if I'm okay without saying anything at all. I'm about to lift my hand and mouth *hi* when a tall guy swoops in and wraps an arm around her shoulder. He pulls her in, and her face disappears from my sight. My eyes open wider. Holy shit. That's Keith Alex. The boy she's had a crush on since seventh grade. And he's hugging her. I can't help smiling. She peeks under his arm for a minute and catches my reaction. I lift up my thumb and grin wider. Penny heaven right there. She smiles, and my heart is stuffed with happiness for her.

Keith pulls her tighter and then leans down and kisses her on the mouth. I barely resist jumping up and down on the spot, as if we're twelve years old and she's reading me what she wrote about him in her diary.

Keith sweeps her out of my view, and I stare at the empty space. Keith Alex and Penny Pierce! I want to rush over to her house later and ask every single detail of how they hooked up.

Except I can't. I miss her so much and hate myself all over again for messing up my right to be her friend anymore. Swallowing to kill my urge to cry, I dart past bodies, needing to get away. A drunken boy grabs me and steers me down a hallway, putting his arm around my shoulder and offering some of his beer. I duck under his arm and keep going until I round a corner and end up inside a kitchen. The ceiling is high and it's huge, probably four or five times the size of our kitchen at home.

The kitchen hidden away in the back of the house suggests Brittney's mom either hates to cook or doesn't want people to see her when she does. A group of kids are standing in front of a stove, close to an open window, blowing smoke outside. Noise from the backyard drifts in, and a smell hits my nose. Skunky pot. I pretend to search around for something, in case any of them cares what I'm doing.

"Yo. You're that girl," a male voice calls. A boy leaning on the counter stares at me with squinty red eyes. The pockmarks on his skin are visible even across the room. "Aren't you the girl whose mom was attacked?" he calls. "She almost died, right?"

I narrow my eyes and give him my filthiest look as my insides jump around. What the hell? Doesn't he know people aren't supposed to say things like that to my face?

"Leave her alone," one of the girls says. She's got dark black hair with green roots. Gothy. I don't recognize her, but she's looking at me with pity in her heavily made-up eyes.

"What?" the boy asks. "That's Allie West's sister."

"So? Do you think she wants to talk about it here?" the girl asks. "Shut the hell up."

I say a silent thanks for her compassion. My thoughts for the boy aren't nearly as generous.

"Whatever." The boy turns back to his friends and reaches for a pipe that's getting passed around.

The girl acknowledges me with a tiny nod. It shakes me though. It's getting harder to breathe. I'm usually fuzzy around the edges, so if people notice me at parties because of my mom, I have no idea. God, I don't want to think about what happened now.

My throat scratches when I swallow, and sweat trickles down my back. My eyes go to the fridge. There has to be alcohol in there. A familiar urge nibbles at my brain. The pleasant buzz from a drink. Leaning against the kitchen island, the counter hard and cool on my hip, I run my hand over the smooth surface. It's marble. My mom hates marble. She thinks it's too showy. My dad likes it for the same reason.

"You looking for a drink?" a girl calls from across the kitchen, a tiny redhead. It's Brittney. She blended in with the other kids. "Take what you want." She's wrapped up under the long arms of a tall boy.

"Thanks," I call. One of the other kids says something, but it's hard to hear what it is. Pushing off the counter, I walk to the fridge and open it. There's an entire shelf of alcohol, and I grab a vodka cooler, pop off the lid, and chug. There's an unexpected noise behind me, and I jump as a boy staggers inside the kitchen.

Great. So not what I need right now.

chapter **thirteen**

J osh Reid stumbles into the kitchen, a big smile on his face, unsteady on his feet. He's wearing his usual expensive jeans and chest-hugging T-shirt. He swims competitively and loves to show off the perks. He has a black hat perched on his head, and there's no doubt, he's a nice-looking male specimen. Too bad we don't have anything in common except hormones. I hope for a second he won't notice me, but of course I'm not invisible, even to drunk ex-boyfriends.

"I thought I saw you heading toward the kitchen." He shakes his finger and heads for me in a zigzag pattern.

"Hey, Reid," one of the boys at the stove calls. "What you doing here? I didn't think you could breathe oxygen."

Josh's eyes are glazed and red, and he's clutching a bottle of Corona with a lime floating on top of the liquid like a dead fish. He lifts his free hand in the air, his middle finger saluted upward at the boy at the stove, but doesn't take his eyes off of me.

"Yo, Jess," he says, a noticeable drunk slur to the *s*. He's a light-weight drinker. "Looking good." He walks over and touches my hip and then pulls his finger back, pretending to have burnt himself. Then he laughs, and it's a silly drunk giggle that reminds me a little of Kyle, and it makes me smile.

Josh misinterprets it. "Want to make out?" He winks and purses his lips, apparently trying to look sexy but barely passing for ridiculous. It's embarrassing that drunk me actually fell for his crap.

"Not really." I throw my cap at him, and it bounces off his chest.

"Hey." He looks like I just farted or gravely injured him. "What's wrong?"

I barely resist rolling my eyes. "I'm too sober," I tell him. Way too sober to talk to Josh Reid. Way over Josh Reid. Sober or not. Good on paper or not.

He frowns. "I haven't seen you in ages. You haven't been to any parties lately. I tried texting you, but Nance said you don't have a phone." He tries to look sexy again. "What's up with that? I miss you."

"Yeah?" I glare at him. "And why is that?"

He frowns. This is not the usual script. If I were in the same state, we'd fight and flirt-insult each other for a while and then start making out. We'd do the whole hooking up thing, and afterward, we'd avoid each other. I sigh, seeing too clearly how pathetic it is.

"You're drunk." I step backward, skimming my back against the kitchen island. "Ouch."

"And you're not." He takes a step and runs his finger along my cheek. I turn my face, but he takes my cooler and holds it up to my lips. "We should fix that. You're way more fun when you're drunk."

I push it back. "Not today," I tell him.

Not today, but every other time. Angry with myself and not missing the irony, I tilt the bottle back and finish half the cooler in one chug to try to bury that anger.

"Hey." He winks in an exaggerated motion. "That's my girl." He moves his gaze slowly up and then slowly down my body, and it makes me feel dirty.

"Not your girl, Josh."

"Totally my girl." He grins and reaches for my hand. "Totally my type."

"You mean female?" I narrow my eyes.

"Burn." He grabs his heart, stumbles a little, and laughs, taking another sip of beer. "My feelings for you are no secret." He tips his hat further down his eye, trying to be sexy. Not succeeding.

"Your feelings for me are fueled by alcohol consumption," I remind him.

He laughs again, but he's starting to look like a priest in a lingerie shop. Things aren't going as planned.

"You're hurting my feelings." He leans down. "I have them, you know. Feelings." He tries to look sexy and seems like he's going to try to kiss me, so I lean back and move my head away from him.

"You okay?" an angry voice interrupts.

I look over. Braxton is in the kitchen. Frowning. I imagine an invisible question mark dangling over his head. He has a vodka cooler in one hand and a beer in the other. "I've been looking for you. I got you this."

Yeah. I am so freaking popular all of a sudden. And everyone wants to get me drunk.

I step to the side so Josh isn't looming over me anymore. "I'm fine. This is Josh. An old friend."

Josh takes a sip of beer. "Boyfriend," he clarifies.

"Ex-boyfriend," I add. "If we want to be generous and call it that."

Braxton walks closer to us. "You sure you're okay?"

"She's fine, man. Who are you?" Josh asks. Even drunk, he manages to give him a superior look. Josh'll be a cutthroat lawyer someday. Just like daddy. His and mine. He never hesitates to go after people's weak spots. "The help?" Josh adds, lifting his chin. He sees through Braxton. Josh drives a Porsche his dad bought him for his sixteenth birthday. He lives down the street from Brittney.

"I'll help you, fucker," Braxton says and walks forward, rolling back his broad shoulders. I realize how big he is. Josh is long and lean and could easily outrun Braxton, which is good, because I'm pretty sure Braxton would kick Josh's ass. Braxton puts his drink down on the island and stalks forward, so I place a hand on his chest, pushing him back.

"Forget it. I said *ex*. And it was nothing dramatic. Josh is cool. We were just talking. I'm fine." I glare at Josh. "You can go away now," I tell him.

Josh stares at me and then at Braxton. "Seriously? You'd rather hang out with this trailer trash?"

I keep my hand on Braxton's chest. "Get out of here, Josh. Don't be an asshole," I say. The two of them are giving me a headache.

Josh stands taller and suddenly looks more sober. "Your taste in friends is pretty questionable."

"Clearly," Braxton says, crossing his arms.

I drop my hand. I have an urge to tell both of them to fuck off.

They've sucked out the last of my positive emotions. I'd rather be in my bed, feeling like an unpopular loser, than here.

"Whatever, Jess," Josh says. "You want to hang out with freaks, that's your problem." Josh stomps to the fridge, opens it, and takes two beers but still manages to give us the finger as he continues his stomp out of the kitchen.

"You okay over there, Jess?" Brittney calls.

"Fine," I call back. "But if you ever want to grow your own dope, try planting Josh Reid."

The group of kids around the stove laughs. At least someone appreciates my humor, because Braxton glares down at me.

"You seriously went out with that guy?"

I shrug. "If you want to call it that."

"Are you still into him?" he asks.

"Obviously not. I like being single." It's a message and not a subtle one, but it's time to make things clear in case he has ulterior motives. Which it kind of seems he does.

Braxton gestures toward the counter where he put down the cooler. "I brought you a drink." He hands it to me. I take it without a word. He holds his bottle up to toast. We clink and he chugs as I sigh. He drinks his beer in silence while I hold mine without taking a sip.

"You know what?" I tell him. "I'm pretty tired. I think I'm going to head home. I can walk. It's nice out and not far."

"Already?" Braxton's cheeks are rosy, as if he's mad but trying not to be. "We just got here."

"I'm sorry." I sigh, not wanting to deal with his crush on me, but

I don't want to give him false hope either. "I guess I'm not in the mood for a party. And I left my mom at home alone."

He furrows his eyebrows. "Yeah? I left mine alone too. But she's a big girl. She's fine."

"My mom…" I start and then stop, sighing, and glance at the kids by the sink, but they're not paying attention. Brittney and her boyfriend are making out. The others look zoned out. "She hasn't been feeling well for a while."

"She's sick?" he asks.

"Long story." I put the vodka cooler down on the counter, done pretending that drinking it is going to happen.

"I should drive you home," he says. "If you really want to go."

I point at his beer. "No. I'll be fine. I'm good walking. Anyhow, I hope you're not going to drive later."

"I have a DD, but I've only had a couple anyhow. And you shouldn't walk alone. Not all guys are as nice as me." He sips his beer, watching me.

"It's all right. It's not far. And it's nice out. I should find Nance first, let her know I'm leaving."

"Your friend with the boobs?" He grins adorably. "Sorry. But it's true." He takes a sip of beer. "I saw her outside, drooling all over Flynn."

My heart races as if I've been hit by a jacked-up defibrillator.

"Flynn?" Without thinking, I pick up the cooler and take a big gulp. "You mean he *is* here?"

"I told you. I ditched Flynn to come and get you. I didn't tell him though, and he left for a while, but he came back." He narrows his eyes, watching my face turn the color of a Christmas poinsettia. "Aw man, for real?" he says, shaking his head. "I thought you two didn't like each other. I thought you were immune to the Flynnster."

"What do you mean?" I blink and cover my hot cheeks with my hands.

Flynn is here? No way I'm leaving now.

"He was a jerk to you that night I drove you home." He shakes his head. "I'm the one who was being nice." His voice has a whine in it, and I understand how it feels playing second fiddle. I've done it for Nance lots of times. It's obvious he doesn't know Flynn and I see each other at New Beginnings.

"We've run into each other a few times," is all I say.

"He mentioned he ran into you and you weren't as bad as he thought." He shakes his head some more. "But I didn't know you were into him."

The kids around the stove burst into laughter, and we both look over, but they're laughing among themselves, not paying any attention to us.

"I kind of hoped you liked me." His face droops, and he looks like he lost his favorite bone.

"I do like you…you know as a…"

"Oh God. Don't say it. As a friend? Please. It's the kiss of death."

"It's nothing personal."

"No? It seems kind of personal to me." He crosses his arms and frowns.

"I'm sorry. It's just…" I sigh. I can't make up a boyfriend to let him down because I'm afraid it will get back to Flynn. Whatever I say to him could get back to Flynn.

My foot taps the tile floor, now aware that Nance is outside flirting with Flynn. I trust Flynn, but Nance, not so much.

Braxton slumps against the counter. "Great. Another female friend." He sips his beer and frowns. "Is there something wrong with me?" His voice cracks and makes me feel bad for deflating his ego.

"Not at all. You're a nice guy."

"A nice guy? That's worse than liking me as a friend." He stares at me and then chugs the rest of his beer and slams the bottle on the counter. "Fuck nice," he says, and then he lets out a huge belch.

"Good one," one of the boys calls.

Braxton and I stare at each other, and then we both start cracking up.

"Gross," I tell him. "But you're still terribly attractive," I add. "With really big muscles."

"Yeah?" He stands straighter and tilts his head. "Whatever. Do you mind if I go after your friend, Jennifer?"

I stare at him. Did I think I was irreplaceable? I laugh harder. "Part of me wants to be insulted."

"What?" he asks, blinking and trying to look innocent.

"Jennifer's kind of…" I try to think of a nice way to describe her. "She usually goes for older guys." *With lots of money*, I don't add.

"Really?" He shakes his head. "'Cause I think she was kind of into me. She was flirting pretty hard."

I laugh again. "You bounce back pretty quickly," I tell him.

"Hey. I held back on your account, but I like to keep my options open." He smiles and he's like an eager little boy again. I decide I do like him. As a friend.

I think about Jennifer. She likes attention. She wants a summer fling. Hopefully she won't eat him alive. "Go for it," I tell him. "It's not as if you need my blessing."

"You're right."

I hand him the cooler. "You want this girly drink?"

"Fuck girly. It's alcohol. And it's free." He takes it and pounds the whole thing back.

"Do you want to go outside?" I try not to look as eager as I feel.

He shakes his head. "Now I get why he agreed to come to this party with me. I thought I'd have to drag him here. Or at least bribe him."

My cheeks warm, but it's pleasure warm, not embarrassment.

"How come girls never go for the nice guys?" Braxton asks.

I happen to think Flynn is one of the nice guys. "I'm pretty easy to get over. It's kind of embarrassing," I say instead.

"Flynn always gets the girl. He should have told me. I may have mentioned you once or twice."

I wrinkle up my nose, hating that a lot. "Jennifer," I remind him.

He smiles. "Jennifer." His lips drooped and he looked away. "You know that Flynn and me, we don't exactly live like…" He waves his hand around the kitchen. "He's got family stuff to deal with. His family is…" He shakes his head.

"I know," I say softly. "And all this doesn't matter so much,"

Braxton rolls his eyes. "Easier to say when you have it."

"Yeah. You're probably right." I shrug. "My family is pretty messed up. If that makes you feel any better."

"Yeah?" Braxton asks as he follows me out of the kitchen.

"Yeah." We walk side by side through the hallway back to the living room.

There are more bodies crammed inside the house now. The music and buzz of voices is louder. Braxton opens the back door and holds it for me. We head onto the deck, and it's packed with people. Even in the dark with all the chatter and laughter mixed with music, my ears manage to pick up on Nance's distinctive laugh. My eyes zoom in on her, and I almost throw up in my mouth a little. She's sitting on the railing of the deck, her arm through Flynn's, and she's gazing at him with her super Nance flirt powers. Full smile, mesmerized gaze, like he's the most fascinating person on the entire planet. I've seen it melt boy brains before.

Fortunately Flynn's looking around, not gazing into her eyes under her spell. Good. I send him a telepathic message: Stay strong. Jennifer notices us first, and she beams at Braxton and then snarl-smiles at me. Nance is so deeply involved in her flirt game she doesn't even notice until we're right in front of them. Braxton immediately forgets my existence and leans toward Jennifer, tapping her hip with his. She bats her eyes at me, and I smile, signaling a silent okay, even though she probably doesn't feel like she needs it. She practically purrs as she turns all her attention to Braxton.

Flynn sees me, and his expression changes. His eyes open wider and he steps away from Nance so she's forced to drop her arm from the crook of his.

"Jess," he says. He smiles.

My heart sings with happiness.

Nance glares at me and then back at Flynn, but it doesn't matter.

"Imagine finding you at a place like this," he says and then he winks, and I know that he came to this party for me.

"Imagine indeed." The gigantic smile on my face may be permanent.

Nance looks back and forth, her lip moving up into a barely there snarl.

"You two know each other?" she asks, but the subtext sounds like, "Why are you talking to *her* when you could be talking to me?"

"We've met," Flynn says and grins. He's holding a bottle, but it's Coke.

"Where?" she demands.

He doesn't take his eyes off me. And I don't take mine off him.

"We met through his brother," I say, which is only half a lie.

My peripheral vision catches Nance's frown, but a grin might as well be tattooed to my face. Nance takes a sip of her drink. This is new territory for her. Losing the attention of a boy to me.

"Hey, Jess. I have to pee. Come with me?" She hops off the railing and pulls on my arm before I can answer, yanking me away from Flynn. I glance over my shoulder at him as she takes me away. He lifts his chin and smiles, telling me without words he'll wait.

I turn back to Nance, who is dragging me behind her. A hand brushes my ass as we pass through the crowd, and I swat it away and can't see who did it. "Assholes," I say to a group of boys cracking up. Oblivious, Nance keeps going, plowing her way through people. As soon as we step inside the house, Nance drops my arm and turns, her hands on her hips.

"So what's up? How do you know Flynn?" Her voice is louder than necessary, and her eyes shine bright. She's functioning on a pretty high alcohol level, but she's got lots of practice.

"Yeah," I say and shrug as if meeting him isn't the best thing that's happened to me all summer. As if Flynn and I don't know each other at a place so different from this party, it might as well be on another planet. As if my dad forcing me to volunteer at a food shelter for the summer didn't turn out to be amazing. Weird. Unexpected. True.

I push her forward. "I saw a bathroom that way."

She digs her heels into the floor in the living room. "Yeah? Well, I want to go for it," she says.

"The bathroom? Yeah. Go," I tell her.

"No. With Flynn. Summer fling. Perfect for fun. You're okay with that, right? I mean, you two are just friends, right?"

"No," I say quickly and so loud it's almost a shout. A boy from the other high school in town is walking toward us, his eyes on Nance, concentrating as if he's practicing what he's going to say to her. He's holding a full beer. Liquid courage. I turn away from him. "No, I'm not," I repeat, just in case the first no wasn't clear.

"What?" She frowns. She gets first pick. That's the way it goes. And the fact she's dragging me off to tell me her plan tells me she's pretty sure we're not just friends. She wants to interfere. But this isn't football. There's no running interference here.

"I already hooked up with him," I say and push on her again so she starts moving. The guy from the other high school stops a few feet away, but he's staring at her. What's another lie added to the hundreds of others I've told in my life?

Girl Code. It's the one thing that will let me lay claim on him. Even with Nance, there's Girl Code. Once lips touch a boy, he's not touchable to the other friend. Girl Code. I've practically peed on him to mark my territory. The image makes me laugh. She scowls at me.

"You did? When? Why didn't you tell me? What don't I know about this?" We're moving toward the bathroom slowly, with me pushing on her back. She digs her heels in and stops.

"Come on." I push harder. "It's not like you've called me. I couldn't tell you," I say with zero shame. "I've left messages on your cell and at home, and you never returned them."

"You know I prefer to text," she says snottily, as if losing my phone privileges was only to piss her off or something.

"I don't have a phone anymore!" I push her toward the bathroom by the front entrance.

The boy who's been watching comes at us from another angle. Nance notices and shoots him a look I do not envy him being on the receiving end of. He veers off and pretends to be looking for someone else. Poor guy.

We stop at the bathroom and try the door, but it's locked. Nance bangs on it. "Hey. I have to pee!" she yells and then turns and pokes me with a sharp fingernail. "I can't believe you found a summer fling before me!" She says it loudly, the way drunk people do, and I glance around, but no one pays us any attention. She frowns. "I need another drink," she announces. "I have to pee!" she yells at the bathroom door.

Finally the door opens and a girl walks out of the bathroom. She's a grade younger than us, and when she sees Nance waiting, her cheeks turn red. "Sorry," she says and scuttles off before she is severely and socially punished for daring to use the bathroom when Nance has to pee.

Nance drags me inside with her, pulls down her pants, and sits on the toilet. I turn to the mirror to check myself out and groan. My hair is a disaster. So is my makeup, or what's left of it from the morning.

"So what happened?" she asks, overly loud and kind of aggressive. "With the fling?"

"Oh. Um. Last weekend. At a…family thing…I was, uh, looking after his brother and, well, things happened." I shrug. As if it's not a big deal. As if I didn't lie to get Flynn off her radar. But she's not going after him. Not on my watch.

Nance's reflection is visible behind me in the mirror. She's got her head in her hands, and when she looks up, she looks foggy and kind of sad. She finishes her business and stands and flushes the toilet. I notice her lower hip has cuts all over it and so does the inside of her upper thigh. When she sees me looking, she turns away and does up her shorts. She comes to stand beside me with an uncomfortable look on her face.

"You okay?" I ask. "What happened?"

She avoids my gaze. "Nothing. It's nothing." Then she turns to me. "Don't get too attached to Flynn. Summer flings end, you know, when the summer does." She leans forward to stare at her reflection and frowns. Her eyes are hooded, and she wobbles on her feet.

"Obviously," I answer and hate myself. I watch her for a moment, wondering about the cuts. "You're sure you're okay?"

"I need a drink," she says. She heads for the door without washing her hands, which is really gross, and I quietly judge her.

When we come out of the bathroom, she throws back her head and spots something and then livens up as if she's on a stage. When I see what she's looking at, I smile. Thank you, Hunter Bell.

"I heard Hunter broke up with his girlfriend last week. I saw a tweet," she tells me.

He graduated a couple of years ago and works for the town. Cutting grass. Shirtless. Pruning trees in parks and boulevards. Shirtless. His longish blond hair shimmering in the sun. Shirtless. He looks good shirtless. She's gone, moving toward Hunter on a mission, but the boy who was trying to get her attention earlier is in her path. Nance gives him a big smile, grabs the full beer from his hand, starts guzzling, and keeps walking without looking at him.

I walk slower, and the boy whose beer she stole watches with me as she reaches Hunter and he greets her with an enthusiastic hug. Hunter smiles at her like she's a Halloween treat and leans down and whispers in her ear. She pets his arm, and I wrinkle my nose and glance at the boy. The heartsick face gets to me.

"Poor guy, she totally didn't wash her hands after using the washroom," I tell him.

He stares at me for a second. And then he laughs.

"Thanks," he says. "That's awesome." And he walks the other way, still laughing.

I make my way through the house, back to the deck party.

My grin starts before I reach Flynn.

"Hey," he says when I'm standing in front of him. "See my friend over there? He wants to know if you think I'm cute." I glance to the side and see Braxton and Jennifer making out. Their hormones seem to be breeding and mutating, fueled by alcoholic substances. I understand their inclination, but at the same time, I want more than a hookup at a party with Flynn. More than hormones and lust. No matter what I told Nance.

"Yeah. Sure he does." I laugh. The smile on Flynn's face is totally sexy and a little bit shy, which of course makes it even sexier. He looks different in this environment, at this party. Not as intense. But still familiar.

"You lost your friend?" he asks.

"She found someone else to salivate over." I try to keep the jealousy out of my voice, but the way he smiles, I don't think it worked. We grin at each other, and suddenly I have no idea what to say. This is so different from being alone together in the greenhouse or at the shelter. "It's weird seeing you here," I blurt out. I could stare at him all day long.

"Can I tell you a secret?" He grabs the belt loop on my pants and pulls me close.

My heart swoops. I hold my breath. Waiting. The buzz of the kids around us laughing and talking loudly fades.

"It's not really my scene," he whispers. We're so close, our noses almost touch. "Usually I hang out at soup kitchens."

I smile, happy he's joking. It must be hard to deal with sometimes, especially at a party like this.

"The only reason I'm here is because I hoped I'd see you."

I press my lips into a smile. "I didn't know about the party until Braxton came to get me. And I only came because he said he brought a friend. I hoped it was you."

"I guess we both abused his crush on you," Flynn says.

I glance over at Jennifer and Braxton. "Good thing for us he's fickle."

We watch them make out like they're madly in love and laugh.

"So what now?" he asks.

Behind me someone drops a bottle on the deck and it smashes. A bunch of kids whoop. No one bothers to clean it up. Instead they kick away the glass and ignore it.

"I'm not really into this party," I admit. "I was actually going to head home. My mom's home alone."

"Can I walk you?" he asks.

"Aren't you Braxton's DD? You'd have to walk all the way back."

He glances over. "Nah. I'll head home too. Braxton's good about taking public transportation if he's drinking. His dad was hit by a drunk driver a long time ago. So…"

I nod. "That's good. I mean, not the accident."

"I knew what you meant." He smiles.

"Yo, Brooks!" Flynn yells and puts his hand on my back. My back likes it. Braxton manages to drag his lips away from Jennifer for a second. "I'm out," Flynn calls.

Braxton stares at him and then at me and nods. Jennifer plants her hand on his neck and drags him back in. Flynn and I laugh again, and he puts pressure on the hand on my back and we start moving. I float past the kids laughing around us, totally unaware of our existence. It doesn't matter. None of it matters.

"You're sure you don't mind?" I ask.

"More than sure."

It makes me want to sing show tunes like Penny used to do when she was happy. Probably still does. I look around for her as we weave our way out the front door, but I don't see her. I look around for Nance and Hunter too but don't see them either. I think about the scratches on her hip for a moment, but Flynn holds the door, and we step into the front yard, and the party noise is instantly gone. It's like a distant echo in the night air.

"Big parties aren't really my thing," Flynn says.

"Me neither. I mean, not anymore," I add because it's true right now and that's all that matters. "You're sure about walking me?" I ask again but not even slightly genuinely.

"Nah. Changed my mind." He turns and goes back and grabs for the front doorknob. "Psych." He turns back to me with a smile.

"Ha ha," I tell him. I can't wipe the grin off my face.

We walk up the driveway to the sidewalk, side by side. We pass a group of teens carrying beer, heading toward Brittney's, but I don't even look at their faces.

"Mmm, smell that," I say. There's a giant lilac bush at the front of the yard. I worry for a second he'll think I'm a big nerd.

"Lilies," he says.

I guess not. I smack his arm lightly. "Those are not lilies; they're lilacs."

"Show-off."

"I know flowers," I tell him.

"Prove it," he says.

"And how do you propose I do that?" I ask.

"Stay tuned," he says in mock seriousness. "A flower test is imminent."

We reach the end of the street, and he waits for me to lead the way. I turn left and he follows. "Tell me," he says as we pass a bunch of shiny clean cars. "Does every kid in this neighborhood drive a brand-new car?"

"Lots," I tell him.

"Your daddy get you one?" He says it lightly, but it sounds a little forced. "I'm surprised you take the bus to the shelter."

I hesitate. "Well, actually I share an Audi with my sister. A hybrid. In his mind that totally makes him green…" I shut up, realizing the joke probably won't be funny to him. "Never mind."

A car pulls into a house across the street. Another brand-new one.

"How come you don't drive it to New Beginnings?"

My cheeks warm, and I watch a spotless convertible yellow Beetle drive by. "I don't know."

He bumps my hip with his. "It's okay. I get it. You don't want to flaunt it?"

It's true. But I don't tell him that at first I was afraid. That it might get stolen or vandalized.

He watches me for a second. "So, what's it like? Being able to get whatever you want?" he asks in a quiet voice.

I think about his question seriously. "I don't know," I tell him as honestly as I can. "I mean, it's the way I've always lived, I guess. We have money, yeah. We have all the material things we need, but that doesn't mean we get everything we want." I think about how unhappy my house is. The people in it, anyhow. "Definitely not."

We walk in silence for a while, staring straight ahead. I want to ask him what it's like not to have money. Are they happier? Do they get by with simpler things, or do they imagine money is the answer to all of life's problems?

"We're so poor, someone broke into our house and left *us* money," he says after a moment.

I sneak a glance at his profile.

"It's a joke," he says and smiles. "I mean, we weren't always like this. We won't be forever. And it's okay. I won't hold your Audi against you. After all, you do have an astounding knowledge of plants."

I snort at the face he makes. The lights from the streetlamp make him look kind of bad ass. He's wearing the shit out of his jeans and T-shirt, even if they're not expensive brand names. He lifts both hands in the air to yawn and stretch, and when the stretch is done, he reaches for my hand.

"That was smooth. Right?"

"So smooth." I grin, and my fingers tingle with happiness as they entwine with his. We walk quietly for a minute. The night air is still and cool. Perfect.

"So, those people at the party. That's who you hang with?" His voice is soft, and he pretends interest in a parked car we're passing.

I shrug. "I guess."

He squeezes my hand. "That girl Braxton's with? She a friend of yours?"

"Jennifer?" I shrug, shaking my head. "More of a friend of a friend," I say softly. "We don't exactly love each other."

"What about Nance?" he asks.

"Nance and I have known each other since we were kids. Our moms used to work together," I tell him. "We've only hung out a lot in the last couple of years though." I pause. "I don't know if I've been a great friend. I'm kind of worried about her," I add, surprising myself.

"Yeah?" he says. "How come?"

I think for a minute about what my mom said about Nance and her "phase" a few years ago. She's never talked about it with me. I think about her hips. The drinking and boob flashing.

"Her dad had an affair with a really young girl, got her pregnant, and married her. And her mom has a boyfriend and is hardly around. I guess she tries handling it. I mean, I've done my share of stupid things, trying to handle my own stuff…"

He doesn't say anything but squeezes my hand.

"Yeah. We find ways."

"Nance and I started hanging out after my best friend and I, well, we had a best friend breakup." I think about Penny. The smile we shared. "She was there tonight," I say softly. "My old best friend. Penny. We were super tight, when I wasn't so…" I try and think of the right word. "Stupid." I sneak a peek to see his reaction.

"What happened?" he asks. He squeezes my hand again, and I feel like I can tell him things. Everything. About how close Penny and I were. How she spent so much time at my house when her dad was sick. We talked about everything then. We had each other's backs.

"I messed up. And now, I've been partying too much, I guess." I fiddle with an earring with my free hand. "I'm kind of crazy when I drink," I admit. That's a big confession to make to a boy I like. "It's embarrassing. Especially the next day." I dip my head, but he reaches over and props up my chin.

"So maybe you shouldn't do it anymore," he says and lets my chin go. He's probably never had time to lay around all day nursing a hangover. Ugh.

"Do you ever drink?" I ask.

"I have. But I have to look out for Kyle so…" He shrugs. "My mom works a lot. She needs breaks sometimes."

"Yeah." The night air is cool and I shiver, but it might be from holding his hand like this. Talking to him. Getting to know him.

"It's okay. He's a good kid. Most of the time. When he doesn't hide from pretty girls looking after him."

I smile and squeeze his hand back.

"I haven't been partying since I started at New Beginnings," I tell him.

"Yeah? You miss it? Your friends?"

"No," I tell him honestly. "I don't. I like my new friends."

He grins. "Like me?"

I swing his hand in the air. "No. Like Wilf. And Kyle. And Martha."

He pretends to grab his heart.

"Okay," I say softly. "You. I like you." I take a deep breath after I say that.

The streetlight we're walking under flickers on and off. He says something, but a car with muffler issues races by and drowns out his words.

"It's not fair," I say when the car is gone.

"What?" he asks.

"Life," I say glumly. "That some people have so much and other people don't."

"Fair is a place that has corn dogs and Ferris wheels. It's not real life."

I wonder if I would be so philosophical about it all in his place.

"It's not your fault," he says as if he reads my thoughts. "That your family has money. It's not even bad. It's kind of the American way."

"Maybe. But still," I tell him. "The shelter is making me see all the things I take for granted. I've done so many stupid things, and I have so much to be thankful for."

"We've all done stupid things," he says.

"Not everyone. What about you?" Another streetlight flickers, and a squirrel runs up a nearby tree and makes a racket.

He laughs at the noise. "Trust me, Jess. I've done my share. I've hurt people."

I'm pretty sure I don't want to think about that. We walk quietly, and I try to think of something to lighten our chat.

"So, how do you know Braxton?" I ask after another pause.

"He lives on my street. When we were moving in, he came over and helped me with the heavy stuff. He's around a lot now. His mom died when he was younger, and he likes my mom."

I nod. "He seems nice. But man, he talks a lot," I add. A car speeds by and a guy yells something out the window, but it's hard to tell what it is.

We watch them drive off.

"Yeah. He does. But he's a good guy. He loves that piece of shit car he has."

"It is a piece of shit," I agree. There are birds making noises in the trees around us, chattering in the night air.

"Hey," he says, stopping abruptly and glancing up. "Did you hear that?"

I look up. All I see are the trees and the black sky.

"What?"

"Who cooks for you, who cooks for you," he says.

I stare at him, wondering what the heck he's talking about.

He looks at my face and cracks up. "Who cooks for you, who cooks for you," he says again.

"Um, Flynn," I say and laugh with him. "What are you talking about?"

"The barred owl. That's his call: Who cooks for you, who cooks for you. I thought I heard it." He drops my hand and walks under a tree, searching, I assume, for his bird friend.

I laugh even harder.

"You think I'm making it up?" he asks. "I happen to know my owls. He could be lost."

I cover my mouth with my hand, but I can't stop giggling. Flynn is standing under a tree, searching for a bird. He throws his hands in the air then and returns to my side. "I'm not crazy. I can't see him, but he's there. Who cooks for you, who cooks for you." He takes my hand and we start walking again, but I can't stop giggling.

"Hey. You know your flowers. I know my owls. That's the barred owl. They hang out in some of the parks around town. Trust me."

"I totally believe you," I tell him, trying to be serious.

"You're bullshitting me," he says.

I giggle and then decide I like him even more.

"That owl has high standards," he says and whistles. "Hanging out in this neighborhood." He swings my hand up and down. "I hate it, you know."

"What?" I ask.

"That you see me getting handouts. I'm not going to live like that forever. I'm going to do things. I have plans."

I think of him coming in early to help out, looking after his brother, looking out for his mom.

"You already amaze me." His situation doesn't make me like him any less. It makes him who he is. And I like that guy very much. "So, what are your plans?" I ask. We're approaching my street, almost home, and I want to take a wrong turn, keep walking with him. Hear all his plans. Every one of them.

He smiles down at me. "Construction," he says. "I'm good with my hands. And I'm not afraid of heights. But I want to move my way up. My dad was a project manager. He did great. I want to do even more."

"Cool," I say, envying him, knowing what he wants to do already.

And secretly, I admire his ambition. I trip on a curb I didn't see coming, and he has to balance me and then stand me upright. We both laugh.

"Thanks," I tell him.

The way he looks down at me makes my insides swoon. His dark eyes sparkle. His bangs hang down sexily. He pushes them out of his eyes. "I'm glad you came to the party," he says softly. I'm the happiest girl in the world.

I take a deep breath. "Me too." I almost whisper it, because everything in me turns warm and gooey, including my voice. "I'm glad you were there." There's so much internal heat burning in me, I wonder if he senses it.

We keep walking but we keep glancing at each other. Grinning. My heart grows and grows and grows until it's so full and so big that I'm afraid it's going to explode right out of my chest.

"So are you working tomorrow?" he asks.

"I don't work weekends," I manage. "This is my street," I add. "That's my house." I point at it, because I doubt he remembers which one is mine from when Braxton dropped me off.

He stares at it and his chin lifts a little. He doesn't say anything.

"It's just a house," I tell him. "I'd trade it in a minute for a happy family." I slow down so we're barely moving.

"What's wrong with your family?"

I stare down at my feet, scared. I want to tell him. I trust him. But I haven't talked about it with anyone. Not Penny. Not Nance. Allie and I don't even talk about it, not really.

"It's okay," he says quietly. "If you don't want to tell me."

"I do." My voice is like a sigh. "I want to." I glance at my house. "It's a long story, and I'm home. And I don't know if I'm brave enough yet."

"Jess," he says. "You're brave. And good. If you could see yourself the way the people at the shelter see you. The way I see you."

"That's not the way I feel," I admit as we reach the end of my driveway.

He turns to me. Faces me. Stops walking and takes my other hand.

"You need to," he says.

But I forget the shelter. I forget my family. The owl. The party. All I can concentrate on is what will happen. The darkness is suddenly ominous. I hold my breath. Excited. Thrilled. Nervous.

It's time to kiss.

"You're going to be amazing when you figure out what you want. And who you can trust."

He lets my hands go, makes a fist, and softly knuckles me on the chin. Like I'm his buddy. His pal. His friend. And before I know it, he's gone.

chapter **fourteen**

H e didn't kiss me.

The house is quiet. It's midmorning already, but I'm still in bed going over it and over and it in my mind. I've rehashed the entire walk home. *Am I not kissable?*

I sit up and cross my legs, feeling like the biggest loser in the world. He should have kissed me. Everything pointed to it. I wanted him to. I thought he would. And then there was the abrupt good-bye, as he left me to walk to the closest bus stop.

I get up from bed, wishing there were someone to call to analyze everything, to dissect every second and figure out what went wrong. Nance is out of the question since (A) I lied to her and said we'd already hooked up, and (B) I know she won't want to hear about me falling for a guy like Flynn. He's supposed to be her fling.

Penny's face flashes in my head, the way she smiled at me at the party. Frustrated, I get up, but before heading downstairs, I tiptoe down the hall to my mom's room, open the door a crack, and see a lump on the bed. She's sleeping.

Downstairs, I go straight to the phone and pluck it off the cradle, staring at the numbers, but I put it back down. I can't phone Penny. It's stupid to expect to go from nothing to everything because of one smile. She didn't call me to chat when she hooked up with Keith.

Instead, I dial Nance's cell number and leave a message. I pour a bowl of cereal but only eat half before pushing it away. Unfairness overwhelms me. I can't even text her. I'm deserted and friendless in my own house. With a sigh, I wander to the living room and try to watch TV, but it's boring reality stuff. I did this to myself. It's easy to hate the person I've been the last couple of years, but I click the remote and it occurs to me—I can change channels. Why not myself?

I throw the remote down and march back to the phone, pick it up, and dial Penny's number. It rings once before my skin breaks out in a layer of sweat and I bang it back down. My cheeks burn with embarrassment. Great. So caller ID just happened. Great.

Chicken. I'm a chicken. I miss Penny so much, but telling her means apologizing. Owning up. It can't be that hard, can it? I think of my sock monkey, the one I gave Carly next door. For bravery. Penny gave it to me after Mom was hurt. I bought her a bigger version when her dad went through chemo, to protect her. Bill the Protector.

A creak on the steps interrupts my thoughts, and Mom walks down the stairs. She half smiles. "You're up," she says as if she's not creeping out of bed at noon. "I was up earlier too," she explains. "But I went back for a nap."

I try to smile, but my lips don't cooperate.

"How are you?" she asks as she reaches the landing.

"Good," I tell her and twist my earring around. What if I could talk to her about Flynn? Would we talk about things like that? If none of the bad stuff happened?

"You worked late last night? Dinner?"

"Yeah. I went to a party after, but it wasn't late when I got in," I tell her. "Before eleven."

"Oh. That's not too bad." She heads to the kitchen and turns on the stove to boil water for tea, then comes back to the living room, plunks down beside me on the couch, and pats my leg. "I remember when I was seventeen. I loved to stay out late. I gave your grandma and grandpa lots of heart attacks. Like you've been doing to your dad lately." She half smiles again. "Don't look so shocked. I wasn't always your mom."

Yeah, but she hasn't acted like one for a long time. I glance down at my fingernails. They're kind of ragged. I haven't had a manicure since I started at New Beginnings.

"Your grandma used to get so angry." She stares off into space. "She'd be angry with me now. She'd be kicking my butt, telling me to get back in the game." She shakes out the memory and turns to me with a smile. "She was a feisty woman. You would have liked her."

Her parents died before I was born, and she doesn't talk about them much. I shake my head though, ready to defend her. "No. You're recovering…"

She pats my leg as she gets up and then walks back to the kitchen to fix up her tea. "You're a good kid, Jess," she calls over her shoulder. "I haven't been nearly present enough for you."

"Mom," I start, wanting to deny it, but from the kitchen she raises her hand to quiet me.

"No. It's okay. Everyone's been protecting me." She sighs and pours water into her mug. She doesn't offer me tea. She knows I don't like it. "I'm getting tired of it. Finally. God," she mutters to herself.

I hold my breath, no idea what to say.

"How's work?" she asks while I freak the hell out.

"Um, good," I tell her honestly. "I like it."

"It is good. What you're doing." She sips her tea and a small shudder visibly clouds her. "You're careful though. Right?"

"I am, Mom."

She droops a little as she returns to the living room, and I wonder if her meds are kicking in. It's like watching her get sucked down a hole. I have no idea how to save her or pull her back out.

"Mom?"

"Yeah?" She walks over, sits beside me, and forces a smile, her hands wrapped around her mug.

"I was thinking about going to Target to do a little shopping. Will you come with me?"

"Target?" Her brows furrow together as if she doesn't know what I mean.

"Yeah. I need to pick up a key chain. I gave the little girl next door my sock monkey one. You know? The one that hung off my purse? That one Penny gave me? Brave Monkey?"

She smiles a smile that tells me she has no idea what sock monkey I'm talking about. Or why I would give it to Carly.

"Anyhow, I want to get a new one. I'll get one for you too. A matching one. We can all use a little Brave Monkey in our lives."

She makes a sound that almost sounds like a laugh. "You want to get me a sock monkey key chain?" she asks and brings her mug to her lips for a sip.

"I do," I tell her.

She stares at me and finally pats my leg. "Okay. Well, let me finish my tea. And then I should change," she says.

It's progress. And Lord knows we could both use a Brave Monkey.

• • •

Mom laughs when I attach her sock monkey to her purse. She looks younger and happier, and she leaves it dangling from her purse over her shoulder, smiling. She stayed close to me while we wandered through the aisles of Target, looking at stuff we don't need. We didn't stay long, not even an hour, and when we walk back in the house, she goes to the kitchen to put down her purse but bats at the brave monkey before turning to me.

"Thanks for taking me," she says. "It was fun." She glances off to the stairs. "Your dad is home tomorrow."

"Okay."

"I'm going to go to my room now."

My heart dips a little.

"To read," she adds. "It's a self-help book," she says softly. "I ordered it online."

I take it as a good sign and silently thank her sock monkey.

When she's gone, I go to the living room and lay on the floor, trying some yoga poses to stretch out my back. The phone finally rings, and I jump up and run to it, checking caller ID before I click the on button.

"Nance," I say instead of *hi*.

"Ugh," she groans. "Don't talk so loud, Jess. My head is a mine-field of agony."

"Hangover? Moaning after the night before?" I tuck the phone under my chin and go back to the living room and hold it in place, lie on my back, and lift my hips in the air to attempt a bridge pose.

"Please," she says. "I can't handle attempts at humor right now. Why don't you text me like normal people do?"

"Um, my dad took my phone for the summer, remember?" I squeeze my thighs together, trying to hold the bridge pose.

"God." She sighs loudly, and I hear water running in the background. "I can't believe you live in a world without a cell phone. I would die. You're impossible to get a hold of. It's super annoying."

I don't say anything. This isn't about the inconvenience for her, is it? I push my hips higher and feel the pull along my back and in my thighs.

"So. Is it super gross?" she asks, and I hear her glugging something. "What?"

She keeps glugging. "That soup kitchen thing?" she says when she's done.

"No." I collapse down slowly, coming down one vertebra at a time, letting out my breath as I go. The phone slips from under my chin and I grab it. "I mean. It's okay. I don't mind it."

I think of Flynn and close my eyes. Her judgmental silence on the other end is heavy, but I keep my eyes closed and let the silence expand. I focus on the people at New Beginnings. They like me. I like them.

"Well, it would freak me out," Nance finally says. She sounds pissed off she was forced to speak first. "And you were pretty lame at Brittney's last night." My eyes pop open then, and the quiet in my head disappears.

"Oh. You do remember me being there?" I say innocently but make a face at the phone. I sit up too fast, and my head spins as the blood rushes away from my head.

"Oh, I remember," she says all bitchy.

"Yeah. So how'd it go with Hunter Bell?" I ask, trying to sound as if I care. I wish it were Penny on the phone instead of Nance. I'm more interested in hearing about Keith. Penny's been in love with him forever. Hunter Bell is a booty call.

"Amazing." Her voice gets a little less cranky. "He's the most amazing kisser in the entire world."

Of course, she's said that about other guys. I stretch out my back and listen while Nance goes on, describing the softness of Hunter's lips in detail. It makes me wonder again why Flynn didn't kiss me. She stops talking for a second as the phone rattles around on her end.

"If my mom saw him, you're dead," she calls to someone at her house. I hear laughter. It sounds like a machine gun. Ah ha ha ha ha ha ha.

Jennifer.

"Your mom wasn't even home last night!" I hear Jennifer shout back.

"Really?" Nance whistles. "I *was* wasted. I passed out on the couch without even noticing. My body hurts so freaking much."

I relax and lie back down, still listening.

"Braxton and Jennifer hooked up over here last night," she says to me. "Just a sec." She covers the phone and says something to Jennifer, but it's muffled. The phone rattles. "She smuggled him into my room last night," she says to me. "Which explains why I had to sleep on the couch. God, Jennifer. So what about the guy you hooked up with?" she asks.

My eyes pop open wide, and then I remember telling her I hooked up with Flynn so she'd back off.

"He was wearing a medical bracelet," she says.

"Yeah." I don't ask if she noticed that while slobbering all over him.

"Is he dying?" she asks, sounding almost hopeful, as if it would be good gossip.

"No," I tell her. "He's not dying."

"Hm. Well, enjoy him while you can."

I chew my lip, reflecting on that.

"No offense, but Jennifer and I were talking about how lame you were acting," she says. She's pissed at me. Or bitchy from the hangover. I have an urge to hang up in her ear.

"I wasn't drinking." I cross one leg over the other and twist in the opposite direction. I remember the cooler in the kitchen with Josh. "Well, not much anyhow."

"Boring. No offense." She glugs some more.

Judging by the twinge in my gut, offense taken. So maybe I am lame. I probably was boring, but it doesn't bother me as much as it would have a couple of weeks ago. Is that who I turned into? A party girl who relies on alcohol to give her a personality?

"Hey," she says. "Speaking of hooking up. Did you see Penny last night? Apparently she's hooking up with Keith Alex."

"Yeah, I saw." I keep the phone tucked under my chin and hug myself. She doesn't know about Penny's forever crush. I kept that secret. Keith is more than hooking up to her, and I'm thrilled for her.

Nance waits, as if she wants me to slam Penny, say something bitchy. I glance over at my purse lying on the chair and smile at the sock monkey hanging off the side. "He's a really nice guy," I say. "I think they're good together."

"Whatever. His dad works at McDonald's. I mean corporate, but still."

I pause to gather courage. This is one of those moments. Those defining moments.

"So actually, I really like him," I blurt out.

"Who? Keith?"

"No," I tell her. "Flynn. I really like him."

"The boy from last night? No, you don't. You're having a fling. He's hot, I get it. But that's all it is. Summer. Fling."

"No," I tell her. "No, it's not." My heart beats faster. This isn't the way I talk to Nance. I can almost see her scowl.

"It's a summer fling," she insists.

I don't respond. The silence over the phone is heavy.

"Jess. I know you're working at that place and being all virtuous and off the grid and stuff, but things go back to normal after the summer," she says, an edge to her voice. "This is our senior year."

"Yeah," I tell her. "It is."

"Do not screw this up," she says. "Things need to be perfect this year."

I think about her dad taking off and her mom's new boyfriend. She's as alone as I am most of the time. I picture her scars. The faded ones on her arms and the fresh ones on her hip.

"There's no such thing as perfect," I say sadly. "It's all an illusion."

I wonder what's going to happen when Nance figures it out too.

chapter **fifteen**

W ow!" Stella says when I walk into her office on Monday. She's at her desk, piles of paper spread in front of her. "You look extra pretty today." She narrows her eyes. "Any special reason?"

"No." I glance down at my favorite jeans. Maybe I took time to curl my hair and apply makeup, and maybe I'm wearing a turquoise top because people say the color makes my eyes pop. It's not a crime.

She stares at me. "What's up, Jess?"

"What?" I say and blink innocently.

"You look like you're going to an audition for a Miss Teen Beauty Pageant."

"Stella, I do not." I want to be offended, but a teeny part of me is flattered.

"Mm-hmm." She looks down at the paper work in front of her.

"Stella?" I ask.

She looks up.

"You called me in here," I remind her.

"Oh, right. Sorry." She takes off her reading glasses, puts them down, opens a drawer, and reaches inside. "This was left for you. On my desk." She pulls it out.

I step forward. It's a thick book. An old, well-worn one. There's a yellow Post-it note on the cover. My name's written on it. JESS.

She nods at it, so I pick it up. *The Book of Plants*, the title says. I know the book, but this obviously is an old and well-loved copy. I open to the first page.

For the Flower Expert.

Just in case.

Flynn. ☺

I smile and trace my fingers over his name. I flip forward and look over a few pages. Notes are jotted in pen at the side in old-fashioned scrawl. I close it and hug the book to my chest, grinning. He is officially forgiven for not kissing me.

Stella clears her throat, puts her eyeglasses back on, and looks down at a paper. A disapproving vibe pulses around the room. I'm about to slink out when she pushes her glasses up on her nose and leans back in her chair, her gaze thoughtful.

"So, Jess," she says. "Only a few more weeks left of summer and then you're back to school. Your dad only committed you to work here for the summer."

"I want to keep coming," I blurt out. "Keep volunteering."

"Senior year is a busy one," she interrupts. "Does your dad know your plans?"

"Not yet." I pull the book closer to my chest.

She presses her lips tight.

"He's not going to stop me from volunteering if I want to."

She leans forward, her hands in a steeple, and stares at me long and hard. Finally she nods. "Fair enough," she says. "But remember you're living in his house under his rules."

"I know that."

She glances at me, her eyebrows raised, apparently done with our conversation. Her eyes go back to her paper.

"Stella?"

She glances up.

"I was thinking about bringing in some plants for the green-house. I used to have a garden of herbs at home. I thought about starting an indoor herb garden here."

She glances up at me over the top of her reading glasses. "Herbs?"

"Rosemary. Mint. Oregano. Easy to grow and take care of. Maybe we could sell some of the herbs to a local grocer and the money could come back to the shelter? Or use the herbs in the kitchen?"

"I don't know about selling anything." She tilts her head. "I like the idea of using them in the kitchen though. Of course, you know the greenhouse is Wilf's baby. He funds the whole thing. You'll need to talk to him about it."

"Yeah. I kind of thought so, but I wanted to check with you first. I don't want to do things to upset you." She stares at me. I think we both know we're talking about more than plants here.

"I know," she says softly, and her eyes lose their angry glare. "You'll have to supply everything you need for the herbs on your own. I mean financially. That's not up to Wilf."

I nod again.

"God knows your family can afford it," she mumbles, trying to sound grouchy.

"I know," I tell her. "They can."

Her expression changes then, and her face looks almost sad. "Wilf isn't going to be around forever, you know. It'll be hard to keep the greenhouse going. After."

I frown.

"Just talk to him about the herbs," she says quickly. "And only if you really plan on sticking around after the summer."

"I do." I frown. "I said I would."

She flashes a quick smile. "Thanks, Jess. I hope you do stick around. You're a good kid." The unexpected compliment from her feels nicer than my comfy jeans. Stoked by her words, I leave her office, grab a lock, and tuck my new book safely away. Smiling as I close the locker door, I hurry to the kitchen. Wilf's already working, training a new volunteer, so I don't get a chance to chat with him about my idea for an herb garden.

I set up my tables on my own and keep my eye on the clock, watching the door for Flynn and Kyle. Before long, the guests arrive and I'm seating them and starting to serve soup, but Flynn and Kyle haven't shown up. Disappointment makes me ache more than usual from the running around. I keep looking up, checking for them, but they don't arrive. When the lunch service is almost over, an Asian woman walks into the dining area, holding hands with Kyle. She's tiny and a little stooped in the shoulders. Her hair is the color of midnight with no signs of gray. There are hardly any lines on her face. She's quite beautiful but somehow looks older and wearier than she should.

When Kyle sees me, his face lights up and he drops the woman's hand and tries running to me. She grabs him and holds him back, a frown lifting her eyebrows.

"Kyle," she scolds. "You don't run in the dining room like that."

The security guard at the door waves at me to tell me to take them to my table, so I walk forward, nerves pecking at my skin from the inside.

"This is Jess, Mommy," Kyle tells her when he reaches me.

He wraps his arms around my legs and I pat him on the head.

"Hey, buddy!"

He grins at me and takes my hand as he turns to his mom. "This is the girl I told you about. The one who lost me."

I almost groan, but she walks toward us and nods her head and smiles. It's quick to disappear and doesn't reach her eyes.

"Nice to meet you, Jess," she says. Her voice is soft.

"You too."

I want to ask where Flynn is today, why she's here, but my tongue feels too big for my mouth. "Have a seat," I tell her, and we walk a few more steps to an empty table. There's only one clean place setting at the table, but I pull out the chair and hold it for her to sit. "I'll go get you a clean plate and cutlery," I tell Kyle.

She sinks down into the chair while Kyle lets go of me and I ruffle his hair.

"I see Wilf over there," he says to his mom. Then he asks me, "Can I help? Can I go get the plate?"

I look at his mom, and she nods.

"Sure," I tell him. "Ask him for a place setting."

After he scrambles off, she looks right in my eyes. "My son is quite taken with you," she says softly.

"He's a good kid," I say, watching him run away. "I like him too."

"Jess?"

I turn back to her. "Yes?"

She blinks slowly. "That isn't the son I was speaking of," she says in her muted voice.

I open my mouth to say something, but nothing comes out. Warmth rushes to my cheeks, but when I see the flash of disapproval shining in her eyes, I struggle for the right thing to say. She blinks again and it's gone—her face is blank, with no emotion at all.

We both watch Kyle run back without a place setting. "Can I go say hello to Miss Stella?" he shouts at his mom.

When she nods, he runs straight toward Stella, and she bends down for a hug and folds him into her embrace like a big mama bear.

"I'll go get another place setting," I tell Flynn's mom. "Would you like a tea or something to start your lunch?"

She nods and lowers her eyes. "That would be nice," she says.

I head toward the kitchen, my ears as hot as my face. It feels like I've done something wrong. Wilf walks by with the new volunteer right behind him, an older white-haired woman with twinkling eyes and funky clothes.

"Cat got your tongue?" he asks me.

If Flynn's mom is a cat, the answer is yes. I fake-smile and pick up a new place setting for Kyle and deliver it to the table. His mom smiles at me when I lay it down, but there's no warmth between us.

It worries me.

• • •

Kyle and his mom are my last guests, and Kyle's cute banter helps make things less awkward. When they leave and I'm cleaned up, I head outside to the greenhouse. Wilf slipped me a key and told me he was taking off to the doctor. I remember I still haven't had a chance to ask Wilf about bringing in herbs.

I'm relieved to breathe the air in the greenhouse, and the leafy creatures inside don't dislike me like Flynn's mom seems to. I start dusting leaves and then take scissors from the cupboard to prune the browned leaf tips, careful to keep the cut natural, following the contour of the leaves.

I fritter around the room, losing myself in the simplicity of green life, and smile at a pot of geraniums, my favorite house-plant in the greenhouse. Soon there's a rush of outside air as the door opens and I turn, expecting to see Wilf back from his doctor's appointment early. My heart pitter-patters when Flynn walks inside.

"Hey!" I say, and a smile takes over my entire face. He's so lovely to look at. I want to be mad at him, for not kissing me last night, for having a mom who doesn't like me, but all I do is smile wider. "Thank you for the book. It's the best gift I've ever gotten," I say and then focus on the plant in front of me, suddenly shy with him. Have I given away too much with my enthusiasm? The quiet air of the greenhouse hums in my burning ears.

"It was my grandma's," he says simply. "I brought it by yesterday so you'd get it this morning." He tucks his hands in his jeans and leans back on his heels, smiling.

"It was your grandma's?" The plants seem to be listening as hap-pily as I am.

"Yeah."

"So that's her writing in the book?"

"Yeah. Weird? Is that a weird thing to give you?"

"No," I tell him. "It's amazing. I love it. A lot. Are you sure it's okay to give it to me?"

"She left if for me. I chose to give it to you. It's okay." He takes his hands out of his pockets and walks closer.

"Thank you." I shift back and forth on my heels and glance down at the ivy. "So where were you at lunch today?" I ask. "I missed you."

"My mom asked me to pick up some things up for her. She wanted to bring Kyle for lunch today."

"Yeah. I met her," I tell him, and my cheeks burn.

"I heard," he says.

I wait for him to say more. Hoping he'll say she liked me. Something. But he doesn't.

"She didn't like me." I hear the hurt in my voice.

He reaches out to touch my arm. "It's not that. My mom just worries." He pulls away and picks up a spray bottle and mists a nearby plant.

I shiver, but it has nothing to do with cold. "Oh."

"It's not about you." He sprays the plant again, watching the water bubbles dance on the leaves. "It's more about me."

"Why?" I ask.

He leans against the counter, watching me, and puts the bottle down. Then he gestures around him. "You work here. I come for free food."

"So?" I put the scissors back in the tool drawer and stare down at them.

"It bothers her."

"Does it bother you?" I ask and look up.

"I don't want it to," he says softly.

"It doesn't matter to me," I tell him. I don't say it, but it would make me feel much better if his mom liked me. I want her to like me.

"We come from different places," he says and stares down at his feet.

"Well." I clear my throat. "I mean, maybe we have different stuff. Maybe our families are in different places right now, but it doesn't mean one is right and one is wrong."

He bites his lip and refuses to meet my gaze.

"We're not that different," I say softly. "You and I."

He doesn't look up.

"Don't give up on me," I tell him and swallow an enormous lump that popped up in my throat. "Flynn, we're not different. Not here." I point at my heart. "Inside." I can't believe the sappy stuff coming out of my mouth. But I mean it. It's true. I can say this to him. Because it's true.

"Maybe," he says. "I want to believe it." Finally he looks at me, and then he grins, and the yucky feelings start to fade a little. "Hey, don't look so bummed. My mom doesn't pick my friends." He picks up the bottle and walks closer and sprays me.

"No, you did not!" I scream and laugh, trying to get the bottle away from him. He sprays me again so I run, and he chases me up the aisle, trying to get me wet. When he catches me, he grabs me by the waist and pulls me in close.

"I could soak you," he says.

But he doesn't lift the spray bottle. He's so close, his breath is in my ear. His lip is almost touching my earlobe. I move a little, and I'm tucked right against him. I don't want to move or let go. He smells like boy. Delicious, beautiful Flynn. We both stay perfectly still, our breaths synchronized, rising and falling at the same time.

Kiss me, kiss me, kiss me, I think.

And then, for the first time in a long time, I decide to be the brave one. For the first time, without alcohol streaming through my blood and giving me false courage, I take responsibility for my actions. Sock monkey style.

I slide my hand behind his neck and pull his face toward me and we kiss. I mean, I really, really kiss him. And it's amazing because he kisses back hard, and it's the best thing that I've ever felt in my whole entire life. If our kiss is any indication, we have enough chemistry to blow up the greenhouse.

"Wow," he says when we finally break apart for a breath.

"Wow," I whisper back, amazed by my bravado. And thrilled by his response. "I thought you didn't want to kiss me," I say.

"Are you kidding?" he says. "I wanted to kiss you very badly." He doesn't let go of my waist.

"So why didn't you?"

"Because I thought maybe you needed to do it first." He bites down on his lip, and I watch, envying it so much. "You think we're not different," he says. "We are, but it's okay, because we understand each other. I want you more than I've ever wanted anyone in my life," he says.

I stop breathing.

"I don't want to scare you off," he says in a husky voice. "Because if we do this. I mean, this. Us. It's not going to be easy. Not for me. Or for you."

I lean forward and kiss him again. It goes on for a delicious moment, but then he pulls back. "You're not the kind of girl who usually gives me a second look."

I snort. It's unsexy, but it doesn't embarrass me. "Are you kidding me, Flynn?"

"I'm not."

"Then you don't know what you have," I tell him in awe.

We stare at each other as if we're really seeing each other. Looking inside and understanding without saying anything out loud. "I want to tell you," I say, "what happened to my mom." My insides seize and I close my eyes and try to get my breath. He tucks a finger under my chin. I press my lips tight and shake my head.

"It's okay," he says. "You don't have to."

He moves his hands to my face and holds my cheeks. I close my eyes and inhale him. Dread courses through me, but I breathe out and then open my eyes. "My mom was attacked," I say quietly. "In the park. Downtown. In daylight. She was running. Alone. She had on an iPod and she had it cranked. She was celebrating a sale. A big commission. She sold houses, real estate. She didn't even hear them come up behind her."

I stop to take a breath, and it's so quiet in the greenhouse, I can hear a fly buzzing at the other end.

"She loved running and hiking. We spent half my childhood doing that, hiking. Me and my sister and Penny, usually. When we were kids, Penny was over at our house a lot. Especially when her dad got sick." I take a deep breath, knowing I'm procrastinating.

He drops his hands from my face and takes my hands in his. He doesn't say anything. Doesn't rush me or tell me to stay focused. He doesn't ask questions. He waits.

"Three guys jumped her," I finally say. "They pulled her off the trail. They searched her for money, but she didn't have anything on her because, you know, she was going for a run. I mean, why would she be carrying money?"

"I remember hearing about a woman who was assaulted," he says quietly. "We didn't live in Tadita then, but I remember it was in the news."

"Yeah. They never named her. But most people know."

Flynn shakes his head. He waits.

"The park was open, but no one heard or saw anything," I continue. Flynn squeezes my hands. "They beat her up," I say and stare at a drooping house plant. "There were three of them. And she's little. She had skin under her nails from scratching them. They never found them. They were wearing ski masks. They had a gun. But they didn't shoot her. They wanted money, and I guess it pissed them off when she didn't have any, so they beat her. She passed out at some point, and they left her. Lying in the bushes. They probably thought she was dead."

I'm shivering now, and Flynn pulls me close, his arm around me. It's meant to be comforting, and I lay my head on his shoulder, letting him protect me. "I'm sorry," he says.

"A boy found her. He was playing hide-and-seek with friends." I shake my head. I often wonder about that boy. If he has nightmares.

"Her face was unrecognizable. They had to wire her jaw shut." I can't stop now. I've held it in for too long, been forbidden to talk about it, and it's been eating away at me. Festering and black. And now it's all rushing out. I push away from him and step back, wrapping my arms around myself.

"She was unconscious for two days. The only good thing we heard during that time was that the rape test was negative. When she woke up, she had to talk to the police. Go over and over it. She was in the hospital for weeks. And when she came out, well, she didn't talk about it anymore. Not with us. I don't think she talks about it with anyone."

"Shit," he says softly.

"She had a doctor for a while. You know, like a psychologist or whatever, and he gave her pills. Pills for pain. Pills to help her sleep. And pills to try to fight the anxiety and depression. She's always tired. She sleeps a lot. But she's never really come back. You know? Not the mom she used to be."

I can feel Flynn watching me. Feel his sympathy.

"It's been over two years. Now my dad works all the time and refuses to talk about it. He's gone most of the time. Traveling for work. And my sister, Allie, she stays at her boyfriend's house. And my mom. She sleeps." I look at him then. He strokes my arm.

"I hate them," I tell him, and the rest of the blackness spills out. The force of my words hurt my throat. "I hate those men who ruined my mom, who ruined my family. And sometimes, I hate my family too."

All the ugliness living and breeding inside me has leaked out, and now I'm exposed for who I really am. "I started doing stupid things to try and forget. I lost my best friend. Most of the time, I don't even know who I am anymore. Except that I'm a bad person." My shame is bared. I'm naked. I've exposed to him the darkness in my soul.

But Flynn only pulls me close, holding me tight. "You're not bad," he tells me. "You aren't. You've been trying to deal. You're a good person, Jess. You are."

I sniffle and blubber, like a little baby, but he holds on.

"I miss them. The way we used to be. The way I used to be," I say to his chest. My face is pressed against it, and it's hard and comforting.

"I know," he says. "I know." I press tighter against him, wanting to crawl inside, wanting him to take away the parts of myself I hate.

He pats my back gently until my crying stops. Eventually I'm only sniffling, and I realize with surprise that it feels lighter. I'm not as afraid. The noise that's always buzzing in my head, the pressure and constant tangible tension, it's gone.

I loosen my hold on Flynn and breathe. Really breathe. Then I lean back and stare into his face. "Thank you," I tell him.

He smiles. I trust him. And it feels better. It's released something in me, freed me.

He bends down then and kisses me gently, and when he licks the inside of my lip, it's so surprising and so delightful, I gasp. We wrap ourselves around each other, and we kiss and kiss and kiss.

And then there's a bang.

The door to the greenhouse is open, and Kyle is inside, staring at us. Stella is right behind him, frowning.

"Flynn, where were you?" Kyle asks. "You were supposed to come and get me at least ten minutes ago," he shouts with five-year-old despair.

Flynn and I drop our arms to our sides and step away from each other, but it's too late.

"You were kissing Jess. You were." Kyle runs over and wraps his arms around my thighs and squeezes me tight. He frowns at Flynn as if he stole his favorite Thomas the Tank Engine.

I pat Kyle on the head. "How's my favorite five-year-old?" I glance at Stella, but her arms are crossed and she's scowling. Uh-oh.

"Me!" Kyle yells. "I'm your favorite five-year-old."

I bend down so I don't have to face Stella, and I'm nose to nose with Kyle. "Of course you are." I lift my hand for a high five, and he whacks it hard so I make an *oof* sound and stand.

He makes a loud humph sound and crosses his arms like Stella. "I thought you were *my* girlfriend. Not his." He points at his brother.

Stella's watching all three of us without a word. Without a pleasant expression.

I ruffle Kyle's hair. "You're better than a boyfriend. You're at the top of my boy-who-is-a-friend list," I tell him. "Like best friend."

He studies me, and his body relaxes and he nods. "Yeah. That's better. I don't like that kind of kissing anyhow," he says.

"Well, good," I tell him. "You're cute, but you're a little young for me."

"That's enough, buddy," Flynn says, holding his hand out toward his brother. "We should go get Mom. She'll want to take you to the park."

"All by myself?" Kyle asks.

"Yup. She doesn't have to work this afternoon," Flynn says. He turns to me and touches my arm. "I'll be back in a few minutes. Wait for me?"

"She's needed in the kitchen," Stella tells both of us.

"Cool. Then I'll meet you there," Flynn says. He ignores Stella's obvious crankiness.

I nod, too afraid to say anything in front of Stella, but he walks by her, pats her shoulder, and whispers something in her ear.

Kyle flies out the way he came in, and Flynn follows behind.

Stella turns to go. "Don't forget to lock up the greenhouse," she says to me, and her voice is harsh.

"Stella?" I call. I don't want her to be mad at me.

My cheeks heat as her disapproval radiates off her in thermal waves.

"There's a lot on Flynn's plate, Jess," she says. "You shouldn't be getting involved in his life. You're just visiting this world. He lives in it."

I don't know what to say or how to say it, so I nod and drop my gaze to my feet. She's trying to protect Flynn. From me. She walks out of the greenhouse, leaving me all alone.

I glance around, still a little shaky from baring my soul. Wrong or not, when I'm with Flynn, it feels like I've found the place where I belong. It's incredible. Amazing. But he feels it too. I know it.

chapter **sixteen**

When Flynn walks into the kitchen with a big smile, some of my worry disappears. The glow on his face dulls my fear that maybe everyone is right about us. His mom doesn't approve of me. Stella doesn't approve. Nance doesn't approve. But when he smiles, it doesn't matter what other people say.

"You almost done?" he asks. "Stella's giving me grief for being back here."

"Yeah." I'm more than ready to rip off my apron and hang it on the designated hook. "I just have to put the cakes in the fridge." I point to the full trays.

"Can you meet me outside when you're done?" he asks. "On the picnic table by the side building?"

When I'm done putting the cakes away, I grab my gear and float to the staff room to punch out my time card. Pulling the plant book from the locker and holding it close to my chest, I hurry outside so Stella won't see me go.

There's a small crowd of regulars hanging outside around the front entrance. Some are early for the dinner lineup, and some hang out with nowhere else to go.

"Hey, Jess," I hear as I slip into the fresh air.

"Hi, George. How's your foot?"

"Better," he says. "Thanks for asking."

"Hey, Chickadee," another broken-toothed regular calls and gives me the thumbs-up. Somehow my nickname with the regulars is Chickadee. Thanks to Wilf.

I smile and tuck my head down, passing by more guests as I move toward the side of the building.

He's there.

Flynn sits on top of a picnic bench. The same kind of bench I've sat on a million times. With my mom at the park, having picnics with Allie and Penny. I jump up and sit beside him, putting my book on the other side. He presses his leg against mine.

"Stella is pissed at me," I say and glance down at rude graffiti on the table. And bird poop.

"Why?"

"I think she believes I'm forcing you to make out with me."

I expect him to laugh, but he puts his arm around my neck, so we're staring into each other's eyes. "It's not wrong. You and me."

"Tell that to your mom." I lift my chin. "Or Nance."

Flynn stares at me. "Nance?" His jawline hardens. "She thinks I'm not good enough?"

I touch his arm. "She's wrong."

"You know, when people tell me I can't have something, I want it more," he says.

I contemplate that. "Is that what this is? Proving you can get the rich girl?" I try and sound like I'm joking.

"No. I'm not trying to prove anything. But I wanted you to know I'm stubborn." He grins.

"I'm glad."

I watch him pull something from his pocket, and then he holds out his hand. There's a small piece of wood on his palm. "I made this."

I peer into his hand. "What's this?" I take it from him. It looks like a tiny squirrel.

"I'm that bad at whittling? It's a monkey."

I hold it closer. "You made it?"

He's wearing a playful grin. "My dad taught me to whittle. He taught me to make cowboy boots first, and then animals. You have a monkey on your purse. I made it for you."

I bump my shoulder against his. "I love it. But now I feel bad. I haven't gotten you anything."

"You haven't?" He pretends to snatch the monkey away.

A dorky giggle squeaks out of me, and I reach for it and a sliver of wood pierces my finger.

"Ouch." A drop of blood oozes out. I lift my finger to my lip and suck it away. "It doesn't matter. It's adorable."

He leans closer. "You're pretty adorable yourself," he whispers in my ear.

A breeze of nerves washes over my skin. My face flushes, embarrassment fusing with pleasure. I'm unable to articulate actual words. I tuck the monkey into the front pocket of my jeans.

"I want to kiss you," he says. "But we're in public. And that's like a Public Display of Affection."

"That *is* a PDA," I tell him and laugh. He glances around. People are milling about the building, but they don't seem to be paying attention to us.

"Braxton says you're out of my league," he mumbles. He picks up my hand and holds it in both of his.

"Stella thinks you're out of mine. And so does your mom."

"No," he says. "My mom thinks the opposite."

I shake my head.

He leans closer. "She does. But you know what?" he asks softly. "I just realized I don't have anything against PDA."

His lips press against mine softly and for only a second, but my head spins and my body melts.

When he pulls back, all the coherent thoughts have officially disappeared from my head. I lean against him, and we kiss deeper and longer. Nothing else in the world matters.

"Get a room," one of the workers having a smoke at the back of the building yells, and the others gathered with him laugh and whoop.

Flynn straightens his back, and we pull away from each other. "Sorry," he says. "I think I got carried away."

"Or was that me?" I ask with a grin.

We sit there like two big dorks, staring at each other without saying anything. We probably look like we're having a staring contest. I smile.

"What?" he asks.

"I don't know. You make me smile," I say. "I feel...connected to you. Is that weird? Do you think I'm weird?"

"Not weird. Well, maybe a little." He holds up his finger and thumb, showing a small measurement. And then he reaches to tuck a strand of hair behind my ear. "I feel it too," he says softly. "So we're both weird."

"Kyle said you had a lot of girlfriends." As soon as it leaves my mouth, I regret it.

He stares into my eyes but doesn't deny it. My belly blazes with jealousy. I chew my lip, trying not to let it bother me.

"I've never had a real girlfriend, you know," he says and brushes my hair back again. "Not a real one. Not like this." He takes my hand and lifts it to his lips. Kisses my knuckles one by one.

"Good," I whisper and link my fingers into his and lean forward. "Me too."

He leans in to meet me, and our lips brush together. I inhale and close my eyes. We kiss and we kiss, and I don't want to stop. I could kiss him until both of us stopped breathing and die happy.

"Jess!" a voice calls. An angry bark.

Dazed, we pull away from each other. I look over and my cheeks flare up. "Shit. It's my dad." I sit taller. "What the hell is he doing here?"

His hands are on his hips, and his face is red and contorted as if it's about to explode off his head.

"It's time to go home," he snaps, completely ignoring Flynn, looking right past him.

"I'm taking the bus," I holler, and my voice sounds stupid, shocked, and embarrassed. My temperature rises from the way he's staring at us like we're doing something wrong. *It's not wrong*, I want to shout.

"I came to drive you home." He looks ridiculous in his expensive suit with the tie that probably cost more than my entire outfit, including my not-cheap sneakers. I notice the way he turns his nose up at the people hanging around the shelter. The way he looks at me and doesn't look at Flynn. I know him, and he's not going to go away.

"Shit," I mumble, picking up my book and tucking it under my arm. I stand up and wait for Flynn to stand with me. He stays seated.

"It's okay," he says. "Go."

I look down and shake my head. "No. Come and meet him."

He glances at my dad, who is busy pretending Flynn doesn't exist.

"Let's go," my dad commands.

"Flynn. Come on."

Flynn looks at me long and hard as if he doesn't want to deal with this, like he wants to walk the other away, but then he jumps to the ground beside me. I take his hand but it's stiff in mine as we walk toward my dad.

Dad's face doesn't change. He shows no expression at all. No reaction or welcome for the boy I'm bringing over to meet him.

"Dad," I say, "this is Flynn."

The redness in Flynn's cheeks and the way he's rubbing at his neck breaks my heart.

I look to my dad and frown, trying to shame him into acknowledging Flynn properly. "Dad," I repeat. "This is my friend Flynn."

Flynn is taller, so Dad has to look up at him. I'm sure this bugs him even more. He acknowledges him with a man nod but doesn't smile.

"Nice to meet you," Flynn says. He pulls his hand away from mine and sticks it out to my dad.

After a second too long, a second that shows his feelings as clearly as if he'd refused to shake his hand at all, my dad presses palms with Flynn. Bubbling rage stands up the hairs on my arms.

"Let's go," Dad commands me.

My stomach burns. Flynn averts his eyes. As if he accepts my dad's treatment of him. My anger reaches out toward him as well. What about his words earlier? It doesn't matter what anyone else thinks. Well, that includes my dad. No matter what an arrogant prick he's being.

I don't know what to do to make this awkward and infuriating situation any better. Other than disown my dad, grab Flynn's hand, and run.

"I'm taking the bus," I say between gritted teeth.

"No. You're coming with me." Dad grabs me by the elbow, and I try to shake him off, but he holds on firmly.

Flynn watches, his eyebrows drawn together. "You okay?" he asks.

"Yeah."

Dad makes an angry sound in his throat, but I nod at Flynn to let him know I'm not about to get physically beaten or anything, because he looks kind of worried.

"Okay. I'll see you soon," Flynn says softly, and he meets my dad's gaze, nods once. "Nice to meet you," he lies and then turns and heads in the opposite direction.

My hatred for my dad grows, but he shoves me, forcing me to walk ahead of him the other way. "What the hell, Dad?"

He keeps pushing at me until we're past the shelter and the curious eyes of the people hanging out and watching. When we're past them, he hisses, "You have no business getting involved with boys like that."

He doesn't look at me as we reach his Tesla Roadster, which he parked arrogantly, taking up two spots.

"Boys like that?" I say. "Oh my God, are you trying to be cliché? You don't even know him."

He lifts his keys to automatically start the engine and unlock the doors.

"Get in the car."

"What are you doing here, Dad?" I ask again.

He grits his teeth. "That woman phoned me. That Stella. Suggesting some inappropriate behavior might be going on." He stomps around the front of his car and opens the passenger door. "Get in."

Betrayal stabs at my soul. Stella called him? Some of my fight knocks out of me. "It's not inappropriate. We like each other."

He waits for me to get in, his hand still on the door. "You are *not* dating a boy from the shelter."

"Why? Because he's poor? Or half Asian?" I ask.

"Neither," he snaps. "You're a volunteer. You don't get involved with these people."

My stomach grinds with anxiety, a sick feeling rolling around my belly. "What are you afraid of?" I ask. "That if I like him, I'll end up on the streets?"

"You're on a short leash, Jess. Don't push me."

"You don't even know him. Or his situation."

"I don't want you dragged in over your head. You're doing this to piss me off," he yells. "Put a stop to it. Immediately." He leaves the passenger door and goes to open his own. He clenches his teeth. "Get. In. The. Car."

"You're giving yourself a lot of credit. Did you ever consider that maybe he's a nice guy? And maybe I like him?"

"No," he snaps. "I haven't."

I consider running, going the other way, never going home. But where would I go? What would I do? Dad has control over me. So I get in the car, my whole body shaking with anger. I slam the door as he gets into the driver seat and pulls on his seat belt.

"You can't tell me who to date," I tell him.

He doesn't answer. He turns the car on, shoulder checks, and pulls out on the road.

"You don't even know him," I say. "He's a good person. You think I can only date boys whose fathers make as much money as you do?"

"Don't, Jess."

"You always like to tell us how you grew up without money. Made it on your own. Maybe Flynn is the same."

"Why don't you ask your mother about boys like him?" he snaps and runs the car through a yellow light.

I gasp and stare at his angry profile, my mouth open. Shocked.

"You have no right," I finally manage. "No right at all to imply that about him."

He's quiet, his mouth tight. He must know he's gone over the acceptable line, but he doesn't take it back. He doesn't apologize.

"Flynn is nothing like the boys who attacked mom. Nothing. His mom and family use the shelter because a *white man* gambled away their money and left them bankrupt. Flynn works and looks after his little brother and helps out around the shelter because he feels so bad about using it."

His lips are pressed together so hard they've disappeared, and he doesn't look at me. I cross my arms and stare out my window, barely keeping in my rage. We drive the rest of the way home in angry silence. I clutch the plant book to my chest and rub the tiny monkey in my pocket.

When he turns onto our street, Dad opens his mouth. "I have to go back out of town for a couple of days tomorrow. I told Stella you would work the rest of your shifts. You are to show up for your assigned hours only and come right home immediately after. I'll be checking in to make sure you're obeying."

I don't say anything. That's what he wants. Silence. Compliance. He thinks he's gotten his way. He hasn't. He pulls into our driveway. The oversized stupid driveway.

He shuts down the ignition, not pulling into the garage. "You may think you can handle poverty, Jess. Welfare. Handouts. But you can't. You have too much going for you to hang out with a boy who believes the world owes him favors." He shuts off the car.

My hands shake with rage. "He works harder than any of the privileged boys who live in this neighborhood."

"You're privileged," he tells me. "You live in this neighborhood. I thought working at that place would show you how good you have it."

"So you're saying you want me to develop a work ethic? Like Flynn has?"

"Don't twist my words," he growls as a car pulls up to the curb of our house. Nance's car. Great. "It wasn't meant to be a dating club," he says. "There are plenty of boys around here."

I reach for my door and open it. I hate my dad so much right now, I can't even.

"If you don't listen to me, you won't be working there at all," he says. "I told Stella you would honor your commitment, but I can take that back."

I get out and slam my door again, holding my book close.

He climbs out the driver side and reaches into the backseat for his briefcase. "Don't tempt me, Jess. I hear anything about you and that boy, and you won't be going back."

The rage inside me explodes. "You are such an…asshole," I hiss under my breath. I can't help it.

I see in his eyes that he heard me as Nance opens her car door and climbs out. "Hey, Mr. W. Jess-I-cup. What's up?" she shouts, not yet aware of the tension between us.

"Watch your mouth," my dad hisses in a low voice. "And that's it. You're not going back to that place."

"Fat chance," I tell him.

Nance bounces up the driveway, holding a plastic bag. She looks back and forth at my dad and me and raises her eyebrows.

"Hello, Nance," Dad growls as he spins on his heels, carting off his briefcase. I lift my middle finger at his back as he goes.

"Trouble in paradise?" Nance asks as he disappears inside the house.

"So not paradise," I snap.

"Apparently not." She thrusts the bag, which has a heavy lump on the bottom. "My mom baked a pumpkin loaf for you guys. I think she's making a peace offering."

"Asshat." I take the bag with my free hand.

"My mom?" she asks.

"No. My dad."

"What's up with Pops-erello?" she asks.

"He's an asshat," I repeat.

"Yeah. You said. But I mean, besides that. What are you two fighting about?"

I peek inside the bag at the loaf. Nance's mom used to send loafs over a lot after Mom was attacked. She's a baker, not a talker.

"He showed up at New Beginnings. Out of the blue. To give me a ride home. Check up on me. Whatever."

"And?" she prompts.

I sigh, some of my anger starting to turn inward. "He saw me kissing a boy."

Her eyes widen. "At the shelter?"

"Flynn," I admit.

"Flynn the summer fling?"

I chew my lip and look at the sidewalk. An old woman with a scarf around her head, as if she has cancer or something, walks on the sidewalk toward us with a small black dog. The dog stops in front of the house and lifts a leg to pee on the lilac bush.

"He came to see you at work? You're actually seeing this guy during the *day*?" she asks. "You never once saw Josh during the day."

I look away from the dog, back to Nance. "Because Josh is a douche bag."

She ignores that. "Why is he hanging around the shelter?" Her voice rises. "Sounds serious for a fling."

"He's not a fling," I say, tired of her using that word, tired of dealing with everyone's prejudices. My dad. Her. Me.

"What do you mean?" she asks slowly.

The little dog starts barking. "Hush, Fredrick," the woman says, and she smiles at me apologetically.

I look back at Nance. "He's more than that. I like him. I like him a lot. And to be honest…" I take a deep breath. "His mom works, and he has a little brother. They lost their house and…everything. Once in a while, Flynn brings his brother to the shelter. To eat."

"What?" Her voice raises into a shriek. The little dog growls, and then the woman pulls his leash and they trot off. "He *uses* the shelter?" She makes a face and sticks her tongue out, disgusted.

"It's no big deal, Nance. It's not their fault. They're getting back on their feet."

"Uh, yeah. It kind of is a big deal." She crosses her arms, glaring at me. "Is that why your dad is pissed at you? God, Jess. I don't blame him. You can do better than a guy like that."

"He's not a guy like anything. You're being judgmental," I tell her.

She raises her eyebrows. "Uh, sorry. I hate to point out the obvious, but hanging out with Soup Kitchen Boy isn't going to win you any popularity contests."

"I didn't enter any contests," I tell her. "I don't care about that stuff." I shove the plastic bag toward her. "And I don't like pumpkin loaf," I tell her.

She frowns and refuses to take the bag. "Take the stupid loaf," she says. Her nostrils flare and her brows furrow deeper. "My mom made it for you."

"Shit." My brain hurts. "I'm sorry," I say. "I like her pumpkin loaf. It's not that." Ugh. I hate myself for trying to keep everyone happy. I have to stand up for myself. And for Flynn.

"It's senior year," she reminds me.

I'm sick of hearing that. I don't want to spend an entire year trying to impress other people, worrying about an image I don't even care about.

"What about Hunter Bell?" I ask her.

Nance doesn't flinch. "He has an expiration date. You have to end it, Jess. Figure out who your real friends are."

I stare at her.

"You're right," I blurt out. "You're so right. And I like Flynn. I don't give a crap about dating the right boys or wearing the right clothes. Not anymore."

Nance looks me up and down, slowly and dismissively. I want to say something to make it better, but I resist. An invisible door between us slams harder than the car door I slammed earlier.

"Yeah, I should go," she says, her voice chilled as if I'm pretty much dead to her. And as if she doesn't mind. "Jennifer is having some people over. I left a message on your house phone. You can go ahead and ignore that. Obviously, it won't work with your plans." She turns to her car. "See you around," she calls.

I watch her drive away, smelling the fumes of smoke from the bridge I just burned as she goes.

chapter **seventeen**

Dad is in his office with the door closed. Mom is in her bedroom with the door closed. Allie isn't home. So, the usual. I take the house phone to my room and place my cherished book on top of my dresser. I pull the monkey from my pocket and gently sit him on top of the book. Despite everything, I smile. They're both amazing.

Sitting on my messy, unmade bed, I stare at the phone, trying to work up my nerve to make the call I want to make. With a deep, deep breath, I finally dial the number and hold my breath, waiting.

"Hello?" The voice on the phone line is quiet.

"Penny," I say.

There's a pause. "Jess?" she asks.

We both know it's me. Caller ID.

"How're you doing?" I ask.

"You know. Okay."

Awkward. So very awkward.

My voice chokes, and I cough. I miss her so much. "Do you still hate me?" I ask, trying to make a joke of it.

She sighs. "I never hated you, Jess."

"Really?" My heart is pounding faster than it should be. "I'm really nervous," I admit. She'll understand. Penny always understood me.

She sighs again. "What do you want, Jess?"

The words sting and my heart sinks. "I wanted to see how you're doing. I mean, talk."

She doesn't say anything, so I forge ahead, wondering if this was such a great idea after all. I imagine her face, smiling at me at the party, and go on. "So, you're with Keith now?"

"Yeah."

That's it. A while ago, every detail would have spilled from her, down to his favorite color. "That's so great. Really great. I'm happy for you. Keith Alex! You've loved him since seventh grade."

"I know." Her voice livens up a bit because we have so many shared memories of her crush on Keith Alex. She sounds a little more like my friend Penny and less like a wary stranger.

"How'd it happen?" I ask.

"Just a second." She covers the phone with her hand. She says my name.

"He's here right now," she says when she comes back to the phone.

"Oh. Well. Ha ha. I guess you can't really talk about him then, can you?" I try to laugh but it's fake and sad. I blink and blink. I'm really not a part of her life. Not anymore. "Listen, Penny?"

"Yeah?"

"I'm sorry," I say, remembering the night I turned on her.

It was after Mom's attack. I'd been feeling restless and reckless. Mom was in bad shape, and I didn't know what to do. Dad told me not to talk about it with people, as if not talking about it would make it go away. So I didn't. Not even to Penny.

But I started wearing tighter clothes and boys noticed, and the attention fed a growing hole inside of me. I liked it. When Nance invited us to a party with the popular kids, I pushed Penny to go. The invite was for me really, but back then, me meant Penny too.

I drank the liquor Nance offered. I drank and drank and for a while, it filled up my blank spaces with happy silliness. The liquor loosened me up, and I giggled and stumbled around, talking to everyone and carrying on like a completely different person. Josh Reid latched on to me.

Penny tried to get me out of there. Away from him. I'd laughed at her. Made fun of her. Called her a nerd. A loser. I used intimate things I knew about her to humiliate her. I humiliated her for other people's entertainment. It went too far. Way too far. She left in tears.

I sigh, heat tingling my cheeks. "I'm sorry for what I did to you. I've never told you that. But I really am sorry. I was such a jerk. And I never said sorry."

She breathes in and out, in and out, but doesn't say anything.

"It's not an excuse, I know. But I was drinking and I didn't mean any of it. Dumb things come out of my mouth when I drink."

"Yeah," she agrees. "They do." And then there's silence again.

I'm crying now, thinking about that night. I had to call Allie to come and pick me up. She drove me home and didn't say a word about me pretending to be sober, even though I hiccupped all the way home. She didn't say a word when I threw up all over the bathroom or in the morning when my face was the shade of white lily. Instead, she left after breakfast and went to her boyfriend's house. Dad was out of town. Mom was in bed. I had my first hangover alone on the couch, curled up underneath a blanket. A messy aching body.

I wanted to call Penny. Apologize. But I knew I didn't deserve forgiveness. So I let it go. I let her go. It added to the already big hole inside me. I turned to Nance. The parties and full force of Nance kept me distracted for a long time.

I sigh, about to tell Penny good-bye, about to hang up, embarrassed and emotionally naked and knowing it doesn't matter. I went too far. She's never going to forgive me.

"Thank you," she says. I take a deep breath and swallow my tears. "Thanks for the apology, but I know things were hard for you." Penny pauses. "Are things okay now? I mean, how's your mom?"

"She's doing better, some days. It's hard to tell. She still sleeps a lot. I think it's the medication."

"That must be hard."

I close my eyes. "It is," I whisper. My eyelashes are wet. It's been even harder without Penny to talk to about it.

"Jess?" she asks. "You still there?"

"I'm here." I sigh deeply. "Listen, I was wondering if we could, you know, get together sometime. Like for coffee or something. To talk? I'm dying to hear about how you and Keith got together. And what it's like, being his girlfriend."

She actually giggles. It's tiny and it's soft. But it's there.

"I met a guy too," I tell her, wanting to share. Wanting her to care the way I do.

"I heard," she says.

"You did?"

"Nance. Telephone. Telegraph. Tele-Nance," she says.

We both laugh. A real laugh.

"I don't think Nance likes him," Penny tells me.

Less now, I think. She likes him less now that she knows the truth about him.

"She doesn't," I tell Penny. "But he's nice. I think you would like him. He's real. He's not fake. Like I've been acting the last while."

Silence.

"I miss you," I whisper. "A lot. I miss you a lot."

"I miss you too," she whispers back. But then she clears her throat. "But you really hurt me, Jess." Her voice is louder now. Clear. I imagine Keith giving her a thumbs-up. Encouraging her to let me have it. I deserve it after all.

"You dumped me," she says. "For Nance. You left me all alone."

"But you dumped me," I say. I never called to apologize. It's just that she never called me either.

"I thought you made your choice. Nance. Drinking. And boys."

I nod. "I don't want that anymore. I think I'm changing," I tell her. "Or maybe I'm just learning to be myself again."

"I hope so," she says.

"Me too." I smile, thinking of Wilf. She would love Wilf. "I'm volunteering," I tell her. "At New Beginnings. I'm friends with a seventy-five-year-old man. And people there."

"That's good," she says. "It sounds good for you."

I nod again. My stomach flops around and I have a sudden

understanding of boys trying to ask a girl on a date. Rejection is scary. "So," I try again. "Do you want to get together? You could come here? Or we could meet at a coffee shop?" I ask.

She clears her throat but doesn't answer.

"Penny?"

"I don't know." She sighs. "I want to trust you, Jess. I do. But..."

"You can't," I answer flatly. My eyes go to the book on my dresser. The monkey.

"I'm afraid of getting hurt again. This is kind of unexpected. I need some time to process things."

"Okay, Pen," I say. It's not what I wanted to hear. But it's something. There's hope. I should have known Penny wouldn't make a snap decision. She doesn't make snap decisions.

"Hey, Jess?" she asks.

"Yeah?"

"What's your boyfriend's name?"

"Boyfriend?" My cheeks heat up and I giggle. "I don't know if I can call Flynn my boyfriend yet."

"It sounds like you want him to be though."

I smile "I do. Yeah, I guess I do." I pause for a second. "He lives in Clover Lawn," I tell her.

"So?" Penny asks.

"Exactly," I say, and my heart fills up.

And that's why I love her. Present tense.

"I think his mom hates me," I confide.

"She probably doesn't even know you," she says. "Listen, I have to go. Keith is waiting. I'll call you back sometime. Okay?"

"Okay." A tear drips down my cheek.

"Good luck," she says.

"Yeah, thanks. Bye." I hang up. My heart is heavy and sad, but there's a thin lining of something new.

chapter **eighteen**

The next morning, Mom is out of bed when I get up. Dressed. She's sitting on a stool at the kitchen island, drinking a cup of tea, her laptop on the counter. Her hair is in a ponytail. She actually has on eye makeup.

"You okay, Jess?" she asks.

"Is Dad home?" I stayed in my room last night and skipped supper because I didn't want to look at his face. No one bothered to call me down.

"No. He's gone to Houston."

"Then I'm fine."

I grab a mug and turn on the coffee. She gets up and walks over, putting her hand on my shoulder. I lean against her hand, watching the Keurig gurgle out hot caffeine. She moves away before I want her to. I want more.

"He doesn't want me going back to New Beginnings," I tell her as she climbs back on the stool. I dump a large amount of sugar in my cup and take a sip.

"He told me," she says.

I blow on my coffee and turn to her, surprised.

"He said you met a boy," she says.

A laugh spurts from me. "He told you that?"

"I asked. I'm trying not to judge until I hear your side of the story."

"Wow." I frown at her and put the coffee down and rub my temples, trying to work out a headache that's forming. "Really?"

She sighs. "I'm trying here, Jess."

I nod. "Flynn is a good person, Mom. I'm not going to stop seeing him because of Dad." I'm afraid of sending her back to her room, but she keeps her eyes on me. Steady. "I don't want to let down the people at the shelter. They expect me back. It's not fair." I lift my chin. "And I'll find a way to see Flynn if I'm working there or not."

We're interrupted by Allie as she noisily walks in the side door of the house, her overstuffed backpack banging against the wall. Mom glances over as if she's surprised, as if she forgot she had two daughters.

Allie slips off her shoes, throws her backpack down on the couch, and walks in looking at us, her eyebrows raised.

"Hey," she says. "I have a ton of laundry to do, but first, I need coffee."

She continues into the kitchen, looks closer at Mom, and does a double take. "You look good, Mom. How you feeling?"

"Fine," she answers automatically.

Allie touches Mom's arm as she walks to the Keurig machine, where I'm still leaning against the counter, and she sets it up for a new cup of coffee.

"What's going on?" she asks.

"Dad," I say. "Tyranny." I take a big sip of coffee and burn the tip of my tongue.

"What else is new?" she says with a scoff.

"Not for you. Since you're never here," I mumble as I put my coffee mug down on the counter.

"Were you at Dana's last night?" Mom asks.

Allie glances at me and then back to Mom. I don't shout out Doug's name to bust her.

"Yeah," she says. "I was. I worked first."

"I met a boy," I blurt out.

"And this is bad?" Allie asks, glancing from me to Mom. "Is he a criminal? Married?" She takes her coffee and sips at it. She drinks hers black.

"Worse," I tell her. "He's poor."

"He goes to the shelter," Mom says.

"Where you work?" Allie asks me.

"Not as a volunteer," Mom adds quietly.

"It doesn't matter," I say, crossing my arms. "It doesn't make him a bad person. And he does help out, by the way. Because he wants to."

"He uses the shelter?" Allie tilts her head, thinking. She keeps sneaking peeks at Mom, as if she can't figure out what's different but knows something is. *She's out of bed, for starters*, I want to yell. Enough pretending. It's not a day for sweeping things under the carpet. "And Dad freaked out," Allie guesses.

"He can't order me around and treat me like I'm five years old. He tried to ban me from going back to the shelter. Flynn isn't a bad person. And it's not his fault. His mom used to have a nice home.

They lost everything because of a deadbeat stepdad who gambled away all their money and then took off."

"That sucks," Allie says.

"You think?"

She has the courtesy to look embarrassed.

"Flynn has a little brother, and he looks after him so his mom can work. He brings him to the shelter sometimes for lunch. But Flynn helps out too. He fixes things. He's a good person. He has goals. And he likes plants."

"He likes plants?" Allie smiles and goes over to sit on a stool beside Mom.

"There's a greenhouse at the shelter," I tell them.

"You like plants," my mom points out. "It's a sign."

The two of them actually start to laugh. It warms my heart even as I frown. "It's not funny," I tell them as they laugh. It almost feels like old times, but I blink quickly. I have to take action. I can't not see Flynn. It's not an option. "So I don't have to quit?" I say to my mom. "I can still work at New Beginnings?"

Allie freezes with her coffee mug at her lips. I don't move either. Neither one of us has pushed Mom in a long time. Asked her to make a decision. To defy Dad.

"You can keep working there," she says and calmly sips her tea. "I'll talk to your father."

I suck in a breath and slowly let it out. "Really? You're sure?"

"Really. Dad's gone for a couple of days. I'll talk to him when he gets home. No need to bother him while he's away. You keep doing what you're doing."

I open my eyes like a deer in headlights but don't say a word.

She turns to Allie. "How's Doug?" she asks.

Allie's eyes open as wide and she quickly takes another sip of coffee, glancing at me to see if I've squealed on her, but I subtly shake my head.

"Good," she says and puts her cup on the counter.

"I'm glad his family has been there for you." Mom reaches for her hand.

Allie and I exchange another look. Maybe Mom has been seeing more than we gave her credit for? Maybe she's getting ready to come back and deal with it?

I leave them and head to New Beginnings early, hoping Flynn will be there helping out and we'll have a chance to talk. About my stupid dad. And his stupid mom.

He doesn't show up though. Not early. Not at all.

chapter **nineteen**

I repeat my steps the next day. I get to New Beginnings early and wait for Flynn and Kyle, but there's no sign of them. Not the next day. Or the next.

Mom is awake when I'm home, but I'm the one hiding in my room. I'm a wreck. I've lost Nance too, but that doesn't even compare to not being able to reach Flynn. He doesn't have a cell phone, and I don't know if he even has a landline. I keep expecting him to show up at New Beginnings with a logical explanation for why he hasn't been there, but I'm afraid. That my dad scared him away. That Flynn let him. I want to yell at him for not coming back. I'm angry. I have things to say. I'm scared. But most of all, I miss him.

"What'd you do to make everyone around here so mad?" Wilf asks on day three when we're carrying dirty dishes into the kitchen. Stella came in for a moment earlier and watched me with her lips pressed together, her eyes disapproving. After a moment she left without saying anything.

"Can I come to the greenhouse with you?" I ask instead of telling him. He's been away for a few days too. I haven't even talked to him about the herbs I want to grow.

"Sure, Chickadee," he says. We put the dishes away and escape the kitchen. I walk beside him, keeping with his slower pace. "Leg is bothering me. Means it's going to rain. I'm more predictable than that nuisance weatherman on channel two," he says as we head through the building. I glance over with a frown, forgetting to smile at his joke attempt. "Kind of like racing a turtle to keep up with me?" he notes.

"I like turtles," I tell him.

"See?" he says. "That. Something is wrong, if you're letting that go without insulting me."

"I don't insult you all the time."

"Only when I'm around." He chuckles.

I try to smile, but my lips fail to make the trip. There's a bad feeling in my stomach. We step outside, down the stairs that lead us to the greenhouse.

"This bad mood of yours have to do with the boy?" he asks.

I frown.

"What? You think I don't notice the way you two are always mooning over each other."

I don't even call Wilf on using the word *mooning*.

"Stella doesn't approve," I blurt out. "Neither does my dad. Or his mom. And now he's disappeared. I can't even talk to him about it."

"That doesn't sound like Flynn." Wilf rubs his chin and frowns.

He's right. And that's the thing. He's right. It doesn't sound like Flynn.

"Want to take my advice?" Wilf asks. "It's not like I usually use it anyway." He laughs to himself.

I really do smile then. For a second. But it quickly fades. "What?"

He stops and pulls the key to the greenhouse from his pocket and opens the door for me. I slip inside.

"Fight for him," he says, following me. "He feels the same way about you. I see it. And I understand. I had to fight for Rhea."

I stare at him, fascinated. He walks to the cupboards where he keeps his gardening tools and keeps talking. "My mother was old-fashioned. And considering how old I am, that's pretty darn old-fashioned. Suffice it to say she didn't believe in mixed marriages. Especially with a poor brown girl whose parents could barely understand English. They worked so hard for so little." He shakes his head. "She had her heart set on fixing me up with one of her friend's daughters. Proper white girls with lots of pedigree and money." He opens the cupboard with his unsteady hands and pulls out shearing scissors.

I watch him, surprised. But also, not surprised.

"Rhea's parents brought her over from India when she was ten. They wanted her to marry a nice Indian boy and give them lots of babies." He puts the scissors down, and I walk over and sit on a stool, watching him. He smiles at me. "I had to work on her parents. Finally I think they gave up because they knew I wouldn't go away. They accepted me. But my mother, she never really gave in. Not even when we married. She wasn't always good to my Rhea. But I let her know from the start. It was both of us or none at all."

"Wow," I say. "That's incredibly romantic."

He sits down on the chair beside me. "I loved Rhea more than anything. I miss her every single day."

"Tell me about her," I say. "How'd you meet?"

219

"She was eighteen. I was twenty and just back from the Korean War. We were at a dance. She was a full foot shorter than me, but I spotted her right away. She had her head back, laughing, and our eyes met. Rhea, she marched right over and introduced herself. Then she asked me to dance."

I smile as he stares into space, as if he's seeing the memory. I wait, intrigued with the story of Wilf and his Rhea.

He looks at me. "She always told people she asked me to dance because she knew I was too shy to ask her. But she was wrong. I wasn't going to let her get away that night. I already knew I was going to marry her. One look, and I knew."

I don't say anything as Wilf sniffles and wipes under his eye. "She lived to boss me around, that little woman. It was funny. No one understood what we saw in each other. But it didn't matter to us. We worked. And people either liked it or they didn't."

His story touches me deeply.

"Fight for him, Jess. I see myself in you."

"But how?" I ask him. "How can I do that if I can't even talk to him?"

Wilf taps the side of his head. "Figure it out. Find a way." He gets up from the stool and hands me the scissors. "Start with the ivy," he tells me, and he reaches for a misting bottle.

There's a tear in the corner of his eye, but I pretend not to see it.

While I'm fixing the plant, I think of a plan.

• • •

Mom is up when I get home. She's in the kitchen with Allie, and they're baking.

They smile at me when I walk into the kitchen. "We're making chocolate chip cookies," Allie says. "For Doug."

"Are you trying to kill him?" I ask. Neither one of them is a baker.

"Hey! Join us," Allie says. "We'll let you sample them first. To make sure they're not poison."

I smile at her joke and promise to join them, but I have something to do first. I take the phone. "I have to make a call," I say and take it to my room. I sit on the bed and dial the number.

No one picks up, so I leave a message.

"Hi, Jennifer," I say. "It's Jess. I'm calling to, um, ask for a favor. I need to get ahold of Braxton Brooks, and I thought you might have his number? Or maybe you could give him a message for me? It's important. Can you call me back? On my landline. It's 587-896-1036. Thanks. Bye."

I join my mom and sister and wait for the call back.

It doesn't come.

chapter **twenty**

The next day, I head back to New Beginnings. When I arrive, Wilf is standing on the steps talking to Martin. They smile at me, and Wilf nods his head and points at the sock monkey hanging from my purse.

"Aren't you a little old for that?" he growls.

"No one is too old for a sock monkey," I tell him. "It has magical powers."

"Good gravy," Wilf says.

Martin blows smoke rings and chuckles. "It's true, Wilf. Everyone knows sock monkeys make you brave," he tells him.

I raise both eyebrows at Wilf. Martin and I already had this conversation. He's up to speed on the powers of Brave Monkey. Martin reaches in his pocket then and pulls out a miniature sock monkey of his own. One that I happened to give to him. I bought up every last one of them Target had in stock. Martha has one too.

I lift my chin. "Brave," I tell Wilf in a haughty voice.

Martin's laugh follows me inside.

The lunch service comes and goes. No sign of Flynn. My bravado sinks.

I rush home afterward but there's still no message from Jennifer. Allie's gone, and Mom is back in her bedroom. Resting.

• • •

On Friday I'm a mess. I can't believe Flynn's given up so easily. I'd even be willing to see Kyle come in with his mom at this point, so at least I could hear Flynn's all right.

I don't want to imagine a world where disapproval from my dad would keep him away. I'm not willing to let other people stop us from getting to know each other better. I don't want him to either.

I want to talk to Wilf, but he doesn't show up for the lunch service again, so I force myself to stop by Stella's office even though I've managed to avoid her all week.

She's at her desk, and when I tap on her door she looks up over the top of her reading glasses. "Yes?"

"Wilf missed lunch. I need to talk to him. Is he going to be here later?" I ask.

"He was at the doctor," she tells me. "He's here now. In the greenhouse." She stares at me over her glasses. There's a thin layer of sweat on her upper lip. The office is stuffy. The small fan on her desk whirs noisily.

"Thank you," I say shortly and turn to leave.

"Jess?"

I spin around.

"Your shift is done," she says. "What do you want with Wilf?" The air in her office may be warm, but her voice is frosty.

"I need to talk to him," I tell her. "We're friends. I hope that's all right," I add with as much sarcasm as possible and rotate on my heels to leave.

"Is this about Flynn?" she says quickly.

That gets my attention. My back stiffens. "What about Flynn?" I ask and slowly turn to face her again.

She takes off her reading glasses, places them on her desk, and sighs. "You know Flynn hasn't been in all week," she says.

"I kind of noticed, Stella." I bite my lip and try to hide my hurt feelings.

She purses her lips tight. "Maybe that's a sign."

If she's aiming for my heart, she makes direct contact. I lower my head but shake it. No.

"Sometimes Flynn brings Kyle here for supper. Not lunch," she says.

I glance up, and she's folded her hands together on the desk in front of her.

"He's come for lunch since I've been here," I say.

She blinks slowly. "Yes, I noticed that too." She lifts a shoulder slightly. "It's not your job to keep tabs on our guests." She emphasizes the word *guest*.

"Whether you like it or not, Flynn and I are friends."

"Close the door, Jess. Come and sit," she says. Her voice is firm, and I want to ignore her, but I can't. My mouth dries and my stomach flops with nerves, but I do what she asks. When I sit, my leg bounces up and down. Up and down.

"Flynn is a good-looking boy," Stella says. I concentrate on the whirring of the fan. It's kind of insulting if she thinks this is about how handsome he is. There are hot boys all over Tadita. I don't care about any of them like I do Flynn.

"I know he's popular with girls," Stella continues. She unfolds her hands and runs one over her hair.

I clench my hands into fists and stare at a pile of papers on her desk. "It's not like that," I say through gritted teeth. "We're different."

She sighs. "We all like to think we're different, Jess. We all think we're going to be the one to tame the broken boy."

I look up, directly into her eyes. "I don't think he's broken," I tell her.

"Well, his family is," she answers quickly.

"They're not broken," I say. "They're mending. There's a difference."

She sighs and picks up her glasses, puts an end in her mouth. "You're right." She sighs again. "Okay. Here's the truth. You deserve that."

My leg stops bouncing.

"Your dad and I have been talking. I told him I was concerned about your relationship with Flynn. He told me he saw you kissing in front of the shelter. He was very angry."

"My dad is always angry," I interrupt. "He has no right to say who I…"—my cheeks burn darker—"kiss."

"Jess," she says quietly. "I think it's sweet. That you and Flynn like each other. I do. But here's the thing. Flynn is a guest here. You are not. He has challenges that you can't possibly understand. You come from different places. He's not in a position to have a carefree summer romance. I don't want to see either of you get hurt. You're both good kids."

"It's not a summer romance. It's more than that. We don't plan to hurt each other. We like each other a lot." I suck in a breath, struggling to keep believing that. Flynn hasn't come back. Doubt is creeping in, starting to find its way in the cracks.

"But he has responsibilities. Much more than you do. He doesn't have the luxury to be carefree," she says.

"I'm not making things worse for him. Maybe I'm making them better." I close my eyes and clench my fists.

"I know you don't want to hear it, but there are plenty of boys in this town. Boys who are more like you."

My eyes pop open. "More like me? You mean messed up? My life isn't the perfect life you seem to think it is," I say with quiet fury.

She leans forward in her chair. "Jess," she says slowly. As if I'm a dim child. "I never said your life was perfect."

"No, but you implied it. We may have money, Stella. But trust me. Things that look perfect on the surface are masking flaws. Big fat flaws. You have no idea about my family."

She frowns as she studies me over the top of her desk. "Is everything okay? At home?"

I glare at her. She's never asked before. She's never tried to find out more about me before. Considered that my life wasn't all fine wine and roses. "It's fine," I say through gritted teeth.

"I'm sorry," she says then. "Maybe I haven't been fair. It's just, well, we both know your dad brought you here against your will." She shakes her head. "And yes, you've proven to be much more dedicated and committed than I thought you would. I know the people here really like you. I think Wilf wants to adopt you. But you and Flynn. You're not meant to be together."

Outside her office a group of volunteers laugh. I want to stand, yell at them to stop, ask them what's so funny. "This shouldn't be about what my family has or his family doesn't have," I tell her. "The way we feel isn't about how much money is in our bank accounts. It's real. Flynn is the first boy I've ever felt this way about. And he feels the same way about me."

She whistles under her breath.

"We get each other," I say.

The people outside her office laugh again. It feels like it's aimed at me.

"Has Flynn told you that he feels the same way?" she says quietly and not unkindly, but her voice is firm.

"Yes." Maybe not in exact words. I look at Stella, and something in her expression makes it hard to swallow, and my eyes begin to burn. Pity. She pities me. She doesn't believe it. That Flynn could feel that way about me. She thinks I'm another one of his girls.

The fight goes out of my body, and I slump down in my chair, suddenly tired, staring down at my feet.

"Your dad told me that he banned you from working here any longer, but that you insisted. That your mom intervened." I glance up at her. "He asked me to talk to Flynn. So I did. I spoke with Flynn early this week," she continues. "I asked him to stay away from lunch for a while. There are other shelters in town where he can take Kyle if he needs to."

The betrayal hits me in the gut. Slams me. I stare at her, shocked. That she would let my dad allow her to do that. That I caused that.

"You let my dad stop one of your 'guests' from coming to your shelter?" I ask her, emphasizing *guests* the same way she did. I get to my feet. "You told Flynn to stay away because of my dad?" I ask. "My dad doesn't have a right to dictate who uses your shelter."

It's not even enough that he's kept him away from me. He's stopped Kyle from coming. Interfered in Flynn's life. I feel responsible and horrible.

"I spoke with Flynn's mom earlier. She wasn't a fan of you two being together either. I'm sorry, Jess. I wish things could be different. I see now that you really care about him. But I called your dad with my concern first. Remember? We don't fraternize with the guests at New Beginnings. It's too complicated for everyone."

"That's an actual law?" I ask. "A rule? Because I don't remember signing an agreement or anything that said that."

Stella doesn't say anything. Tears burning behind my eyes fight to escape. One slips down my cheek, and I wipe it away with a tight fist. My chest hurts. "I don't want to have to quit working here," I tell her, struggling to keep in sobs. "I like it."

"You don't have to quit," she says with a sigh. "We can juggle schedules. School starts soon, and you can work nights. We'll work things out."

"I can't be responsible for keeping Flynn's family away."

She sighs. "You're not. We'll work it out. I can talk to his mom. Let her know when… It's an unfortunate situation, Jess. And I understand what you think you feel for Flynn, I do. But you're so young. It's best to keep you separate."

"Do you have any idea how patronizing that sounds?" I demand. "Or how archaic?" One of us has to stay strong. I need to find Flynn and tell him it doesn't matter to me. What my dad says or what Stella wants to enforce.

She sits up straighter. "I'm sorry. I'm not without sympathy. But I already talked to Flynn. I asked him not to come around when you're here," she continues. "He gave me his word. No trouble."

The heat of my anger evaporates my tears. I swivel away fuming and stride to the door. "Maybe he *should* make trouble," I say, and then rush out of Stella's office, ignoring the curious stares of the volunteers in the hallway.

I run outside to the greenhouse. The door is unlocked, so I run inside and stop, panting as I try to catch my breath. Wilf is standing in the middle, his back to me. He's bent over, not moving. He doesn't seem to have heard me.

"Wilf?" I walk closer, trying to shake off a bad feeling. Trying to forget Stella's hurtful words. "You okay?" I can't keep the panic from my voice.

He's stooped over, and from behind, with his gray cardigan sweater and his wispy gray hair that circles his head like half a bowl, he looks feeble and older than I've thought. A flash of fear makes me frown.

When I reach him, I see his eyes are moist and red. His lip trembles.

"Wilf," I say softly and put my hand on his back. "Are you okay? What's wrong?"

"Argh. I'm an old man feeling sorry for himself." He wipes under his eye and sniffles loudly and stands straighter, batting away my hand. "I'm fine."

My own troubles fade. "What's wrong?" I demand. There's a box of Kleenex on the workstation, and I go pull out a few tissues and hand them to him.

He takes them and blinks a few times as if he's confused. "Nothing. I miss my wife. I'm old. It takes me five minutes to pee." He blows his nose loud enough to chase away the mice that live in the walls in the building next door.

"You're sure? There's nothing else wrong?" I ask.

He shrugs. "Nothing else? You ever try to pee and can't do it?"

"Stella said you were at the doctor again. Are you sick?" I ask. I'm done beating around bushes. So done.

"Sweetheart. Of course I'm dying."

I inhale a deep breath.

"Oh, don't look so worried," he says quickly. "We're all dying. We're like time bombs ticking. Waiting to go off." He makes an explosion sound and flicks open his hands.

I frown and squint my eyes. "That's not even a little bit funny. Are you sick? For real?"

A fly lands on my arm and I swat it away.

"I have an old-age problem. Is that a disease? Call me in about sixty years or so when you have the same thing. We'll make a decision on that together," he grumbles and shuffles off toward Rhea's azaleas. "Of course, by then I'll be long gone, so we'll have to do it by séance."

I watch him, staring at his back as he sticks his finger in the dirt to check moisture in the soil. "So you're okay? You're only sad?"

He snorts. "That's what I love about you, Chickadee. You're not all soft about the sad stuff."

"Maybe I am," I tell him. "Maybe I've just learned to hide it."

"Maybe you have," he says and moves to the next plant. "And maybe it's time you started facing things."

"Maybe you should drink more water instead of giving it to all the plants," I tell him. "To help with the peeing."

He snorts again. "Maybe you should be politer to your elders?"

I walk closer to him. "Wilf, I'm worried about you, okay?" I say softly.

He looks up at me for a moment. His eyes are watery. Sad. They see a lot. But then they twinkle. And then he winks. "I like you too, kid. But that's how you worry?" he asks. "That's how you show concern, bugging me about my peeing? You definitely need to work on that."

I cross my arms and try not to laugh. "Well, you started it," I say.

"I liked the old days when young people were seen and not heard. You kids today are so damn lippy." His voice is gruff, but he's hiding another smile.

My heart swells. "You're kind of cranky sometimes, Wilf, but I like you too."

He pretends to huff and puff. "That's what all the girls say when they want something." The annoying fly lands close to Wilf on a table, and he reaches out and smashes it under his palm.

"Holy reflexes for an old guy," I say. "And it so happens that I do want a favor," I add.

He wipes the fly remains on his pants. "And I thought you were coming to see me because of my good looks and charm. So what is it, Chickadee? What do you want?"

I walk over and pat his arm. The skin is wrinkly and thin, but it doesn't matter. He's my friend. "I want to help you in the greenhouse," I tell him. "I want to tell you about my plans for starting an herb garden in here. And I want to hear more stories about Rhea and figure out how she could be so in love with such a grouchy old man."

He laughs. "I wasn't old or grouchy when I met her. And I used to cut quite a cloth."

"You're speaking in old-manism again," I say. "That's another reason I love you."

"Huh." He snorts again and grabs a clipper from the table. "But what's the real favor, young lady? Emphasis on the *young* and not on the *lady*. It must be big the way you're sucking up to me." He snips at the air.

"I need Flynn's address," I blurt out.

"No," he says abruptly.

Wilf turns away and starts fussing with a leaf on a plant.

"Please? I mean it, Wilf. I can't get ahold of him. I don't know where he lives. Or if he even has a phone. I have no way of talking to him."

"Maybe he doesn't want to talk to you," he says. He snips the leaves a little too aggressively.

"You told me to fight. You told me you fought for Rhea," I remind him.

His shoulders slump and he stops cutting leaves, but he doesn't turn around.

"Stella told him to stay away. My dad and Stella. But they're wrong about us. They can't tell me who to fall in love with. My dad can't control my life. I'm not a little kid anymore."

Wilf turns slowly, his eyes softer, his lip trembling a little. I watch him, and my worry about him adds to the pain in my chest. He doesn't look so great.

"You barely know the kid. You think you should be throwing around the word *love* so loosely?" he asks.

"You knew right away when you met Rhea," I say to him. "Boom. Just like that." I snap my fingers.

"Yeah." He smiles, but he's looking over my head at something I can't see. "From the moment I laid eyes on her. From the moment she stepped on my foot, trying to lead when we danced."

"Well. Maybe it's the same for me. I need to go and see him. To see if he wants to fight, because I'm willing to fight with him."

Wilf makes a low growling sound and coughs. He grumbles under his breath about his privacy and other people's privacy.

"Wilf." I grab his hand. The soft skin is loose on his old bones. "Please? If I don't talk to him, I'll die."

"Spare me the teenage drama," he says. "You're not going to die."

"Please?" I repeat. "It feels like it."

"How do you know I even know where to find him?" he asks, yanking his hand away from mine with surprising force.

"You do," I say. "You know his whole family. I know you know."

He sets down the clippers. He sighs and runs his hands over what's left of the hair on his head.

"It's not a nice neighborhood," he tells me.

"I don't care," I tell him.

"My point is I want you to be safe. I don't want you traipsing off there, and I know you're going to."

"I'll be safe. I know Tae Kwon Do."

He frowns. "Do you really?"

"Okay, no. But I have pepper spray in my purse. And my sock monkey who makes me brave."

He glares at me.

"I have spray. My dad makes me carry it."

"Of course he does." He rubs his chin. "I shouldn't be encouraging you. You're an impetuous thing. You're stubborn and hardly worth all this trouble for Flynn."

I hold my breath, waiting.

"I'll think about it," he tells me.

"If I don't talk to him," I tell Wilf, "I won't come back. I can't work with Stella if she's the one who made him go away."

"You're like a thorn," he says.

"But you'd miss me."

Wilf sighs.

chapter **twenty-one**

The bus ride to Clover Lawn doesn't take much longer than going to Tuxedo, but it's in the opposite direction, and in many ways, it's like traveling to a different town. I stare out the smudged bus window at houses that need paint jobs. Some have rotting or broken-down fences. Many have unmowed lawns and dirty toys and bikes that look abandoned and sad, lying in tall grass and weeds. There are nice lawns too, of course, and houses properly looked after, but it's nothing like the rows of shiny big houses in Tuxedo with manicured lawns and long driveways. I fight the fear and anxiety filling space in my head.

When I pull the cord at the stop Wilf instructed me to, I glance around before hopping off the bus to the sidewalk. The napkin in my purse has directions on it. Walk down Oak Street, turn right at Walnut, and then left to the address: 298 Home Street. I walk quickly toward Flynn's house, ignoring the sick feeling in my belly.

There's thumping and cheers across the street. A group of boys in a park are playing basketball. They don't pay any attention as I pass, and I breathe out, relieved. I don't want to be noticed. A group of moms pushing strollers approach the sidewalk I'm on and kind of force me onto the road as they pass in their little gang.

A few minutes later, I'm standing in front of the address on the napkin. I stare at the house. I hate it. I hate everything about it. I hate the judgmental thoughts. The voices of my dad, Nance. The house looks like a rejected cardboard box. Beaten up and abandoned. The wood's dull gray color is fading and chipping away. On the tiny lawn are two small and equally unhappy evergreen trees drooping down at the top, the sagging branches brushing up against a tiny screened window.

It doesn't matter, I remind myself. Everything I have, everything I expect without even knowing, it boils up inside me. My hands are clammy and cold, and I tuck them into my hoodie pocket. It's still early and the weather is warm, but I'm freezing.

Sitting on lawn chairs in front of an identical home a couple of doors down are three or four boys my age or a little older. They're smoking and laughing, and when they notice me, my stomach drops. I promised Wilf I wouldn't come alone. I outright lied and told him my sister would meet me. *It's safe*, I tell myself. Flynn is nearby. Braxton is nearby too.

I walk up the short path to the front door. The paint is chipping off that too. I push the doorbell, but there's no sound so I knock in a quick pattern. There's nothing from inside.

"Yo!" one of the boys calls. I can only assume they're talking to me and look over. "You looking for Flynnster?"

I nod but realize that's useless. "Yes," I call, but it comes out too quiet. "Yeah," I call louder.

"Man, I can't figure out how that guy gets so many good-looking chicks," another boy says. I stand straighter, trying to erase the way it makes me seem insignificant.

"Hey," the first boy calls. "Do you know what would look good on you?" He waits a fraction of a second. "Me," he yells, and his friends crack up. "There's a party over here and you're invited," he calls, clearly on a roll. "Yo, and it's in my pants."

"Small party," I yell back, trying to sound tougher than I feel. The boys laugh even harder, and then the door opens. Flynn stands in the doorway, staring down at me. He doesn't look happy, but I can't stop a smile from breaking out on my face.

"Looks like someone's going to get lucky," calls one of the boys.

Flynn takes a step so he's beside me on the porch. He puts his hand on my back and sort of moves me behind him. "Yeah. Your mom," he calls, and the boys hoot and laugh some more.

In a swoop he moves me so we're inside the house, and he closes the door behind us. He stares down at me as if he can't believe it's me and brushes his hand along the side of my face and then quickly pulls it back. "What're you doing here?" His voice is low. "You shouldn't have come here."

I take a deep breath. We're standing in an entrance. It's small. In front of us is a tiny living room and a kitchen to the right. There's a teeny hallway to the left and a closed door. The house is cleaner on the inside. There are pictures on the wall. And plants. I smile at all the potted plants on tables. He follows my gaze.

"My mom likes plants. Shit," he says and runs his hand through his hair. "Why are you smiling at me like that?"

I can't help it. I duck my head to hide my expression. "You never came back," I say, and then there's a pout in my voice. "I had no way to get ahold of you."

He glances behind him.

"Come in," he says. I slide off my shoes and follow him. Flynn nods his head at the couch. It's brown corduroy and well worn. I ignore how old and lumpy it looks and sink down on it. I don't want to be the type of person who cares about things like that. He sits on an old chair across from me, covered in some sort of vinyl. With holes. I hate the poverty in his house.

His knee bounces up and down. Up and down. I fold my hands in my lap.

"You don't look like you belong here," he says.

Neither do you, I think, but I don't say that out loud. He waves his hand around the living room. His face is tense. "I hate that you're seeing this."

"It's not so bad," I say. "I hate that you let Stella tell you to stay away."

He drops his gaze to the floor and glances back behind him at the closed door. "Kyle is napping," he says. "My mom will be home soon."

"Will she kick me out?"

He glances up for a second and half laughs. "Probably not. But she won't be happy. How would your dad feel if he came home and found me on your couch?"

"My dad is an asshat," I tell him.

He doesn't disagree.

"He made Stella tell you not to come back," I say.

He waves his hand. "They're trying to protect you."

I laugh, but it's bitter. "You sure about that? I think Stella was trying to protect you. It's not fair though. To tell you not to go back. I'll leave."

He puts out his hands, face up. Giving up. "No one wants us together."

"I do," I tell him. "I do."

He rolls his neck out. "Shit, Jess. So do I. But I hate this. You being here is embarrassing. I don't want it to be. I don't want my mom to be right."

A clock on the wall ticks loudly. It sounds like it's saying his name over and over. Flynn. Flynn. Flynn.

I hold my breath. "Right about what?"

"That it matters. That you care. About this stuff."

"Oh my God, Flynn." I try to imagine myself living in a house like this. And fine, it does, it makes me uncomfortable. Maybe even a little afraid, but being in a big house doesn't stop me from being afraid either. I'm just not used to this. I can get used to it. It's only stuff. I close my eyes and think of my house, all the nice things inside, but how has it made me feel for the last couple of years? Alone.

"The thing is," I tell him. "It's you. When I'm with you, I'm happy. It doesn't matter where we are. The shelter. My house. Here. It's being with you." My bottom lip quivers, and I try not to cry.

He stares at me, his lips pressed tight.

"For the last couple of years, in my big fancy house, I've felt all alone." My sniffles start. I breathe deeply, trying to stay in control. "I lost my mom. Then my sister. Even my dad. I lost Penny, my best friend." The tears are spilling out now.

He's up in a flash, sitting beside me, pressing his leg against mine, his arm around me.

"I'm happier with you," I manage to say. "I thought I meant something. I thought I mattered to you." There. I've laid it out. He can reject me if he wants. But at least I'm being honest.

"Shit," he says. His chin rests on my head. "You do. I'm sorry, Jess."

I cry harder. "I don't want you to be afraid of my dad."

"I'm not," he says. "I'm not afraid of him. It's Stella. She said I would mess things up for you. And I don't want to do that. I'm sorry. Don't cry, Jess. I'm here. I won't stay away anymore."

I push back, tears running down my face, my ugly cry in full gear. "She said you would mess things up for me?"

He nods.

"That's not what she said to me. She told me I didn't matter to you. That I was like all the other girls."

"Not even a little," he says. "You matter. A lot."

I wrap my arms around him and hold him tight, and for the first time in days, I finally breathe properly. There's a sound behind us. The front door opens, and his mom walks inside. She looks at me, and I pull away from him and try to smooth myself out.

"How's Kyle feeling?" she asks Flynn, her eyes still on me.

I sniffle and wipe under my eyes, and she squints, looking closer at me. She's carrying a plastic bag in one hand.

"He's napping," Flynn tells her. He doesn't look concerned at being found with me in his arms.

"How long?"

"Not very. He'll probably sleep a couple of hours more."

"Mrs. McCarthy gave me some homemade bread," she says to Flynn, holding up the bag. "We have leftover fish. We can eat at home tonight."

She glances down at me again, studies my face. "You like fish, Tess?"

"Jess," Flynn says, and he gently unwraps himself from me and stands. "And don't tell me you didn't know that." He faux glares at her.

"I love it," I lie and stand up and walk toward her, my hand out to shake hers. "Hi, Mrs. Carson."

She stares at my hand and starts to laugh, but she takes it in hers. "You're a determined little one, aren't you?" She shakes my hand and lets it go, laughing some more.

"Not usually," I admit. "Usually I'm a chicken."

She tilts her head, studying me. "You must really like my son then."

My cheeks heat up.

"Fine," she says. "You do. Okay."

She walks to the kitchen. "Go on," she calls to Flynn. "I can see you've finally stopped moping now. So take the girl somewhere." She looks at me. "And you don't need to eat fish when you don't even like it. Crazy girl." She puts the plastic bag in the tiny refrigerator. "I need to have a nap before my next shift. I'll go lie down with Kyle." She shakes her head at us and heads off toward the bedroom. "Be back in two hours, Flynn."

Flynn walks me to the front door.

243

I slip my shoes back on. "How did she know I was lying about the fish?" I whisper.

He starts to laugh. "Never underestimate my mom," he says. "Come on. Let's walk to Nellie's."

He takes my hand, and when we walk by his neighbors, the boys hoot, but Flynn gives them the finger and they all laugh. I'm tempted to say something about the other girls they mentioned, but I don't. He says I matter. I trust him. I look around at the trees on the street. They're mature and full. Beautiful.

"Are you hungry?" he asks as I run my hand along the bark of a tree we pass.

"Kind of." I'm starved.

"Nellie's has awesome pizza. I know a place where we can go to eat it. And talk."

It sounds like heaven, but I frown and shake my head. "I don't need pizza. We can just go talk."

He laughs. "It's okay, Jess. I help the owner out with odd jobs. He gives me free pizzas. It's a win-win situation."

I smile. "You're a pretty resourceful guy."

"I like pizza."

The walk to Nellie's is short. The restaurant turns out to be an old house with only four tables inside. A man with a big round belly stands behind a counter smiling when we walk in. He yells at someone in the back to cook up a loaded pizza.

"Flynn," the man says. "And who is your fine-looking companion?"

Flynn introduces me to Pete, the owner. While the pizza cooks, Pete tells me a funny story about trying to fix a leak in the roof on his own and how he ended up soaked from head to toe. I laugh and smile, listening to the two of them joke with each other about odd jobs gone wrong.

"Pete knows pizza. But he doesn't know fixing," Flynn says.

When the pizza is out of the oven, Pete puts it in a box and hands it to Flynn. "Check back soon," he tells him. "There's something wrong with the hinge on the oven door."

Flynn assures him he'll be back and holds the box up in the air. We leave Nellie's and head toward a back alley and a stretch of bushes. Flynn points to a pathway that's concealed by a bunch of overgrown branches and bushes. "Come on. This path goes to the water," he tells me. "Follow me."

He leads me down a narrow path. I hear water lapping on the shore and smile. In a moment, the pathway opens up to a small pebbled beach. It's narrow, not very long. Tiny white-capped waves crash and splash to the shore, as if they're playing with each other.

"It's beautiful," I say. I wonder if he's brought other girls here.

"Yeah," he agrees. "The best part of Clover Lawn. Someone told me they used to have summer homes out here and then the town started settling farther away from the water. I guess this beach got kind of forgotten and lost."

"It's really cool." There's litter around the edge of the beach, fast food boxes and cups lying in the dune grass, proof that other people know about the area.

Flynn walks a little farther then kicks off his shoes and sits. I tilt back my head, close my eyes, listen to the sounds, and inhale the scent of the water.

"Eat first and then talk?" he says. "I'm starving."

He opens the pizza box and pats the spot beside him, so I sit, pulling off my shoes and pressing my bare feet against his. There's so much to say, but it doesn't feel necessary to rush. My stomach grumbles, reminding me that being with Flynn is many wonderful things, but it doesn't fill an empty stomach.

His hands me a slice of pizza, and I fold it and take a big bite, and my mouth is instantly delighted by an amazing sauce and crust.

"Mmmm." I smile at our toes and chew, loving the feeling of sand on my feet.

We eat in silence. A seagull squawks above us, and I watch it swoop around us in a circle.

"You cold?" There's a breeze from the water. Flynn notices when I shiver and he pulls off his hoodie.

"No. It's okay. Really." I shake my head, but he's already wrapping it around my shoulders.

He takes another slice of pizza and inhales it while he stares off at the ocean. A moment later, he turns to me. "I really am sorry," he says.

Another seagull swoops in, joining the first one that's now on the shore, not too far in front of us. "I told my mom about you. She thinks it's cool."

"Really?" He smiles, understanding the significance.

"Yeah. She's been up and about more lately."

"That's awesome."

I nod. "We're not doing anything wrong." I watch his profile. "It's not wrong to like each other."

He's chewing, but he looks at me and smiles. "I know." He leans closer and kisses me, but it's a short and friendly peck. "Do you want the last piece?" Flynn says, gesturing to the pizza box.

I shake my head and smile. Flynn ate two pieces for every one of mine. He takes the last piece from the box, but instead of shoving it in his mouth, he rips it into small pieces and then throws them ahead of us, scattering them around for the birds circling us, the birds who've been enviously watching us eat. They swarm down to the shore and devour the pizza in a noisy feast.

"Figured they were hungry too," he says like it's no big deal to give up the last piece to a bunch of birds, and then he sits back beside me, relaxing against me on the sand.

He reaches for my hand, and we entwine our slightly greasy fingers. The sensation makes me tingle all the way to my heart. It's hard to tell where his hand starts and my hand ends. I lean against him, calmer now. I'm not afraid. We'll find a way to make things work.

"I don't want to sneak around," he says. "Not with you."

I shake my head. Our palms are sweaty as they press against each other, but it's a nice mushy sensation. We kiss again, but instead of building up like a frantic song that needs a climax, a splashy ending, it slowly winds down. It's not a kiss of passion but a promise.

"It's going to be okay, Jess," he whispers. We stay like that, wrapped up in each other's arms.

"Do you think I'm crazy?" I ask him. "For coming to see you. What if you had turned me away?"

He laughs. "I guess you knew I wouldn't."

The water and the wind and the birds play an unchoreographed song in the background.

"Kiss me," he says. I lean back and enjoy the flavor of him, the slightly tangy taste of pizza on my lips.

"Mm," he says. "You are delicious, but we should go." He gets to his feet and holds out his hand. "I need to get home before my mom goes to work. I'll walk you to the bus stop and wait with you so you're safe."

I take his hand, stand, and slide my shoes on. "I don't want to go home," I tell him.

"I know. But your dad already hates me. Let's not make it worse."

"My dad." I shake my head. Some of my anger returns.

"Don't worry," he says as he puts his shoes on. "I'll wear him down. I'll find a way. I won't stay away. Not anymore."

We walk to the bus stop holding hands. Most of all, I'm happy. When the bus approaches, I let his hand go reluctantly and watch out the window until we turn a corner and I can't see him anymore. I wish we could have stayed on the beach forever. But we have to get back to real life and find a way to make it work in a world where people don't think we should be together.

It can't be that bad now that we have each other.

chapter **twenty-two**

I'm practically floating up the driveway, trying to contain my megasmile. When I open the door and step inside the house, the atmosphere hits me immediately. It's not empty, and it's not quiet. Dad stands in the living room, his face a scary mask. Behind him, Allie is sitting on the couch, her face all pinched up and worried. My happiness bubble splats, and my smile disappears. I immediately feel like I've done something wrong.

"We've been looking for you. Where were you?" he demands.

I start sweating and glance at Allie for a clue about what's going on. "Nowhere," I automatically say.

Boom! He smacks the wall beside him with his hand, quickly getting my attention fully back. I jump and step back from him.

"What the hell?" I yell.

"Watch your mouth, Jess," he yells back. "Were you with *that boy*?" he asks.

"I was working," I yell. "And it's true. I *was* working. Before I was with that boy.

He taps on his watch as if he's trying to break the glass on it with his finger. "Until this time?"

I press my lips shut and glance at Allie. Her back is straight, her eyes are open wide, and she's biting her lip the way she used to when she was a kid and she'd done something wrong. She shakes her head, but I don't get her meaning.

"I was at New Beginnings," I repeat. "Working."

"Not this entire time. Lunch doesn't last that long."

I shrug.

"I told you I didn't want you working there," he says. "And I certainly didn't want you traipsing off to Clover Lawn on your own."

My blood stops flowing and my body freezes. How do they possibly know? "You've told me lots of things," I snap. "You once told me you'd never let anything bad happen to this family."

Allie's eyes open wider. I'm playing dirty now.

"You are *not* to see that boy. Or go to that neighborhood."

"What did you tell him?" I turn to Allie, seething. She's sitting on the couch, watching this happen. Not even trying to stick up for me.

"Jess," she says. Her head is tilted, and if she were a dog, her ears would be pulled back. "It's for your own good. You're caught up in something that isn't good for you."

"My own good?" I make a growling sound and stomp my foot. "You don't know what you're talking about!" I shout. "Who do you think you are? You're barely part of this family anymore, and suddenly *you* know what's best for me? You don't know anything!" I yell.

Dad grabs me by the shoulder. "Your sister is trying to save you from a huge mistake."

"Huge mistake?" I shake him off me and back away from both of them. "Flynn is the only thing in my life that isn't complete crap. For the first time in ages I have someone to talk to."

"Jess," my dad interrupts.

"What?" I yell as loud as I can, the anger bubbling in my throat. I want to hit a wall too. "You think I'm making that up? How would either of you even know? Neither one of you is ever here. You"—I point my finger at his face—"are always flying off, disappearing for days at a time. And you." I turn back and point at my sister. "She is not at Dana's house. She's practically living with Doug. She sleeps at his house, and everyone knows it except you and Mom. This family is a mess."

"Jess!" she shouts, jumping to her feet, her eyes wide and tears flowing.

"What? You think you can tell on me but I have to keep covering for you? Doug's mom is more of a family to you than we are." I scoff and swivel back to my dad. "You really don't know where she's staying? You're that removed from what's going on you don't even know?"

My dad stares at Allie, his eyes wide. His perfect daughter isn't so perfect after all.

"I won't be banned from seeing Flynn. His family may not have money or live in the nicest area, but at least his mom isn't home hiding in her bedroom so hopped up on pills she doesn't have to deal with reality."

Allie's eyes open wider. She's staring at something behind me. I close my eyes for a second, and my stomach drops. I open them and turn. Mom is standing at the bottom of the stairs, her hand on the railing.

Her mouth is open in an *O* shape.

"Mom," I say quickly, walking toward her. "I'm sorry. I didn't mean that. I'm sorry."

She lifts her hand. Shakes her head. "No," she says. "No, I deserve that."

The house is suddenly too quiet. The clock on the wall ticks too loudly. The hum of electronics is deafening.

"Fuck," my dad says, and my ears almost fall off. The self-control is slipping away.

"Martin," my mom says, her voice quiet but not weak. "It's okay."

"No, it's not." He turns from all of us, slides on shoes, grabs a jacket, and storms out the door.

The three of us stare at the closed door, shocked.

"Fuck," my mom says.

"I'm sorry," I tell her again.

She stares back at me. "I'm the one who's sorry." And then she starts to laugh.

I move closer to her, worried. Allie walks toward us too.

"Mom?" Allie says. "You okay?"

Mom lifts her hand and covers her mouth, but a giggle sneaks out.

"Fuck," I say.

"What's wrong with you?" Allie shouts at me.

I giggle then, realizing why Mom's laughing. Because we're ridiculous. All of us. It's actually kind of honest to freaking laugh about it.

"She said it first," I say as if I'm five years old again.

Mom puts an arm around me and holds out her other arm for Allie. Allie scoots under, and Mom embraces both of us. She's not laughing anymore, but she smiles and shakes her head.

"Jess is right. We're a mess."

Allie cries louder, and Mom lets me go and pulls her close. They stand like that for a while, and I go to the couch and plop down, exhausted.

Mom pulls away from Allie first. "It's okay, Allie," she says. "Your dad will be back soon. He's having a hard time believing you girls are actually growing up without his say-so. And he certainly doesn't know what to do with me. He's gone for a walk. To get some perspective."

I stare at the door my dad walked out of. Allie comes to the couch and sits close beside me, pressing her leg against mine. We may be mad at each other, but we're still all we've got in this crazy parent scenario.

"I'm sorry, Allie," I tell her. "But what the hell did you tell Dad about Flynn? I've been covering for you for over a year."

I glance at my mom. She's gone to the kitchen to fix a cup of tea.

"For the record, I knew where you were," she calls to Allie as she puts a cup under the Keurig. "But I trust Doug's mom."

Allie and I exchange a wide-eyed look. All sorts of truths are coming out now that we've opened up the gaping wound that is our family.

Allie sighs. "Nance called. She sounded really concerned. She said you were in Clover Lawn and that she was really worried. That you were in danger. She made that boy sound awful."

"Flynn? He's not dangerous! And how'd she even know I was there?"

"I don't know. But she kind of implied you were going to walk in on him making a deal or something. And that you could get hurt."

"Oh my God!" I yell as loud as I yelled at my dad earlier. "She said that? That is a lie. He was babysitting his little brother. I was not in danger."

"Good Lord, Allie, why didn't you tell me if that's what you were afraid of?" Mom calls from the kitchen.

Allie and I exchange another look.

"Or at least tell your father," she concedes with a sigh as she walks out of the kitchen toward us, holding her mug.

"I'm sorry," Allie says. "I did tell Dad. But not everything. He would have freaked."

"It wasn't true anyhow," I remind them. "Flynn is a good person." I look at my mom then. "I'm sorry for what I said. I didn't mean—"

"No," she says, cutting me off. "It's true. I've been neglecting you."

"But you have a reason," I tell her.

She sips her tea, standing very still, watching us closely. "I'm going to try," she finally says. "Try harder. But, God, I need help."

"Oh, Mom," I say. "Of course."

Allie jumps up and runs to Mom's side. She's so much better at things like this. Or she used to be. "I'll be around more if you want."

Mom puts an arm around Allie and puts her tea down on the coffee table, and they walk to the couch and sit beside me.

Allie looks as terrified as I feel. It's scary to hope and scary to think this won't last, this glimpse of old Mom. I don't want her to disappear again.

"What about Dad?" I ask.

Mom sighs. "He's having a hard time, you know. He doesn't know how to fix me. He wants to fix all of us. Keep us safe. But he doesn't know how, and it overwhelms him that he can't. I think that's why he's been away so much." It sounds like she's thought about it before.

"Control issues up the wazoo," I mumble.

"I'll talk to him." Her features have a long-forgotten fierceness.

It's kind of selfish, turning the conversation back to me, but it's eating away at me. "Mom, Nance lied. I have no idea why."

"Nance is an idiot," Allie says. "I don't know why you hang out with her. Penny was always your best friend. You and Penny only put up with her because of Mom."

My eyes fill with tears.

"What?" Allie asks.

"I miss her. I messed up with Penny. A long time ago. I embarrassed her, said bad things about her," I whisper. "And I never told her I was sorry. Not until a couple of days ago."

"Oh, Jess," Allie says. "I didn't know. Why?"

I close my eyes. "I guess I didn't want to deal with it."

Mom pats my back and then rubs in a circle. I twist my earring. "You two went through so much together when her dad was sick. You can give it another try, can't you?"

"Some things aren't fixed by sorry," I add. As the three of us sit quietly contemplating that, the doorbell rings. We all stare at the door, and then Allie makes a guilty face and jumps up and runs to it and peeks through the peephole.

"Um, Jess." She turns to me, her hand on the knob. "It's for you. Don't be mad, okay?"

I frown and sit up taller.

"When Nance called, all worried, the first thing I thought to do was call Penny. She's here." She turns back to the door and opens it. "Come in, Penny," Allie tells her.

Penny steps inside and sees red-eyed, blotchy faces on all three of us. "Um. What's wrong?"

"Family drama," I tell her. "Don't step any further if you want to stay out of it."

Penny closes the door behind her and steps inside.

I get up and run at her, throwing my arms around her and hugging her tight.

chapter **twenty-three**

Penny comes to my room and sits on the bed. I sit across from her. She glances around. "I've missed this room. Talking with you." She picks up one of my pillows and hugs it close.

"Me too," I tell her. "I'm sorry. I've wanted to tell you every day how sorry I am. But I was too scared." I look down at my comforter. The purple is fading. "It got easier to avoid it. I've been such an asshole."

"Well, things were kind of messed up," she says. "At home."

"You think?" I say and look up and smile. She moves so she's leaning against my headboard. I sit beside her and we stretch our legs out. Wiggle our toes.

"I don't know how I'd handle things if it happened to me. To my mom," she says without looking at me.

"Well, you handled your dad's illness with a lot more grace."

"We were younger," she says.

"Yeah. Well, you wouldn't have gotten drunk and hooked up with Josh Reid."

She makes a face and sticks out her tongue. "Ugh. You're right about that." We both start laughing. It feels good. "Josh Reid," she says and punches my arm.

"Ugh," I tell her. "He's not that bad, you know. He's kind of inse-cure with girls. Except when he drinks. Kind of like me and guys. Until I met Flynn."

"Really?" She tilts her head. "Huh." Then she sticks out her tongue again. "But still. Ugh." And then she smiles. "But what about Flynn? Your face lights up like a Christmas tree when you say his name."

I grin and then frown. "Nance lied about him, you know. To cause trouble."

"I'm gathering," she says.

"My dad doesn't want me to see him."

"That sucks."

"I know. But he doesn't know him. Flynn is an amazing guy." I jump off the bed and go to my dresser. I smile at my plant book but pick up the carved monkey. "He made this for me." She puts out her hand and I place it inside. "He made it because he noticed my sock monkey on my purse."

"Oh my God. That is so sweet." She looks up. "Was it the one I gave you? Brave Monkey?"

I smile. Almost true.

"I still have Bill," she says. "My sock monkey. The one you gave me when my dad was sick. The Protector."

We both laugh, and then I ask her a zillion questions about Keith, and she tells me and we giggle and squeal and giggle some more. There's so much we have to say. But for the moment, we talk about boys, and it makes both of us happy. I can't believe how much has happened in this one day. I've been on an emo roller coaster.

"Are you hungry?" I ask when we have a lull in our conversation. Penny always had the metabolism of a small country, and she nods. When we go to the kitchen, Mom and Allie are sitting at the kitchen table, drinking tea.

"Sit," I tell Penny and walk past and open the pantry door and spot a bag of ripple chips. Penny's favorite. When I grab them and hold them up, she smiles.

"Is Dad back yet?" I ask.

Allie and Mom shake their heads. "Don't worry," Mom says. "He'll be back soon."

I grab a bowl and dump the chips in and take them over to Penny.

"Are you and Keith heading to the Thompson bonfire tonight?" Allie asks Penny as she shoves a handful of chips in her mouth.

"Um. Not anymore," she says between bites.

I glance at the clock on the wall. It's only eight thirty. "You're not going because of me?" I ask. I realize I didn't even know about the party. And that doesn't bother me, but Penny missing a date with Keith because of me does.

She shrugs.

"You have to go," I tell her. "You're going with Keith Alex!"

Penny and I giggle when I say his name, like we're in seventh grade again or as if her relationship is brand-new. It's not. But it is to us.

Penny takes another chip. "Why don't you come with us?" she asks and glances at my mom.

I shake my head.

"Doug and I were going to go," Allie says, but she glances at Mom too. "But I don't think we'll go now."

"It's okay," I say to her. "You go. I'll stay home with Mom."

"Oh please," Mom says. "You don't need to sit around and baby-sit me. Your dad will be home soon anyhow, and we need to talk. Privacy will be good. Go. Both of you." She smiles at Penny. "I like seeing you two together again. Go have fun." She waves her hand in the air to shoo us away.

"But…" I start.

"Take your skinny little chip-eating butts and go and have some fun."

"You're sure?" Allie and I both say.

"Go!"

"I'll text Keith, and he can pick us up from here," Penny says. "It's a bonfire party, so we don't have to do anything fancy. Maybe you can you lend me a hoodie?"

"Keith Alex," I squeal and jump to my feet, jumping up and down. Penny smiles while I jump up and down and pogo without a pogo stick.

Mom and Allie laugh and then we sit, and even Allie reaches for a chip as Penny texts Keith.

I think about Flynn. At home, babysitting his brother. How great would it be to be able to text Flynn? Or even call him. Ask him to join me at a bonfire party. I wonder if it will always be this way? Together, but not.

I don't care. He's worth it.

chapter **twenty-four**

Keith arrives at my place in a hatchback. It's new and clean but not over the top. Penny kisses his cheek when she climbs in the front beside him. I sit in the backseat, watching the two of them. They're so cute together, it makes me jealous. Happy for her. Really happy. But jealous.

Penny insists we drive to Wendy's before the bonfire. I guess she wants Keith and me to get a chance to talk before the party. I wonder if she's nervous. I've known him for years, but never as Penny's boyfriend. And he's probably heard lots of things about me lately. Lots of them not nice. And probably true. The two of them order enough food for three people twice their size.

"It amazes me how much this little girl can eat," Keith tells me proudly as we sit in the parking lot, stuffing our faces.

We make jokes about how much food Penny can consume, and then finally he's done and he tells Penny he's driving to the party and fires up the car, does a U-turn at a set of lights, and starts driving toward the country road that leads to the bonfire.

"Hey? Does it sound like upsexy in here?" he suddenly asks Penny.

"What's upsexy?" she asks.

"Not much, what's up with you?"

Penny punches him on the arm, and I giggle. It's not funny; it's just so freaking adorable, and I'm still getting used to them. PennyandKeith!

"Does she always punch people?" he asks me. "Or is it just me?"

"She always punches people," I tell him.

He looks at Penny and then at me in the rearview mirror. "Penny missed you a lot," he says.

"Don't tell her that." Penny punches him again. "She's not off probation yet." She's kidding. But she's not.

My heart aches a little. "I missed her too," I tell Keith, but it's meant for her.

I love that Keith isn't threatened by our old friendship. That he's trying to make things better, as tentative as they still are. The guys Nance hooked up with always hated having me tag along with them, as if I was a competitor for her attention or something.

"Did you know she used to write things about you in her diary?" I ask Keith, leaning forward and sticking my head between them and grinning.

"Jess," she says. "Do not tell him my secrets. Because remember, I know yours too."

I laugh and lean back in my seat. "Not anymore, you don't."

"I'd like to read what she writes now," he says. "It would be X-rated."

She punches him one more time.

By the time Keith reaches the farmer's field, it's getting dark. Cars are parked in uneven rows. There's a big turnout, not a huge surprise for a bonfire party as summer is winding down. The farmer's field is owned by Greg Thompson's family. He's a senior next year and the last of three brothers. There have been lots of parties out this way. They sometimes end up getting busted by cops if things get out of control. I've been to a couple of the bonfire parties, but I try not to think of the last one. Mostly because I only remember the beginning of the evening. There was beer. Lots of it. And the end of the party is kind of a blank. Of course, it involved waking up at Nance's. And Josh.

When Keith parks, we climb out of the car, and Penny asks me to grab a blanket and chair from the trunk. I drape the blanket around my shoulders and take a lawn chair. Keith pulls out a six-pack of beer from the trunk and a chair.

"You're sure you're going to be okay?" Penny asks as she takes the last lawn chair. "Not drinking?"

"It's fine," I tell her. "I really don't want to."

She hesitates for a second. "Okay. Well, good. I'm kind of glad."

"It won't happen again, Pen," I tell her. "What I did to you. I promise." I have no desire to get messy drunk and risk the friendship I want to rebuild.

She nods. "Okay." She grabs a six-pack of Coke and slams the trunk down. "We can have these. I'm Keith's designated driver. That's the only reason he takes me places."

He bends down to kiss her on the lips. "Not even close," he says.

The three of us walk toward the noise and the smell of smoke and bright flames shooting up from the fire. The party sounds like it's in second gear. It'll go up a few more notches before the night is over.

Keith holds Penny's hand and carries his six-pack in the other. I think of Flynn's hand and hope sometime the four of us will hang out. Keith drops Penny's hand to check his phone. "Keep your eye out for drunk creeps," Keith says to us both. "And don't wander off anywhere alone or take a drink from anyone. Cale texted me earlier and said there are a few assholes here."

Penny and I make the same wrinkly face.

He shoves his phone in his jacket pocket and takes back Penny's hand. The music gets louder as we get closer to the swarm of bodies buzzing around the fire. My stomach does a nervous little dip. It's weird. I'm not with Nance; I don't have to do anything or impress anyone. Boring me is fine. As if she senses my nerves, Penny grabs my hand and squeezes. "You okay?" she whispers.

I nod.

She unfolds her lawn chair, and I do the same. Then she sets out a blanket and Keith puts down his beer and pulls one from the case and pops it open. I watch him.

"You want one?" he asks

"No, thanks."

Penny leans closer. "Keith is cool to go off on his own for a while. I'm not going to leave you alone," she tells me.

She remembers how nervous I get at parties. Got. Without alcohol. Get. I can do this. "Thank you," I tell her and mean it so much.

On cue, Keith bends down and kisses her cheek. "I'm going to find Cale. Don't go far from here, okay? I'll be back," he says. He disappears in a twist of bodies moving around us.

Penny plops down in the lawn chair. "Want to people-watch?" she asks. It feels so good having her to talk to. I have some proving to do, I know that, but it definitely feels like we're on our way. I plop down beside her and look at the kids sitting around, some on lawn chairs, some on blankets, and some closer to the fire on long log seats. The flames from the fire light up the face of a boy heading toward us, a smile on his face.

He pushed glasses up on his freckled nose, his hair a mop of messiness.

"Cale!" Penny jumps up to hug him. "Keith just went to look for you."

He walks forward and lifts Penny off the ground in a bear hug. I guess they've gotten closer because of Keith. "Penster," he says.

Penny laughs as he puts her back down. He pushes his eyeglasses up on his nose.

"Do you know Jess?" Penny says.

"Hey, Cale." We had a class together early in high school. Freshman year, before I started taking easier classes.

"Hey, Jess," he says, lifting his hand.

"You still the smartest guy in high school?" I ask.

He looks away, as if I'm making fun of him.

"No. I mean, it's cool. That you're top-of-the-class smart."

Penny puts an arm around him. "He's not only brilliant, he's the sweetest boy on earth."

"Sweet as a Nerd," Cale says. "And I do mean the candy."

"JESS-I-CUP!!" a voice calls from behind Cale. I recognize it immediately and cringe. Great. Everyone turns to the staggering mess approaching us. Nance. Loaded. It's apparent before she opens her mouth to say a word.

"I'm schtill mad at you." She stumbles right into me and attaches herself to my side. She's wearing a tank top cut low to show off her boobs. Around her neck are neon glow stick necklaces. "But I'm *so* glad you're here." She throws both arms around my neck, even though one is holding a plastic cup of beer and it spills all over my hoodie. Nice. She tugs on my neck, almost pulling me over. "Let's party, gurl. No one parties like my Jess-I-cup." She lets go of me and starts dancing, but despite all those dance lessons, she still has no rhythm.

I can't meet Penny's eyes. I stare at the ground, embarrassed for Nance, embarrassed for me because this is what I used to look like at parties too. Is it too much to ask for the ground to open up and swallow me whole?

"Ugh. You!" she says to Penny. "Are you here with *her*?" she yells in my ear. "I thought you two were best friends for never."

I glance at Penny and try to apologize through my eyes and then glare at Nance. "Why'd you tell my sister those things about Flynn?" I demand.

She makes a very unattractive face. "Oh, that boy. Braxton saw you in Clover Lawn with him, and he told Jennifer. I was worried." She drags out the last word and giggles, immediately forgiving herself for lying to my sister. There's no use getting into it now. She makes another face at me. "I told Jennifer to stop with her summer fling. And she listened." She turns to Cale and pokes him in the chest. "Hey, Cale. Got a smoke?"

"Sorry," Cale says. "Last time I smoked, my hair was on fire."

She tries to take a sip of her beer but misses her mouth and it slides down her top, soaking her in the front. She laughs, and my cringe grows in intensity. "You're mad at me?" she slurs.

"I don't want to talk about it now," I say in a low voice.

"Well, la dee da." She makes a rude gesture with her hips. "Go ahead. Surround yourself with losers. Your dad will kill you." And then, as if a switch turned, the way it goes with drunk people sometimes, Nance starts to cry. And because she's drunk, it's not a tiny, sad little sound—it's loud and wet and messy. "Don't hate me, Jess."

"Oh God," I say and pat her arm as she throws herself on me, sobbing.

"Oh God," Penny repeats. "I'd forgotten the drama." But she helps her off me and shushes her.

Cale moves in, blocking her from other kids starting to look over at the train wreck.

I bend down to her level. "What's wrong?" I ask. "Why are you crying?"

"My mom." She slides to the ground. "My mom doesn't love meeeeeee."

"There's some strong stuff floating around here," Cale says. "Did she take anything?"

"It's possible." I sigh and kneel down beside her on the ground. "Nance?" I say. "Did you take anything? Besides alcohol?"

Despite what a jerk Nance is, Penny kneels down on her other side and strokes her arm and reassures her.

"I don't know," Nance mumbles to her knees. She grabs my hand and squeezes pretty hard, considering. "She's always gone. With her boyfriend." Mascara runs down her cheeks and circles her eyes. "Why doesn't anyone love me?"

"Your parents love you." I try to wipe away the mess on her face. Despite everything, my heart aches for her. She's got a lot of things bubbling under the surface too.

"No," she says. "They don't." And then she sobs some more.

"I should get her home," I say to Penny. "I need to find Allie. She'll be pissed off, but she'll take her home."

"Don't be silly," Penny says.

"No. I have to get her home. She's a mess."

"I know that. I mean you don't have to get Allie." She stands up and reaches for her phone. "I'll text Keith. We'll take her home." She's so nice, it almost makes me cry myself.

"Are you sure?" I stand up. "You guys just got here."

She rolls her eyes. "She can't stay here like this. There will be more parties. It's okay."

Nance cries on, and I look around. The party keeps on going. People are talking, laughing, smoking, and drinking from plastic cups. It's noisy and only getting louder.

"Want me to go find Keith?" Cale offers.

"Do you mind?" Penny asks. "He's the worst at checking his phone."

"Course not. I'll bring him back." He disappears into the crowd.

"Thank you," I say to Penny, my voice small. "This isn't your problem."

"Let's just get her home."

"Wait." Nance gets up. "I don't want to go home." She slips on her ass but manages to stand. "I'm not going home," she repeats. The sadness is gone from her voice, and now she's mad.

"Jennifer!" she yells loudly. "Jennifer!" She staggers a little as she tries to leave us, but I grab her by the arm and try to hold her back.

"Nance," I say. "We're going to go."

"Jennifer!" she yells again.

A body crashes into me. "There you are!" Jennifer yells at Nance. "I was looking for you." Jennifer is holding a beer cup and wearing an outfit similar to Nance's, but it's obvious she's not nearly as drunk.

"She's pretty out of it," I say, gesturing to Nance. "We were going to take her home."

"Home? The party's barely started." Jennifer links her arm with Nance's. "You don't want to go home, do you, Nance?"

"Course not," Nance shouts and stumbles as Jennifer tugs on her arm.

Cale appears from the dark, Keith at his side.

"She should really go home," I say to Jennifer again.

"She's fine," Jennifer says over her shoulder. "I take care of her now. Not you."

The two of them stumble off.

"That is not going to end well," I say.

"It's okay," Penny says to me. "You can't make her."

Keith is at her side, his arm around her shoulder. "Not if she doesn't want to," he adds.

"I have some experience with girls of this nature," Cale says wryly. "Trust me, somehow they end up fine. It's usually the people around them who pay."

"You still want to go home?" Penny asks, touching my arm.

I do. I want out of this place and away from the horrible feelings.

I don't want to be that girl anymore. "You and Keith probably want to stay though? We just got here."

"Meh." She glances at Keith.

He shakes his head. "I have to work in the morning. It's no big deal," he says.

"I feel bad though. Leaving Nance too."

"I'll keep an eye on her. I'm going to stick around," Cale offers. "Jennifer's not as wasted either. I was talking to her earlier. We'll look after her."

"You're sure?"

"No problem," he says. "I'll make sure Nance gets home. She lives down the street from me."

Keith and Penny fold up the lawn chairs.

"You're sure? Don't leave because of me," I tell them.

"We'll find something to do," Keith says, and Penny smacks him on the arm.

I blush but laugh. Keith dumps his beer on the ground and sticks the empty bottle back in the case.

"Jess!"

A deep voice calls my name. We all look over. My heart starts to pound.

chapter **twenty-five**

Flynn stands by the fire. The reflection of the flames dances around him, and he looks wild, gorgeous, and completely unexpected.

How is it even possible he's here? I left him to babysit hours ago. It seems like the longest day of my life.

"Flynn?" I ask and walk toward him. And then we're moving toward each other, and it's like I'm in a dream sequence. We're facing each other, standing nose to nose. I start to laugh. "What are you doing here? How did you get here?" I glance around for Braxton, but it's just Flynn.

He puts out his arms, and I slide inside, smelling him and hugging him as hard as I can.

"I came," he says, "to see you."

The party goes on, and people laugh and talk as if everything is completely normal. But it's better than normal. Flynn is here.

Allie and Doug are behind him, walking toward us, holding hands. Flynn looks back at my sister and her boyfriend.

"After you and Penny left, he showed up at the house," Allie says. "He came over to talk to Mom and Dad. And then Doug and I brought him here."

"You were at our house? But how? Why?" I have no idea what's going on. The fire crackles behind us, and the sound of people having fun fills the night air. The area around is lit up from head-lights of cars still arriving. But all I hear is Flynn.

"You're supposed to be babysitting," I tell him.

"My mom unexpectedly got the night off," he says. "So she let me come out. To find you. Braxton dropped me off at your house. I was going to take a bus home."

"You should have heard him," Allie says. "What he said to Dad."

I hug him harder. He went to my house? I still can't believe he's here or that he spoke to my parents! This day has been too much.

"He totally made his case with Dad. He told him all the reasons he should be allowed to date you," she tells me. She's grinning at both of us.

"Wow," says Penny. "That's pretty great."

"Cool," adds Keith. He unfolds the chair he's holding and sets it down. "I guess we're staying now."

I realize they're still standing behind me, staring and trying to figure out what's going on. Keith steps forward though and pounds fists with Flynn. "Nice work, bro," he says with a grin. "Reeling in the parents." He imitates throwing out a fishing line and reeling it back in.

Penny puts down her chair and crosses her arms. "Listen to the big talker." She turns to Flynn. "My parents read Keith the riot act the first time they met him," Penny adds. "He totally sucked up. He was super cute though. It worked."

"Sorry, guys," I say. "This is Flynn, and this is Penny. And Keith."

"Penny Penny?" Flynn asks, smiling at her.

"Penny Penny," I tell him.

The three of them laugh, and Penny starts elaborating about when her parents met Keith, and he laughs and tries to make himself sound much more macho than she's doing. While they're joking around, I turn to my sister. She drops Doug's hand and steps closer to me.

"He really stood up for himself, Jess. And for you," she says softly. "He told Dad he really liked you and that he would treat you well. He told him he was a hard worker and that his family was going through tough times because of his stepfather but that he was nothing like him."

Flynn laughs with Keith and Penny, and I watch him, my heart swelling.

"He asked Dad if he could date you," Allie says. "Asked permission. And Dad actually agreed." She holds both hands together and lifts them to her heart. "I kind of fell in love with him too."

Doug rolls his eyes and reaches for her hand. "Let's not get carried away, Allie."

She gives his hand a little smack. "Don't be jealous, Doug. Anyhow, that's when I asked him if he wanted to come to the bonfire with us. To surprise you."

I reach out to hug her too, grateful she believes in Flynn. Grateful she's looking out for me.

Flynn moves to my side and puts an arm around me.

"Definitely staying?" Keith asks with a smile and plunks back down in his chair and reaches for a beer.

I'm in a blurry kind of heaven and don't let go of Flynn and watch the people I care about starting to get to know each other.

"I'm so glad you're here," I whisper as the others talk.

"Me too," he whispers backs and kisses the top of my head. "I wouldn't want to be anywhere else."

My sister smiles at Flynn like he's the best thing that ever happened to me. I bury my anger with Nance for the lies she told about Flynn, because things worked out kind of great. My worry for her settles into the back of my mind for later. For right now, all I want to be is in the moment with my friends.

Allie's phone buzzes in the middle of an animated story, complete with hand gestures from Keith about a hiking trip he and Penny went on. I watch Allie still smiling at Keith as she reaches in her hoodie and pulls out the phone. She glances down, frowns, and then lifts it to her ear.

"Hello?"

Doug puts his arm around her as she listens, but she's frowning and shrugs him off and then turns her back and walks slightly away from us, one hand over her ear to block out the party noise.

When she turns back, her eyes are on Flynn, and they're wide and alarmed. He notices at the same time I do, and his body stiffens. Allie abruptly ends the call.

We've all stopped talking, and we're all watching her.

"Flynn," she says. "We have to go. Right now. There's been an accident. At your house. Your friend Braxton called Mom and Dad. It's your brother. He's been hurt."

• • •

When I climb inside Doug's car, I realize I've never been in it before. He and Allie have been together almost three years and this is the first time. Beside me, Flynn is vibrating, his face pale, his eyes wide.

"We're about twenty minutes from the hospital," Doug says, turning around to look at Flynn. "I'll get you there in fifteen."

He takes off out of the farmer's field at full speed. We drive in silence for a while, and then Allie's phone rings again and she picks it up before the first ring ends. She nods, listening, and then she turns to the backseat, lifts the phone, and hands it to Flynn. "It's your friend Braxton."

I watch his face as he talks. Asking questions, closing his eyes, listening. Finally he ends the call and hands the phone back to Allie. Doug speeds through a yellow light.

I put my hand on Flynn's leg, and he looks at me, puzzled. "My stepfather, I mean, my mom's ex, he showed up at our house. Looking for money." He presses his lips together and stares at his hands. He's making a fist, pressing it against his leg. "He went after my mom. I guess Kyle tried to get in the middle and he got hurt. Thrown against the wall. His head hit the edge of the coffee table. He lost a lot of blood. He was unconscious."

"Oh shit" is the best I can manage. "Shit. He'll be okay," I say. "It'll be okay."

"Will it, Jess?" Flynn snaps in a low tone I've never heard before. I shrink back in my seat. "Just because you said so?"

"She didn't mean it like that," Allie says quickly. "She's trying to help." I see Doug look at us in the rearview mirror.

The air in the car is charged but quiet. "Sorry," Flynn says after a moment, but his teeth are gritted and his hands are shaking.

"No," I say. "No. It's okay. You're worried. Of course."

He turns away from me, staring out the window at the flashing lights of traffic and streetlights as Doug speeds toward the hospital. "I should have been there. If I'd been there, this wouldn't have happened."

I want to throw my arms around him but reach for his hand. "Flynn, it's not your fault," I say, but he doesn't look into my eyes. It's subtle, but after a moment, he pulls his hand away.

"We're almost there," Doug says, his hands on the wheel, driving his heart out.

"Braxton's at the hospital with my mom. Kyle will be okay. But ambulances and hospital visits. They're not okay for my family. I know it's not something you guys have to worry about, but my family…we don't even have insurance."

"He'll have to pay," Allie says, lifting her chin, her eyes flaring with outrage. "Your stepfather."

"Ex-stepfather," I tell her.

Flynn laughs bitterly. "Yeah. The thing is, he has no money. None. That's why he went to find my mom. He's not even her ex, not legally. They're still married." He looks like he's going to rip the throat off someone with his bare teeth.

"Well, we'll find a way," Allie says, "To make him pay. Our dad's a lawyer, Flynn."

Flynn shakes his head. "You don't understand." He doesn't say it unkindly, but Allie and I stare at each other over the top of her seat. He's right. We don't.

"Okay," Doug says from the front. "We're here. I'll drive straight to the emergency entrance. You two go."

"No." Flynn turns and looks me in the eye. "I know you want to help, Jess, and I appreciate it, but no. I need to go myself. I need to talk to my mom alone. Kyle's going to be okay, so I'll be fine. Please? Okay? I need to do this myself. Braxton'll make sure we get home."

Doug stops the car, and he and Allie pretend to look out the windows and not listen.

"Are you sure?" I ask, not convinced. "I can stay with you. Help."

"I'll call you as soon as I know more about Kyle. I'll call you at home."

He slides over to the door and opens it. "Thank you," he says to Doug and Allie. "I didn't mean to be a dick."

"No. Of course, you're worried," Allie says. She glances at me, and her eyebrows are furrowed, concerned.

Flynn leans over and kisses my cheek. "I'll call you," he says.

And then he's gone.

• • •

When I wake up, my first thought is about Flynn. And then Kyle and his mom. They're home. At least I know that from the abrupt call from Flynn late last night. Kyle has a concussion, but he'll be okay.

My insides ache, wanting to be with Flynn, wishing he'd let me stay with him. I get up and go to the top of the stairs, and based on the murmuring voices, Mom, Dad, and Allie are up and in the kitchen. I stop, watching the three of them talk. It looks almost normal. Like we're a normal family.

Mom turns as if she senses me and stands as I walk down the stairs.

277

"Jess." She comes over to meet me and puts her arms around me. The hug is good.

We walk to the table, and I and plunk down in the empty chair. Mom sinks down again too. I can't help but notice that it's been a long time since we've all been around the table at the same time.

• • •

Everything is supposed to be back to normal. But I forget what normal smells like, tastes like, or even looks like. I'm in this weird place in my head, with no way to reach Flynn. I want to go to his house, but everyone in my family suddenly has an opinion about my life and advises me to give Flynn time. Give him the weekend with the family.

Mom spends most of Sunday making appointments with therapists. Sounds like she's booking time for all of us. Dad doesn't pull out his work once, and Allie sticks around all day too, not spending every moment at Doug's. It's hard to breathe, sharing the space with everyone again.

"I'm supposed to work tomorrow," I say to my dad on Sunday night after a long day hoping Flynn would reach out to me and hearing nothing.

He nods. "Go."

I need to go back to New Beginnings. I need to see the people and talk to Wilf.

Of course I also have the not-so-secret hope that maybe Flynn will show up too. It's the place that brought us together. Maybe it can bring us back.

chapter **twenty-six**

Sunny sees me when I arrive. Her lips are pressed tight, and she avoids looking me in the eyes. "Stella wants you to go see her first thing."

I go straight to Stella's office.

"Hey, Jess," Stella says when I step inside. She doesn't look very happy to see me, and she looks frazzled. Tired. Her fingers are on the keyboard, but her eyes are on me.

"You heard about Kyle?" I guess, not about to beat around the bush. Forget small talk.

"What about Kyle?" She frowns and presses her lips tight.

"His dad. He showed up at their house. Kyle got hurt."

"Oh my gosh," she says. "Is he okay? Is Flynn okay?"

"Kyle will be fine, and Flynn wasn't there. He was at a party. With me," I say. Her eyebrows bunch together. "He talked to my parents. They're okay with us now."

She's shaking her head and leaning forward, watching me, as if she's trying to figure out how I managed to get Kyle hurt.

"They can come back now, right? You told Flynn he'd mess things up for me. It's not true. Keeping them away. It's not fair."

Stella rubs her chin, not looking at me. She lets out a big breath.

"Stella?"

She raises her hand and shakes her head. "I have some other news."

Her tone surprises me, and I forget the speech I was about to make.

"It's Wilf," she says softly, and I realize that her eyes are sad. Not tired. Sad.

The hairs on my arms stand up. My body goes cold.

"I'm sorry," she says and sighs again. "I know you liked each other."

Liked. Past tense.

"Why are you sorry, Stella?" Hot tears bunch up behind my eyes.

"He passed on," she says. "Last night."

I blink, imagining him working in the greenhouse beside me. Twinkling eyes. Growly voice. The eyes won out. Every time.

"He's been sick for a while," Stella says. "It wasn't totally unexpected. But it was fast."

I bite my lip, refusing to cry. "He didn't tell me. I even asked."

"Probably he didn't want you to worry." She leans over and takes something from a drawer in her desk. "He left this for you last week. Said to give it to you when it was time."

"He knew? He really knew he was dying?"

"I don't think he knew it would happen so fast. But I think he was ready."

I stare at the envelope in her hand, not wanting any of it to be true. The tears biting at my eyes are hot. They hurt.

Even though she could hand the envelope across the desk, Stella stands. She walks around, tucks the envelope in my hand, and pats me on the shoulder. "There's going to be a service for him. Thursday. At Deerlodge. A few of us are going to go together if you want to join us."

I nod. I do. I want to join them.

"You okay?" she asks.

I gnaw on my lip and stare at the envelope in my hand. "I only knew him a few weeks. You knew him a lot longer."

"With a good friend it's not always how long you knew them, but how well you did."

The truth of that simple statement tugs my heart. I glance up at her then. "What about you? You okay?"

She smiles, but it's a sad smile. "At my age you see people go. It is easier to see people Wilf's age go. Easier than when young people are taken too early."

We look at each other. Something in her eyes makes me ask. Invites me to ask. "Did you lose someone, Stella?" I ask softly.

She leans against the corner of her desk. "I had a son."

My mouth opens.

"I didn't raise him," she adds quickly. "I was young when I had him. Only fifteen when he was born. He was adopted. He contacted me when he was twenty-one. We saw each other from time to time. He was a lovely person. Brought up by a lovely family. They did a fine job. He was good to me." She sucks in a quick breath. "He was killed in an accident. Too young." She shakes her head. "It's hard when people leave us."

My chest feels like it's been pried open, but my heart beats hard with sorrow for the son she had to give up. The son she got back and then lost. And for Wilf. My grouchy old friend who will be missed. I glance down at the envelope in my hand. On the front is my name in shaky penmanship.

"Wilf was a good man," she says. "He told me a while ago he'd be remembering New Beginnings in his will. I have no idea what he left. But I'm hoping we can use some to keep the greenhouse going."

"Cool," I say softly. "That's cool."

She folds her hands. "Wilf was ready. He planned his exit strategy, tied up the loose ends. Even arranged his own memorial. He loved his wife so much. He wanted to be with her again. I think he's happier now."

I nod, trying to smile. She's right.

"You know he was a wealthy man."

"He was?" I glance up, surprised.

"I'm pretty sure he didn't leave you his fortune, so take that notion out of your head," she says with a wry smile.

I can't help laughing. Because for a moment, it did pop in my head. But no. He knew it's not what I needed from him. He wouldn't do that.

She smiles sadly and then stands and walks around her desk and sits. "I have to get this paperwork done," she says. "You're okay?"

I stand. "Can I have the key to the greenhouse? Check up on his plants?"

She waves a hand at me, telling me to take it.

"Jess?"

I look at her.

"Keep that key, okay?"

I do my best not to cry.

She nods at me. "Sometime, when you're ready, if you want, I'd like to talk about what happened to your mom."

Surprised, I can only nod. I start to leave and then turn back. "Can I keep volunteering? Fit it around my school schedule?"

She leans back in her chair. "I'd like to put you in charge of the greenhouse. You want to do that? You can still work in the dining room sometimes. Some of our regulars would miss you."

"That would be great."

I leave her office, clutching the envelope in my hand, grabbing the greenhouse key from the hook where it hangs.

When I walk to the greenhouse, the tears I've held inside run freely down my cheeks. I walk straight to Rhea's azaleas. "Oh, Wilf," I say to the air around me. "Why'd you have to leave me too?"

"It's not about you this time, sweetheart," I almost hear him say.

I take a stool and move it to the azaleas, holding the envelope close to my heart.

Dear Jess,

Dear is an old term of endearment. In case you didn't know that. And since I'm old, it works. You are, you know. A dear. A strong girl. A good girl. A dear.

You're going to be all right, no matter what you did to land yourself in this place. In some ways, I suspect that my Rhea had a spiritual hand in it. Bringing you here. I've no doubt she's up there, an angel, looking out for me. I think she wanted us to meet. The daughter I never got to have. Or maybe the daughter of the daughter I never got to have. That's confusing.

Anyhow. If you're reading this, it means I'm departed.

Don't be sad for me. I was ready to go. Ready to be with my angel again.

I need to ask you a favor. I would like you to look after the greenhouse when I'm gone. Another reason Rhea brought you to me. Because you can carry it on. In her name. With the right amount of love and appreciation. I hope you can do this, and then when it's time for you to move on, let it go with no regrets. I've left funds to keep it running for as long as it can.

So good-bye, dear Jess. Remember you have your whole life ahead of you. Fight for what you want. Choose well. Be brave.

Love,
Wilf

chapter **twenty-seven**

The church where Wilf's memorial is held is the biggest non-denominational one in town. Even though there are probably about sixty or seventy people there, it doesn't seem full because of the large, echoing size of the room. I wish every seat was taken by people who knew how awesome Wilf was and how much he'll be missed.

At the front of the church there's a stage with bouquets of flowers in each corner. The front of the stage is lined with potted azaleas. I'm seated in the middle in a row with staff and volunteers from New Beginnings. It's hard because Flynn and his mom are visible from where I'm sitting. They're near the front of the church. Flynn's mom is on one side of Kyle, Flynn on the other. He's bent over, reading Kyle a book. I plead with the back of his head, hoping he'll turn around, look for me. But he doesn't.

We haven't spoken in six days. I've given up hope that things are okay. My insides are gutted. I've gone over different scenarios hundreds of times. What if I decided not to go to the party? What if I were still home when Flynn arrived to talk to my parents? What if his stepdad wasn't such a complete asshole?

People around me talk in hushed voices, but it's hard to pay attention so I sit quietly and don't say anything at all. My emotions are being pulled in one direction and then in another. My eyes keep going back to Flynn's head.

I think about Wilf, wishing so hard he were sitting beside me, talking to me in his growly deep voice, making fun of the people talking about him with such quiet reverence. I didn't know him long and only got to see a tiny part of who he was, but in our short time together, we had something special, Wilf and I both knew it even if we didn't talk about it. Me and the grouchy old man. Keeping it real.

At the front of the room, below the stage, someone begins playing the piano. The service begins. A female minister walks to the podium and speaks in a clear, soothing voice. I smile at that. I've never seen a female minister before. The minister talks about God and about Wilf's life. My heart soars and aches, hearing things about him I didn't know. He was a successful business-man. He published a book of poetry. He played the bagpipes. He took Spanish dance lessons with Rhea. And oh, how he'd loved Rhea.

When she's done, the minister introduces an older woman, a friend of Wilf and Rhea. The woman tells stories about Wilf. People sniffle and wipe their eyes and noses, and when she's finished, the minister announces a family friend will sing a song for Wilf, a song Wilf requested and dedicated to his wife at his memorial.

My heart begins pounding hard when I realize it's Flynn stand-ing. He walks to the front, picks up a guitar leaning on a wall near the podium, takes it, and faces the crowd. I didn't know he even played guitar. What else don't I know? He begins to play. Tears flow down my cheeks. Flynn's voice is beautiful and emotional. At the end of the song, his voice cracks and he looks over, and for a moment, our gazes meet. For a briefer moment, he smiles. Then it's gone and he puts the guitar back and walks to his seat.

The minister finishes up a short, sweet service and announces snacks and beverages will be served in a room in the back of the church, outside the sanctuary. The crowd begins to file out, row by row. Flynn and his family stand and walk down the main aisle toward the back of the church. When our row is up, I follow the crowd into the main hallway of the church.

When I'm in the hallway, a hand grabs my arm. Flynn. He pulls me off, away to the side, out of the crowd. We're standing close to the washrooms but far enough away, the traffic flowing in and out doesn't interfere.

"Hey," he says.

"Hey." My heart pounds harder as I stare at him with so much I want to say. My words trip over each other in my head, but nothing leaves my mouth. I've no idea where to start.

"How you doing?" he asks.

"Wilf would have loved your singing. I mean, I loved your singing too. I didn't even know you played guitar." I sound formal and weird.

"I guess we don't really know all that much about each other," he says.

I want to find out, I think. I want to know. He nods at someone across the room, and I turn and see his mom and Kyle. Kyle's back is to us, but his mom moves away, swept toward the room where the snacks are.

"How's Kyle?" I ask.

"Okay. He'll be okay," he says.

I nod again. Gnaw my lip. Twist my earring. Wish I could find the right words. He smiles, his lips tight, not showing his teeth. His expression worries me.

"I've missed you," I blurt, and then words uncork from my brain. "I've wanted to come and see you, see Kyle, but wanted to give you time too. You can come back to New Beginnings. Stella doesn't mind. Not anymore."

He's looking across the room though. Not at me. "I've missed you too, Jess," he says, still not looking at me. "It's just…" He pauses.

Just?

"I should have been there."

"I can help you look after Kyle if you want," I say in a rush. "We could take him to that beach. My turn to get the pizza." My voice sounds desperate. Clingy.

"Timing," he says softly.

It sounds like good-bye.

Definitely good-bye. My back stiffens. A hot flush leaks sweat from my body. I almost place my hands over my ears. Run away.

"Timing?" I manage to say.

He doesn't answer and stares off in the distance.

"So that's it?" I ask him. My voice shakes. "We're done?"

"I have to think about my mom. I mean, I should have been

there. I shouldn't have been, you know, partying like I have no responsibilities. I do. I have to be around. For my mom and Kyle."

My sadness is drowned by a flood of anger. "That's not fair." I don't try to keep the anger from my voice.

"Ferris wheels and corn dogs," he says. "Fairs."

That makes me furious. I know there's no use arguing. But it's ridiculous. Giving up on me so easily. "You're not responsible for what happened."

"Maybe not. But who is if I'm not there?" he asks.

"That doesn't mean you don't get a life of your own too."

"I can't. I can't be the boyfriend you need me to be."

"I don't need you to be anything, just you."

He smiles at me, but he's already gone.

I drop my gaze. "I thought I mattered," I say with more hurt than I've ever felt before.

"You do," he says quietly.

"Then fight for me," I plead. "You are allowed to have both."

He doesn't say anything, and the silence lands like a punch to my stomach. I'm robbed of air. It's almost as if he's breaking up with me, but we never even really established ourselves as a couple in the first place.

"Fine," I say. But it's not fine. It so far from fine, it's in a completely different time zone from fine. I spin on my heels, hurrying for the bathroom.

"Jess," he calls but doesn't come after me. He doesn't fight.

I hurry to the church washroom, and amazingly, it's not lined up with women. I'm able to run straight into an empty stall and sit down on the toilet, gulping air and trying to keep tears from dripping down my face. My head droops to my chest. Keeping the tears from flowing is a lot of effort, but I sit still and will them not to come. Heels click on the floor, and I realize there's a lineup starting outside my stall, so I take a deep breath, wipe under my eyes, flush, and walk out. I ignore the other women and walk to the mirror and stare at my reflection. At least I don't look out of place, with my red eyes and blotchy face and sniffly running nose.

If Wilf were still alive, he'd give me hell for crying about my own problems at his funeral. *Perspective, Jess*, he'd tell me. Thinking about Wilf makes me miss him even more. I turn on the tap and run water over my hands, pool it up, and splash it on my face. My makeup is already ruined. It doesn't matter.

While I'm drying my hands and face with the rough paper towel, the door opens. I glance up. Flynn's mom gazes at me in the mirror. I blink fast.

"Jess," she says.

"Hi," I manage but can't think of what to say next.

Neither can she, apparently.

"I'm sorry about what happened," I finally say.

"I am too."

I look at the sad stoop to her shoulders. The old black skirt she's wearing. The slightly frayed sweater. *I need him too*, I want to tell her. And I thought he needed me. Is it right for Flynn not to have a life of his own? Does he owe her that? Should he sacrifice his life or his happiness so his little brother can have more than he does?

I don't know. I don't know the answer.

She married Kyle's dad. And now she's paying for it in more ways than one.

And so is Flynn.

My tears are threatening to roll again, so I start walking. I pass her and open the door. "Good-bye. Good luck."

I walk into the main area. Some people are leaving, some are hanging around the door, but most have piled into the room where they're serving snacks. I spot Stella close to the exit and hurry toward her.

"I'm leaving," I tell her and give her a hug.

She watches me, pity in her eyes as I hurry out as fast I can move in my high heels. When I'm safely inside the Audi, I drop my head to the steering wheel and let myself go. I cry as hard and as loud as I want to.

"Good-bye, Wilf," I whisper when my tears are finally dried. "I hope you're with Rhea now," I tell him. "I hope you're happy."

I turn the key in the ignition.

I have no idea where I'm going. Or even how I'm going to get there.

chapter **twenty-eight**

Penny and Allie are sitting on my bed, jumping up and down to bounce me around, trying to get me to laugh.

"Come on," Allie says. "Get your lazy butt up. We're going to take you to the new frozen yogurt place. It has every kind of topping you can imagine. No one can feel bad when they're eating frozen yogurt with gummy bears and chocolate."

I want to lie back on my bed and moan, but there's no use arguing with these two. I see in their faces they're not giving up. I've already lain around in my bed all last weekend, and based on the way she keeps checking up on me, it's starting to freak Allie out. Even Mom was up more than me, after a slight relapse. Now she's getting outside for walks and going to a therapist almost every day.

Nance came to see me after the party. She didn't remember most of it, but she laughed it off, like blacking out was another highlight of a great summer bonfire party. I didn't say anything about Flynn and neither did she. When I tried to talk to her about her parents and how she felt, she brushed me off. "I don't care about what they do," she said. "Don't be lame."

After that remark I told her Penny and I were talking again and trying to make up.

"You're a loser" were her exact words. "You deserve each other." She left without saying good-bye.

Since Wilf's funeral, I've been working back at New Beginnings regularly. I keep at it, because I have to look after the greenhouse now. I've potted and built up an herb garden like I promised Stella. The cooks are trying to incorporate herbs into the meals we serve, but it's hard when they're bulk-sized and the dinners are usually donated. Still, I love having the herbs at the greenhouse, and no one else minds.

Allie pulls me to my feet.

"Fine," I say. "I'll eat some stupid yogurt."

The two of them only complain a little that I don't change out of my oversized, slightly stained T-shirt over my short shorts. My hair is in a messy bun, and there's no makeup on my face. At least I brushed my teeth. That's as much as I can care.

Allie drives and I tell Penny to ride shotgun and sit in the back-seat. I listen as they chatter the whole way, trying to engage me. I pretend to smile and try to hide the extent of my disinterest in everything they're talking about.

When we get to the yogurt place, I take a container and force myself to add gummy bears and candy sprinkles to piles of yogurt that don't appeal to me and pick a bright-green teddy bear spoon after the girl weighs my cup. Allie pays for mine, but not even that or the bright colors and candy can dent my mood.

The girls try extra hard, but I barely eat.

And then it happens when we leave.

"Oh," Allie says and steps in front of me and tries to turn me around, shove me back inside the store. "I forgot I should take one home for Doug," she says.

But it's too late. I've seen him.

Flynn is walking through the parking lot. He has an arm draped over a girl's shoulder. He's pulling her head close to him, and they're laughing. He leans down and kisses her. She's tall. Thin. She's wearing a tiny shirt that shows off a brown flat belly and shorter shorts than mine. Her hair is long and luxurious. She's gorgeous.

My first urge is to throw up. My second urge is to run at her and gouge out her eyes. My third is to punch him in the stomach. Penny grabs my hand, and Allie pins herself to my other side. And then, Flynn glances over and sees us. Sees me. The smile on his face freezes. His eyes open wider, and he pulls his arm away from the girl. She looks at his face and then follows his gaze over to the three of us. Me, looking like a hot mess, and Penny and Allie clinging to the side of me like I'm a pathetic loser. All of us staring at them.

My face is on fire.

"Jess," he calls. "Hi." He walks away from the girl, glances at Allie and Penny, and tries to smile, but it doesn't work so well. "Hey," he calls.

The girl narrows her eyes. I want to hate her. He says something to her and then starts walking over to us. I watch the girl walk away, her head held high. And then I recognize the car she's heading for. Braxton's piece of crap. Braxton is leaning against it, and he waves at me. Beside him, under his arm, is Jennifer. She looks embarrassed for me, but she lifts her hand.

Then Flynn blocks my view. He's standing right in front of me. I can't ignore him, though I really want to. A lot.

"Hey, Jess," he says softly. Penny and Allie don't leave my side. "Girls," he says to them. Allie and Penny don't say anything. "Can I talk to Jess for a minute?"

"Go ahead," Allie tells him.

"Alone?"

I nod my head. "It's okay."

"You sure?" Penny asks.

"It's okay."

They each squeeze a hand and glare at him and slowly walk away. Not too far.

"How're you doing?" he asks. He runs his hand through his hair.

"Not as good as you, obviously." Screw being civil. "That your girlfriend?"

I want to sound like I don't care, but my voice cracks and betrays me. I shouldn't have said anything.

"She's not my girlfriend," he says.

"No? You're just sleeping with her?" I look straight at him. "That's what you wanted? Easy?" I clench my hands into fists at my side. "Do you even know how embarrassing that is for me? That I thought I meant something? I heard it enough times. That you have lots of girlfriends. Everyone told me. Even Kyle."

"I never lied to you," he says.

"Whatever." My fingernails press into my palms. "Does she think she's special too?"

He reaches for me, but I pull my hand back.

"Don't," I tell him.

He glances toward the girl. She's watching us but pretending not to. "She doesn't mean anything."

"She does. She's a person. She deserves to be treated like one."

He drops his gaze. "Jess?"

"Go," I tell him. "You've made things more than clear."

He doesn't move. "I'm sorry."

"Go!" I say again, but this time I yell it.

Allie and Penny are quickly at my side, but Flynn is already walking away. The girl is gone from Braxton's car.

The three of us move in a straight line back to Penny's car. Jennifer stands by it. Why didn't I see Braxton's car when we pulled into the parking lot?

"Hey," she says to me. She half smiles at my sister and Penny. "I'm glad you two made up," she says. "You were such good friends." She looks at me. "You okay?"

"Fine," I say through clenched teeth.

She glances over at Braxton's shitty car. Braxton's watching us. Flynn is gone too.

"We're seeing each other now," she tells me. "Like dating. He gave me an ultimatum. After the bonfire party I went to with Nance. All or nothing."

"I thought he was a summer fling," I say.

Jennifer shakes her head. "Turns out, not so much. Turns out I kind of like him." She glances back at Braxton. "Flynn's been a mess about you."

My skin crawls. I shake my head. "I can't do this," I tell Jennifer.

She nods. "Yeah. Okay. I get it."

She lifts her hand then, to block out the bright sun. There should be dark clouds. Rain. "Nance is going to make life hell for us. At school. Me with him. And you, with her. You know that, right?"

"I don't care," I tell her. I look at Penny. She nods.

Jennifer turns to go back to Braxton.

"We'll have your back," Penny calls. "If you want us to."

Jennifer glances back. "Yeah? Thanks."

I sigh deeply. "You're a pain in the ass, Jennifer," I tell her. "You know that?"

"At least I have one," she says.

"See you at school," I say. I don't trust her completely. Not yet.

I hop in the back of my sister's car and squeeze myself into a ball.

Penny and Allie get in. "Oh God," Penny says. "That was horrible. Are you okay?"

"No," I admit. It's really over.

He's with someone new. I was wrong about him.

chapter **twenty-nine**

M onday afternoon, I'm in the greenhouse.
"Hey guys," I say to the azaleas. "Looking good. Wilf would be happy."

I mist and water and fuss over them. When I'm all done, I head to the area where I've lined up the potted herbs. I bend down to inhale the peppermint leaves, and when I stand, I grab my chest and scream. Flynn is right in front of me. Holding a small plant.

I clench my hands into fists and only just resist punching him hard on the shoulder. "You scared the shit out of me."

"Jess!" Kyle calls and walks out from behind the counter. "Soap!"

"Sorry, Kyle," I tell him. "I didn't see you." I force a smile. "You look good. You feeling better?"

He holds up his hand. "I got a new train," he tells me. "A girl. Annie."

"That is awesome, dude," I tell him.

"Kyle, can you go and water those plants?" Flynn puts down the plant he's holding and picks up a water bucket and walks Kyle far away from the herbs and starts him watering a row of flowers.

My hands flitter around. I feel like throwing up. *I don't care*, I remind myself. *I don't care.* When he returns, Flynn touches my shoulder lightly.

"Please don't touch me!" I say, gritting my teeth and moving away. He doesn't have any right. Not now. Not ever. He can't touch me again.

His hand hovers over my arm and then he pulls it back. "I'm sorry," he says.

"Yes," I agree with him. "Yes. You are."

He picks up the pot with the cactus. He holds it out. He's giving me a cactus? A thorny plant that sucks the life out of the ground around it. Seems appropriate.

I frown and focus on my anger. Anger is better than hurt. I turn to my herbs. "What are you doing here?" I ask and angrily pull a piece of thyme out by the root.

"I need to talk to you. Explain some things." He's staring at me. "I hate that you're so angry with me."

I hate it too. But I don't tell him that. It's none of his business.

"I brought you a cactus because it symbolizes endurance and adaptability. And finding ways to survive even in tough circumstances."

Behind us Kyle is singing a rhyming song about purple stew.

"And that's supposed to make everything better? A cactus?" I frown. "I don't want anything from you, Flynn," I tell him.

"No." He inhales deeply and puts the cactus down. "I want to tell you the truth. Even if it hurts."

"I kind of want to punch you in the stomach until it hurts," I tell him. "That's me. Being honest." I pull a peppermint leaf too hard, and it rips in two.

"I don't blame you," he says.

I scrunch the leaf up into a ball and bring it to my nose and inhale. I don't want him to hurt me anymore. I don't want to give him that power.

"My way of dealing, not getting hurt," he tells me. "It's always been to keep things locked down. Not let people in. Do it alone, you know. But you came along. And Kyle loved you, and then, well, it was different."

I turn my back on him and watch Kyle. Holding the watering can, chattering away to the plants, and singing.

"I blamed myself, Jess. For not being there that night. For not protecting my family."

I sigh. "I know that. You think I don't know that? But you can't always be there. You know?"

"That's what your dad said too."

I freeze to the spot, not sure I heard that right. "My dad?"

"Yeah. He came to see us. Talked with my mom. He's helping her get her divorce done so it's official. So Kyle's dad has no right to come near her again."

"My dad?" I frown. What the hell? My forehead wrinkles deepen from my angry frown. Since when does my dad talk to Flynn's family?

"He said he would have one of his partners, the one who handles marital law, draw up the papers. He's making sure my stepdad signs them." He looks over at Kyle, who is belting out a verse in his song. "He refused my offer to pay him back whatever it costs."

"Let him do it," I say, and some of my anger for my dad, the constant thing that's still between us these days, shrinks just a little. "He can afford it. If he wanted money for it, he would have said so."

He nods. "I went to see him."

"My dad?"

"Yup. At his office. Fancy place."

I haven't been to my dad's office since I was a little kid. I try to imagine Flynn in the corporate setting and almost smile at the contrast.

"I told him I wanted to work it off. He refused. He told me it was karma. His way of dealing with things he had no control over. Bad people. And then we talked a little bit," he says. "About feeling responsible. He told me how he felt. About not being there for your mom. He told me he feels responsible every day for what happened."

"That's crazy," I say. "She went for a run."

"Still, I get it. It's a thing. Feeling responsible for your family."

I concentrate on my feet, shaking my head. No. No. He is not allowed to get along with my dad. He is not allowed to have the sympathy of my family. I've worked hard to get to the place where I am. I don't want to forgive him. It doesn't excuse the girl.

"I'm sorry you saw me with her," he says. "With Lindsay."

I barely resist my urge to grab a nearby spray bottle and attack him with it. Yell at him and curse him while I hose him down. Lindsay. She has a name. I loathe it.

"It doesn't matter," I whisper and focus on Kyle. Watching him. So innocent still.

"It matters a lot." His voice cracks. "She doesn't live in Tadita. She was visiting for the weekend. It was stupid. A mistake. I was trying to forget you."

"Yeah. Well, I was doing the same. Only I chose yogurt instead of a boy. And you should be more careful with people. How do you know it didn't mean something to her? Maybe she thought you cared."

"She has a boyfriend," he says. "In Seattle."

Kyle's sweet voice dances in the air. I shake my head. Back and forth. Back and forth, focusing on Kyle, watching him.

"I wanted to be the same way I was before I met you. Not involved, you know. Not caring. But it didn't work." He pauses. "It made it worse. Because no one else is you, Jess. No one."

I shake my head. No. He is not allowed to say these things to me. I have worked hard to make myself believe that we will never be. That he is bad. Wrong. Gone.

"And then I realized something else. I want to be like Wilf," he says. "I want to fight for you."

I reach for the nearest bottle and spray him. I spray him again. And again. "No," I tell him as I'm spraying him. "It's too late. You screwed up. Wilf would be furious with you too." Tears run down my cheeks, and my hand drops to my side, limply holding the water bottle.

"Did you hear?" he asks softly. "Did Stella tell you what Wilf did?"

My heart flutters, and I put down the bottle. "You mean besides die?" I ask.

Flynn winces, and that secretly makes me smile. Wilf would have appreciated my dark humor. Even if he thought it was rude. Flynn, on the other hand, looks horrified.

"I'm only kidding. God. What?" I ask impatiently. "What did he do?"

"He left my mom his house. We found out from his lawyer. They had to get a relative to sign off on it before they told us."

Pow. That gets my attention. I almost hear Wilf's voice in the greenhouse. Laughing. I turn and finally look Flynn right in the eye. God, it hurts.

"He did?" I ask.

"Yup. We have to pay inheritance tax and there are bills to look after and stuff, but there's no mortgage. He left me a note."

"Wow," I say and glance down. My sarcasm and bitterness are corked by the hugeness of what Wilf did for Flynn's family. "That's pretty great." I look over at Kyle.

"I know. It's an old bungalow in Heritage Point, old but in great shape. It's a better neighborhood with a better school for Kyle. He starts first grade this year."

I glance across the greenhouse at Kyle again. He's still singing and slopping water all over the floor as he tries to water the plants.

I smile. What a great thing to do. What an amazing old man. I miss him. Wilf. I miss Kyle. God. I miss Flynn too.

"I miss you," Flynn says quietly, as if he really does see inside my head sometimes.

I bite my lip and look away. No. I can't do this. I can't hear him say things like that. I've been working hard the past couple of weeks to file him away in a part of my brain that I don't ever have to visit. Far, far away from the shredded thing that used to be my heart.

He takes a step closer to me. He's looking down at me with an expression he's not allowed to use anymore. "I really screwed up, Jess. I messed up bad."

"You're only doing this now because you have a house. Well, Wilf didn't give you the house so you could screw me over. I hate you." I start crying full on then. "I hate you so much."

"It's not the house," he says. "I've been trying to get the nerve to talk to you. I'm so afraid, still afraid, that you won't be able to forgive me."

I close my eyes but I don't move away.

"I'm sorry," he whispers. "I've been miserable trying to figure out the right way to reach you. I thought I should give you time. To get over being mad." He puts his hand on my arm. "I was stupid."

"It didn't work," I whisper. "It made me madder."

My hand betrays me though. When he puts his hand on top of mine, I don't move away. He slowly moves forward, tentatively, and then I'm crying against him. Drenching his T-shirt with my tears.

"It's the truth, Jess. I don't want anyone else. Only you. Spoiled. Rotten. You."

"I can't stand seeing you with anyone else," I say and cry on his shirt more.

"I know. And I'll never screw up again. I want this. I want real. I want scary. Please. Forgive me. Take me back."

"I've been working so hard to let you go," I tell his chest.

"A chance," he says. "One more chance. Let me fight for you. Let me try."

I'm gripping his shirt in both hands, staring up at him, tears still running down my face.

"What about your mom?" I ask. "What will she say about it?"

He rests his chin on top of my head. "She knows I'm a mess

without you. She wants what I want. She hopes you'll go and talk to her. When you're ready."

I can think of a million reasons why I don't want to talk to his mom.

"Are you two done hugging yet?" Kyle asks. He wanders closer, holding the empty water bucket, and he's smiling at me, like it's the most normal thing in the world, seeing me hugging his brother again.

"He missed you," Kyle tells me. "Like a girlfriend. I missed you like a friend."

I laugh and wipe away the tears collecting all over my face.

"We want to take you somewhere, Jess!" he says to me. "For a hangover."

"To hang out," Flynn clarifies and smiles at me.

"We want to show you the flowers," Kyle says. "Will you come?"

I run my hands through my hair, trying to catch my breath. I'm dizzy, disoriented. Nothing feels real. Flynn stares at me. Waiting.

"It's the turtle place!" Kyle blurts out. "Flynn wasn't sure if you would come. But I was. How can you resist turtles?"

"It's an indoor atrium," Flynn adds. "There are flowers and plants and ponds with fish and turtles. It's in one of the buildings my mom cleans. People are allowed to visit."

"I don't know," I say, afraid. Hopeful, but still so afraid.

"Please?" Flynn asks. "Come?" He holds out his hand.

I stare at him and open up another little crack. And put my hand inside his.

"You're sure?" I ask. "Really sure?"

"I'm so sure. I'm the surest. Surely."

Kyle runs ahead of us.

"Stay where we can see you!" Flynn calls to him. "Wait for us."

"We have to go slow," I tell him. "I have to be sure too."

"As slow as you need," he tells me. "I want you sure. Why do you think it took me so long to kiss you the first time?"

I take his hand. There's a sound in the air, almost like a sigh. "I kissed you," I remind him.

I think of Wilf and smile, imagining him giving me a thumbs-up.

I grab my purse from a shelf and take out the greenhouse key to lock up behind us. When I throw my purse over my shoulder, my sock monkey hangs from the handle down my back.

"Hey." Flynn points at it and smiles. "You've got a monkey on your back."

"You're right." I laugh and unhook it from my strap and hold it in my hand. "Not anymore," I say. "Hey, Kyle!" I shout. "You want this sock monkey? He has special powers."

Kyle runs to us and squeals over the monkey. I think of something else and turn to Flynn. "What did the note say?" I ask. "From Wilf."

He smiles. "It said, 'You better be fighting for her.'"

And then he holds up his fist and I bump it with mine.

Acknowledgments

Thanks to my mom for inviting me along to volunteer at Siloam Mission in Winnipeg for Christmas dinner, which gave me a place to base my setting on and gave me a peek at how one shelter operates. Bravo to volunteers at Siloam and everywhere!

Thanks to Aubrey Poole, my new editor at Sourcebooks, who helped massage this book into shape. Thanks to Sabrina Baskey and Elizabeth Boyer for stellar edits and EVERYONE at Sourcebooks who all work so hard to make beautiful books with beautiful covers and get the books into book stores and libraries. Thanks also to my agent, Jill Corcoran, for getting me this far on my publishing journey.

Also thanks to everyone at Raincoast Books in Canada. Let's grab our Chapters/Indigo and Indie bookstore friends and go play some hockey and hang out at Tim Horton's after. You're all welcome to visit my igloo anytime you're in Calgary.

Special thanks to Linda Duddridge and Denise Jaden for early eyes and helpful advice while writing this book. And to Linda for the hot yoga and writing sessions. Thankfully not at the same time. Ew. Sweaty keyboards.

I'd also like to give a shout-out to book bloggers and librarians everywhere, who love books so much and help spread the word about their faves. Having my work read is an honor. You can have the last cookie from my cookie jar every time.

I'd also love to give special thanks to people I've met or corresponded with over the years whose kind words and/or encouragement have meant more than they probably know. For Aly Phanord, Fifi Islaih, Kim Baccellia, Amanda Pedulla, Amy Mueller, Hannah Doermann, Michelle Arrow, Ashley Morrison, Lindsay Robertson, Julie Goldbeck, Lisa McManus, and Jean Vallesteros: big hugs! And to all of you who I should have mentioned and forgot to because my brain is getting old and kind of mushy…give me a virtual smack next time you see me around, okay?

To my favorite son, Max Gurtler, and my favorite husband, Larry Gurtler, thanks for putting up with the weird things that happen around me when books are getting written. And the piles of dust and take-out food that follow. Thanks for long rides to BC and threats to take off your seat belt when the parents are getting too embarrassing. For the big garage that still keeps filling up with stuff and the swim meets that numb our butts but make us proud. The good, the bad, and the ugly. You're my family and I cherish you.

Lastly, to everyone who touches my life just by being in it. Go you! Hugs and thank you. ☺

About the Author

A Rita Award Finalist and Crystal Kite Award Finalist, Janet Gurtler's young adult books have been chosen for the Junior Library Guild Selection and as Best Books for Teens from the Canadian Children's Book Center.

Janet lives in Okotoks, Alberta, Canada with her husband, son, and a chubby black Chihuahua named Bruce. After her latest haircut, Janet's son told her she looked like a mom from an '80s TV show.

BOYS LIKE YOU

Juliana Stone

USA TODAY BESTSELLING AUTHOR

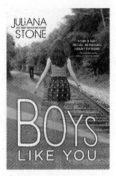

TWO SHATTERED HEARTS ARE ABOUT TO COLLIDE IN SMALLTOWN LOUISIANA.

Monroe Blackwell is sent from New York to spend the summer at her grandmother's in the sleepy town of Twin Oaks, Louisiana. There, she attempts to reconnect with the person she was before her younger brother's death.

Nathan Everets also knows heartache firsthand. A terrible car accident has left his best friend in a coma. As Monroe and Nathan are thrown together in the small town, they each slowly begin to heal—and fall in love. But for both of them, finding happiness means first facing their past and hopefully, finding their future.

SOME KIND OF NORMAL

Juliana Stone

USA TODAY BESTSELLING AUTHOR

PERFECT ISN'T ALWAYS WHAT IS SEEMS...

Golden boy Trevor Lewis had everything—until his best friend made a stupid mistake that landed him in a coma for six months. Now he's trapped spending the summer with perfect, stuck-up Everly Jenkins as his tutor.

With a family that's falling apart, Everly's scared that spending time with Trevor will reveal her secret. And yet they quickly realize that sometimes the struggle is what makes you strongest.

THE SUMMER AFTER YOU AND ME

Jennifer Salvato Doktorski

WILL IT BE A SUMMER OF FRESH STARTS OR SECOND CHANCES?

For Lucy, the Jersey Shore isn't just the perfect summer escape, it's home. As a local girl, she knows not to get attached to the tourists. They breeze in during Memorial Day weekend, crowding her coastal town and stealing moonlit kisses, only to pack up their beach umbrellas and empty promises on Labor Day. Still, she can't help but crush on charming Connor Malloy. His family spends every summer next door, and she longs for their friendship to turn into something deeper.

Then Superstorm Sandy sweeps up the coast, bringing Lucy and Connor together for a few intense hours. Except nothing is the same in the wake of the storm, and Lucy is left to pick up the pieces of her broken heart and her broken home. Time may heal all wounds, but with Memorial Day approaching and Connor returning, Lucy's summer is sure to be filled with fireworks.